HOUSEBOATING IN THE OZARKS

HOUSEBOATING IN THE OZARKS

A novel

Gary Forrester

Dufour Editions

First published in the United States of America, 2006
by Dufour Editions Inc., Chester Springs, Pennsylvania 19425

© Gary Forrester, 2006

Cover: *Monarch Wing* intaglio design by
Rosalind Faiman Weinberg. Printed at Mad Dog Press.

Paper ISBN 10: 0-8023-1341-8
Paper ISBN 13: 978-0-8023-1341-6
Cloth ISBN 10: 0-8023-1342-6
Cloth ISBN 13: 978-0-8023-1342-3

Library of Congress Cataloging-in-Publication Data

Forrester, Gary.
Houseboating in the Ozarks : a novel / Gary Forrester.
  p. cm.
ISBN-13: 978-0-8023-1342-3 (hardcover)
ISBN-10: 0-8023-1341-8
ISBN-13: 978-0-8023-1341-6 (pbk.)
  I. Title.

PS3606.O7486H68 2006
813'.6--dc22

                                        2006001815

Printed and bound in the United States of America

Acknowledgments

I would like to thank several people for their support during the writing of *Houseboating in the Ozarks.* Phil Deaver and Paul Freidinger were generous with their advice and enthusiasm, providing models of diligence and persistence. Darlyn Finch and Herb Budden helped me, at an early stage, to defer to the story's unfolding. And Christopher May's thoughtful editing and steadfast encouragement greatly improved the novel's final form.

I am happily indebted to each of them.

Foreword

My name is Finbar Studge. I am a writer.

Many years ago, I wrote a collection of short stories that achieved modest critical success in America, and even more modest sales. Encouraged by the critical response, I embarked on a novel in which I meditate on the human condition, based loosely on a series of reflections on the death of my father when I was seventeen. As I began, I was much older than my father had ever been, which caused me to see his life in a more sympathetic light. When the novel was finally finished, I called it *Groin Damage*.

In both the short stories and the novel, a character named Christian Leonard Hooker pops up now and again. He is based on a boy I grew up with in Illinois. I last saw him more than forty years ago, but we continued to correspond occasionally through the years, most recently by e-mail.

I was wary as I developed this character, because I knew that once the stories were published, the real Christian Leonard Hooker would read them sooner or later. My concern was that I hadn't painted a very pleasant portrait of my former friend. The word I found myself using most often to describe him was "mean." In private correspondence with readers and publishers, I also referred to my Hooker from time to time as an "asshole."

In a review, *Publishers Weekly* observed that Christian Hooker had a peculiar "genius for meanness." The reviewer surmised that the essence of his meanness was "not in outright lies, but in the brutal administration of half-truths." Hooker's attitude to truth was described as "one of benign neglect - he rarely tells malicious lies." I re-read my sketches, and had to agree. Yet the reviewer had a grudging fondness for Christian Hooker: "He alone, of all the men in Studge's stories, has not been ambushed."

Much to my surprise, most readers found my anti-hero to be romantic and idealistic, in a rakish sort of way. They liked him and wanted more of him. Through sheer persistence, his meanness garnered an air of integrity, almost endearing in its familiarity, a pit-stop of certainty on the race-track of life. You could *count* on Hooker to be Hooker. And if a working definition of genius is the ability to hold two completely contradictory concepts in the mind at the same time, with total conviction as to each, Christian Hooker was gifted far beyond meanness.

As I delved into this fictional character, or let him delve into me, I became increasingly attached to him. I hoped that my childhood friend would understand that my Hooker, however brutally portrayed, was cared for by his creator.

I need not have worried. When Chris Hooker read the thinly-disguised accounts of himself, he was ecstatic. He was flattered beyond words that he was the subject of fiction. I seemed to have unleashed in him some primal need for re-creation. And sadly, he began to be lost in the character I had drawn, offloading whatever remnants of normal human feelings he still had, crawling deeper and deeper into the persona of the solipsistic miscreant I had conceived.

By this time, he was living in Australia. "Living in exile," he called it grandly. But by all accounts, a more accurate description was what we used to call "living in sin." Chris progressed through a series of wives with a variety of ethnic backgrounds, and numerous children, some out of wedlock. He became embroiled as the central figure in the longest-running defamation suit in Australian history, and single-handedly brought the government of Victorian Premier Judith Kennan to its knees. I didn't have to take his word for this, because he sent me regular clippings from *The Age,* Melbourne's daily newspaper. Chris was on the front page for weeks, with weird stories about the blood of pet ducks on bicycle seats and seances with a government minister's dead child.

He seemed hell-bent on living up, or down, to the standards I had established for his fictional counterpart. I felt like a prophet, for I had written:

Hooker was a razzle-dazzle guy. He could unan-
swer more questions in a week than most men in
a lifetime. It had become a pattern in his life.
Give him a relationship and a couple of months
on his own resources, and Hooker could bring
more ruination than whole defoliation programs,
whole societal collapses, whole holy wars.

And this was *before* the murder trial. Chris became a suspect in the disappearance and presumed homicide of a well-
known Australian model and "television game-show hostess," as
The Age quaintly described her. Chris admitted to an affair with
her, but denied any knowledge of her disappearance.
Eventually her husband was tried for her murder and acquitted.
Chris was the prosecution's chief witness. It was all so sordid.

And then Chris slipped from my radar. For seven years, I
heard nothing but rumors from Australia, by way of Chris's
estranged relatives in Illinois. Apparently he had dropped out
completely, and was living somewhere near the outback in
the charmingly-named Wombat Forest, with a new wife
twenty years younger and new-born twins, a boy and a girl.
They lived in a twenty-room house made of mud-brick,
wood, and tin, built by a back-to-nature religious community
who sold it to Chris when they broke up in a fight over a cassette player. Chris bought the house and eighty surrounding
acres of eucalypt with the proceeds of his defamation suit.
They had no running water, no heat, no electricity. Chris
pumped shower water from the Loddon River, collected
drinking water from the corrugated roof, chain-sawed huge
amounts of wood for cooking and winter fires, hooked up a
set of solar panels to the roof, fenced in an organic garden to
keep out the kangaroos, hauled human waste into the forest
for burial, and grew his hair.

I had very little contact with Chris until the beginning of
2000, when he moved with part of his international entourage
back to America, to take a teaching job at Sand River
College. One day in late 2003, he e-mailed that he was about

to start an "autobiographical novel" of his own, and he wanted me to edit his work.

He just had to get it all down, he said. No one had to read it. It didn't have to be any good. He just had to get it all down. He would never forgive himself if he didn't get it all down. I had no idea what "it" meant. He made it sound like a bodily function. It was in him, and it had to come out.

He proposed to "novelize" certain things that had actually happened on a recent vacation, "just like Kerouac and *The Dharma Bums*," he said. (I refrained from reminding Chris what Truman Capote had said about Kerouac's work: "That's not writing. It's typing.") Chris said he would work in third person limited, "to give it objectivity." He wanted to build on my Hooker sketches, but to "flesh him out" (his words). His working title was *Miraculous Pet Recoveries*. I found all of this alarming.

In the hope of maintaining some measure of control over the situation, and perhaps to encourage Chris to use the writing process as a re-entry to the human race, I reluctantly agreed to his request. I had only one condition: that he *not* send me excerpts as they rolled from his printer in the white heat of creativity. I knew that he would want instant gratification, and I wasn't about to give it. I insisted that I wouldn't edit his work until he had completed the entire novel in draft form. I doubted that he would ever finish.

Chris accepted my terms. He e-mailed that he was establishing a "modus operandi," which he described in great detail. He would write in stolen moments, in a room in his home or in the Café Kopi in downtown Sand River, whenever he got a break of fifteen minutes or more from work and family. Whenever possible, to clear his head, he would warm up at his piano. This way, he said, he could begin writing without words.

No one would ever hear these inspirational sessions at the piano, said Chris, except his wife Kazzie, his step-daughter Kristen, and the twins. There would be no recordings, no sheets of music. The notes would just come together in a disappearing series of fragmentary moments, with a long silence after each improvisation. He wanted the same for his novel, he said. "Stasis in motion" is how Chris described the whole process, but that didn't make any sense to me.

Much to my surprise, six months to the day after Chris asked me to be his editor, a brown package containing 70,000 words of would-be novel arrived on my doorstep in Florida. He'd changed the title to *Houseboating in the Ozarks.* Obviously he didn't intend for this to be his final version, because he'd scrawled directions in the margins, such as "over" and "put this in later," with long rambling passages of circled handwriting on the backs of the printed pages. He'd penciled in agonizing word-changes with no obvious reason. "Pronounce" became "declare"; "elusive" became "ambiguous," then went back to "elusive" again. There were arrows indicating that entire sentences were to be transported elsewhere in the manuscript.

For the most part Chris's spelling and grammar were very good, especially for a draft. And I wasn't surprised, or even particularly disappointed, to find that he played fast and loose with inconvenient facts from his chosen summer of 2003, probably hoping that no one would notice. Chris had never been one to let the truth get in the way of his story-telling.

The exasperating aspect of Chris's manuscript was that his 70,000 words seemed to add up to nothing. It was about what you'd expect from fifteen minute snippets in a coffee lounge. A fast-food novel. What was the point? I wondered. What was it he just had to get down? Was this it? Or was this just a failure to communicate, a *Cool Hand Luke* moment?

In keeping with my promise, I made a few comments on these self-indulgent meanderings parading as a novel, sent them back, and waited with something like bemusement. I observed that the Christian Hooker in *Houseboat* wasn't nearly as mean as my Hooker character had become over the years. "Maybe you've mellowed," I wrote, cautiously. Seven years in a eucalypt forest must have had some effect. This new Hooker was still wrapped up in self, but more remote, less intrusive. This change, if true, made the world a better place, but did not result in any perceptible improvement in the body of Western literature. I had hoped, for starters, that Chris would learn to see through someone else's eyes.

"I have trouble relating to a piece of work that is purely process," I wrote, "that is only a slice off your psyche, where whatever comes out is all right. If this is only therapy, I'm against it on principle. If it's photos from your wallet, I might as well fly to Sand River to chat with you over espressos at the Café Kopi."

That was probably too harsh. Privately, I had to admit I found his total self-absorption a bit mesmerizing. Chris had no meaningful external references. And to be honest, I felt some joy as I found myself wondering, every page or so, "Christ, is this guy for real?" I was fascinated with the notion of one of my own characters struggling to be born, or reborn. I felt energized at the border between art and life. I was looking forward to Hooker's next draft.

Feeling somewhat guilty over my initial comments, I e-mailed Chris some constructive criticism. At least I hoped it was constructive:

> If you persist with this project, would you please give a little thought to whether you really want to write a novel (however you choose to define the term)? If so, why? And which of your chosen requirements remain unmet by this first draft? How do you propose to meet them in your next shot?

> A novel tells a story. Maybe you don't want to get it published. You just want to pass it around to a few pals at Sand River College. That doesn't let Christian Hooker off any hooks. If you want to tell a number of people exactly the same thing in exactly the same words, that's enough. There has to be a reason for that thing and those words, over and above the level of a one-way conversa-

tion with piano accompaniment, and that's saying quite a lot.

For starters, there has to be significance in the form. You can put that in by what's happening, and that's probably the easiest, or you can put it in by the balance in the words, and that's been done about twice in the history of the world (see James Joyce and Virginia Woolf), and I wouldn't count on it happening again - at least not in *Houseboating in the Ozarks*.

I'm not asking you to write my kind of novel. (I'm suggesting it's a helluva lot easier, which it is.) I'm saying that whatever kind of novel, whatever kind of whatever you write, the odds are immense against its being any good, and you're going to have to be prepared to criticize it harshly. You're the last person in the world who should like it. If you can't see what's wrong with it, you're not doing your job.

My index finger hovered over the send button for several seconds. Once the finger dropped, my comments would be off to Chrisland, no turning back. I started to re-read what I'd written, but after about ten words decided what the hell, and pressed the key. "Your mail has been sent," said my screen, which was fine with me. I pressed ok.

But before I heard back from Chris, before even an acknowledgment that he'd received my words, the sad news came from Illinois that Christian Leonard Hooker had disappeared under what the Sand River police were calling "suspicious circumstances." Wherever he was, he didn't have a single thing with him - no money, no wallet, no car, no passport, not even any clothes from his closet. After six weeks of half-hearted canine patrols and aerial searches, the police declared that Christian Leonard Hooker was presumed dead.

I felt empty for days afterwards, sadder than I ever could have imagined. His vanishing did not change my daily routines, as I hadn't seen him since we were kids. But it messed with my head. Something I hadn't even known was there was suddenly gone, and there was a big hole in the universe.

He was not even sixty years old. There would be no further drafts, no finished Hooker novel. I would never learn whether Chris might have overcome the beginning novelist's curse of autobiography, and moved beyond the immaturity of his first draft.

For some reason, I felt honor-bound to find at least a small audience for his novel. I'd made no promises along these lines, but I felt as if I'd made one. Chris was gone, probably lying in some ditch somewhere, unable to execute his hieroglyphic changes, unable to send e-mails of future drafts. Although I had long ago abandoned the idea of God and an afterlife, my feelings of obligation were akin to something sacred. I decided to publish Chris's work privately, for distribution to family and acquaintances.

I tried my best to follow the sprawling road-maps from Chris's manuscript. I have not edited his work beyond those changes he had indicated. The reader is invited to speculate as to the final product - what might have been.

Chris's chapters are titled according to nine consecutive days in the summer of 2003. The reader will note that chapter numbers are followed by references to certain "mysteries." Chris did not mean to suggest that anything particularly mysterious happened on any given day, or indeed anywhere in his novel. It was just that he was in the habit of saying the daily rosary, and the rosary is divided into sets of so-called "mysteries" or meditations built around the life, death, and resurrection of Jesus, who plays a small but significant role in Chris's story.

He is gone, and it cannot be undone. And yet, it saddens me to remember my childhood friend sitting in a gently-rocking boat at Patterson Springs, near the old Chautauqua grounds, with his father Leonard. In this snapshot from my memory, Christian Hooker is only twelve years old, and his whole life stretches before him endlessly, for ever and ever. In my remembrance, he smiles as the sun catches the ripples on the water, and the lake seems alive with a thousand twilight fireflies. In his high pre-adolescent voice, and higher spirits, he sings with his father, round and round and round:

> Row row row your boat
> Gently down the stream
> Merrily merrily merrily merrily
> Life is but a dream.

Finbar Studge, editor

SATURDAY: JOYFUL MYSTERIES

We can never know what to want, because,
living only one life, we can neither compare
it with our previous lives nor perfect it in
our lives to come.

Milan Kundera, *The Unbearable Lightness of Being*

To get to your home in the Wombat Forest, you drove inland
from Melbourne through Digger's Rest, Woodend, Tylden,
and Spring Hill. You'd stop at the Glenlyon General Store to
fill up with gasoline or grab a newspaper, then turn to the for-
est for the final few miles. At least twice a year you'd lay down
some rock on the path, after the rains had come, and level it
with a bulldozer.

On the way in, you'd take a mental inventory of the euca-
lypts that had fallen to the ground not too far from your path.
These would be accessible for the jeep and the wagon, so you
could go after them later with a chainsaw. As you rounded the
first dam, the two-storey house would come into view, sev-
enty-two squares of mudbrick and timber, shining tin roof and
solar panels, set to the south of the six-acre clearing, two hun-
dred feet down from the vegetable garden. Rollie, the pony,
would be grazing near the tool shed, and the twins would be
jumping on the trampoline. The chickens and goats, inside the
ten-foot fence that kept out the kangaroos, would lift their

heads from the garden grass.

Josh would be shooting basketballs at the hoop near the parking lot, and the little Pomeranian, Bear, would run to the edge of the clearing to greet you. In the springtime, Tadpole Creek would flow behind the house, first into the nearest dam, then along through the blackberries and into the Loddon River. But in the summer, the creek and sometimes the river would run dry and stay empty until winter.

Sean and Jeshel would be in the kitchen with Kazzie and Kristen and the cats, painting and reading and spinning yarns. Usually one or two overseas guests, from Holland or Korea or Japan, would be working the property for room and board. As you came to a stop in the driveway, the stones would grumble beneath your wheels and the sulpher-crested cockatoos would squawk in flight from the habitat tree. Your eyes would follow them through the azure sky, across the clearing and into the northern perimeter, then watch as they circled back for home.

You'd check to see if your clothes were hanging on the line, the ones you'd need for court, and you'd count the stacks of wood to see how many weeks you were ahead. And you'd wonder how you ever got to be here, and how many more years you'd stay.

At night, before sleep, you'd look north through the window into the darkness for the headlights that never came, the beams you always thought would one day flicker through the gum trees. But much to your surprise, the job was never finished.

* * * * * *

These were the thoughts of Christian Leonard Hooker in 2003, on his fifty-seventh birthday, in his living room in Sand River, Illinois. It was the Fourth of July, and it occurred to him, finally, that he had lost his immortal soul. In a moment of epiphany, he knew he was alienated from the Tireless Watcher, and had been for some time.

Two weeks passed, and on a Saturday morning he drove his wife and her fourteen-year-old daughter to Chicago

O'Hare for their flight to Australia. This had nothing to do with his soul. The trip had been planned for more than a year. They lived now in the flatness of the American Midwest, and Kazzie was homesick for the seas and hills of Australia.

So Chris loaded the family Windstar and eased down the driveway of their home. He glanced at St. Anthony's School across the street, where the twins would soon start the fourth grade. They sat in the back seat with Kazzie. Chris's twenty-year-old son Sean sat next to him in the front. Kazzie's daughter Kristen had the middle seats to herself. It was seven a.m.

About an hour later, just north of Ashkum on Highway 57, Chris saw a big black van overturned on the shoulder across the median. It was burning. The Windstar was the fourth vehicle on the scene. A fat blonde woman in front of Chris pulled her car over, jumped out, and ran across the highway. Chris slowed to let her pass, took a final look at the smoke and the flames, and moved on. There was a plane to catch.

Kazzie and the kids looked out the back window as Chris gathered speed. A brown-skinned woman was standing next to the burning van holding a child. "That was bad," said Kazzie. "I wonder how many people died."

As they reached the outskirts of Kankakee, they saw two ambulances heading south, followed by a police car. "They're too late," said Sean. "It'll be half an hour by the time they get there."

Kazzie opened a Japanese children's book, *Seashore Story*, and read to the twins. Kristen listened to her Discman, chewed gum, and read a teen magazine. Sean stared straight ahead. He was wearing bright red industrial ear protectors, the kind used for chain-sawing. He called them his headphones. He'd been doing this for a year, ever since he'd burned some of Chris's old bluegrass compositions onto CD's for posterity. The exercise left Sean with a ringing in his ears. For weeks he was borderline suicidal, convinced he would never be able to think clearly again, that his philosophy stud-

ies at Sand River College were doomed. But gradually he
came out of it, settling nicely into metrosexual eccentricity.
    Chris eavesdropped on *Seashore Story*. He'd read Taro
Yashima's tale many times, but he never tired of it, and
Kazzie's soft Australian accent was soothing. A fisherman
leaves his village and rides on the back of a giant turtle to the
bottom of the sea. A magnificent palace lies, brightly-lit, upon
the ocean floor. It has everything the fisherman wants, so he
stays there year after year. But one day he asks the turtle to
take him back to his village. When they arrive home, the
landscape is the same, and the seashore follows familiar lines.
But nothing else is recognizable. The villagers have no idea
who this strange old man is, with his long white beard. He
has been away too long.
    When Kazzie had finished, Chris glanced at Sean. Chris
hated the red headphones. They embarrassed him whenever
he and Sean walked along the streets of Sand River. And
now, beneath the headphones, snug in Sean's ears, were
sound-deadening plugs Chris had bought for him at the
Landen Hospital hearing center. Chris hoped the earplugs
would solve the problem, and for a while they did. But then
Sean started wearing the earplugs *and* the headphones, and
Chris's irritation doubled.
    "Isn't the ringing on the inside?" Chris would say. "How
can the headphones help the noises on the inside?"
    Sean would explain, over and over, that outside noises
made the inside noises worse, so the headphones and the
earplugs kept both kinds of noise under control. Even so, you
couldn't play a car radio when Sean was with you, and you
couldn't watch t.v. at home or go to a restaurant or a movie,
and you couldn't speak above a whisper in his direction. If
Sean heard a sudden clap of sound, he'd put his hands to his
cheeks and wilt, even if the red headphones were on and the
earplugs were in. Something about it made Chris think of the
Little Prince on his tiny planet, tending to his special flower.
    Another thing that perturbed Chris, besides the embar-
rassment of it all, was that he had to repeat everything he said

to Sean. Chris would say something, anything, and Sean would always say "Huh?" and then Chris would have to repeat whatever he'd said. And then Sean would respond, but because he couldn't hear his own voice, he would talk way too loud, making Chris wince. This went on and on and on.

If Chris spoke to Sean on the telephone, it was the same thing. Chris would say "Hello," and Sean would say "Huh?" and Chris would say "It's your father," and then Chris could hear Sean say "Oh hi" as if he were far away in a tunnel, because Sean would be holding the phone about a foot from his ear. This meant Chris could hardly hear Sean's voice on the phone. In about thirty seconds, Sean would say "I've gotta go," even if they hadn't reached the point of Chris's call, or any point at all, and by that time Chris would have forgotten what he called about anyway because he was so agitated.

As they passed through Kankakee, Chris asked out of the blue whether it was moral to torture a known terrorist if by doing so you could save innocent lives.

"Huh?" said Sean.

Chris growled to himself, then repeated the question. Chris hated repeating questions to anyone, and most of all to Sean.

"Of course it's moral," shouted Sean. He said "of course" a lot when he talked to Chris. He was in his Jeremy Bentham phase, telling everyone who would listen that he was a reform evangelical utilitarian. Sean believed in the greatest good for the greatest number.

Chris wasn't so sure it was moral to torture the terrorist, and said so. "Maybe a civilized society has to draw the line," he said. "Maybe there are some things we can *never* do, no matter what happens." A fat bug splashed onto the windshield. Chris turned on the wipers, but that only made the smear worse. He growled again.

"Because if we do this," he said, "if we torture, if we assassinate, we have lost everything." Chris gazed through the bug-goo at the highway ahead, feeling pretty pleased with himself. He felt that he'd staked out the moral high ground. Sean thought he was an idiot.

"What if," Chris continued, "you had to do the torturing yourself? Would that still be ok."

Sean sighed. He sighed a lot when Chris talked. He replied that Chris was confusing morality with squeamishness. Just because Sean wouldn't do the torturing didn't mean it shouldn't be done.

Chris sensed victory, and moved in for the kill. "So it's ok to let somebody else do your dirty work for you?" This was a line of argument Chris had used many times, in many countries, in many languages, in many small triumphs. It always seemed to work. It was the same argument he had used for twenty-five years in favor of vegetarianism and against capital punishment. If you're not ready to kill the animal, you shouldn't eat the meat. If you're not ready to flip the switch, you shouldn't support the death penalty.

Unfortunately, Sean's only reply, even louder than usual, was "Huh?" It started to rain, and the bug-smear got worse, and Chris wasn't about to repeat another question. A long time passed. They took the exit off Highway 57 to I-80, then entered the toll-road to O'Hare. Chris chomped on a low-carb Atkins almond brownie bar and fiddled with the radio dial, trying to get a Chicago sports station that would give Friday night's baseball scores. He got nothing but static, then remembered that he shouldn't play the radio anyway with Sean in the car.

At the first toll-booth, Chris threw forty cents in the coin basket, and Sean said softly, "It's not about dirty work." He was trying to be patient. He really was. "And it's right to torture the terrorist, no matter who ends up doing it."

Chris had lost interest in the terrorist anyway. What he really wanted was to connect some dots back to the burning van south of Kankakee. He had something he had to get off his chest, something for his oldest son, some passing of a Hooker torch.

As usual, he started indirectly, telling Sean about an old Anthony Quinn movie, where Anthony Quinn is an important man in a village occupied by the Nazis or somebody. The Nazis divide the villagers into the cooperators and the non-cooperators. Anthony Quinn was a cooperator. But one day, the Nazis decide to shoot some of the trouble-makers. They line them up against a wall, and the head Nazi hands a rifle to Anthony Quinn, cooperator-in-chief. Anthony Quinn's face fills the screen. If he refuses, the Nazis will go ahead and kill everybody, including Anthony Quinn and his family. If he obeys, at least he can buy some time. He aims the gun at the villagers lined up against the wall. But then the Nazi shakes his head. He takes the rifle from Anthony Quinn and turns it around, butt forward. Anthony Quinn's face fills the screen again. The idea is that he is supposed to club the villagers to death, one by one.

"I can't remember what happens after that," said Chris. "I think Anthony Quinn refuses, and the Nazis kill everybody." Chris looked over at Sean, who had fallen asleep and was snoring loudly.

"Almost there," said Chris to no one in particular, looking every bit of his fifty-seven years. Kristen was still listening to her Discman. Kazzie was reading another Taro Yashima story to the twins, *Crow Boy*. Only a few miles to go.

Chris was naturally inclined to use old films as short-cuts in conversation, because his own life felt like a movie. As far back as he could remember, he was able to flip a switch inside his head and soar to a lofty perch, where he could watch himself go through the motions of the day. And even when he floated back down to his skin, he could still sense an unseen director, somewhere, monitoring his every move. Someone was keeping secret tallies, and filling wicker baskets with unused footage.

He wanted to tell Sean that this was not the first time he'd passed a burning car without stopping. He'd wanted to say that he, Chris, could feel this alienation from the Maker of Heaven and Earth, and this was nothing new. They were all living in Australia when Chris passed his first burning car, Chris and Sean and Sean's younger brother Josh and their mother Elspeth. Kazzie, the future mother of Chris's twins, was only twenty-two years old, and Chris wouldn't meet her for another five years.

And besides Sean and Josh, Chris had a daughter nobody knew about, a little two-year-old named Jeshel. Her mother, Miriam Slade, was an opera singer turned Buddhist nun, not a hair on her head, the kind of person who didn't take painkillers when she had a tooth drilled. Chris met her at a music joint called *The Piggery*, in the western suburbs of Melbourne, where his bluegrass band played once a week along the banks of the polluted Maribyrnong River. Miriam was using her show-biz connections to recruit musicians for a fundraiser to restore the Maribyrnong.

It was November when he met Miriam Slade, Chris recalled, and Josh was a month from being born. He felt radiant in anticipation of his second son. As he sang his own songs and played his own melodies, he felt invincible. Miriam could see his aura. Anyone could see it.

Between songs, she handed him a poem, written in pencil in her own hand on the back of an envelope. In place of a signature, Miriam had sketched a feathered dreamcatcher. Chris read her poem secretly, more than once, before he saw her again:

> He who is born before his day,
> dies while he waits. But you did not
> know, did not live your dying.
> Your prophets made no prophecies,
> yet you fulfilled them: yours was
> the voice that focused what they
> could not say.
>
> This is that moment, that eternity,
> and you have seized it, standing off,
> standing apart.
> And then there was nothing.
> You are the end, the emptying.

The third day was a long time coming;
you are with us despite yourself.
Any room wherein we speak becomes a church.

Chris was smitten. Who wouldn't be? He waited three days, convincing himself that he deserved whatever Miriam Slade had to offer. They met, as she directed, in a servant's cottage behind a Toorak mansion. Chris brought a bottle of red wine for the occasion, a Cabernet Sauvignon from South Australia, but Miriam had other rituals in mind. She lit a dozen red candles and a stick of hand-dipped incense, pressed a button on her stereo to start Ravel's *Pavane for a Dead Princess,* and asked Chris to listen to her musings on purity as he tasted her kiwi fruit.

"I was performing in Rossini's *Tancredi,*" she said, "hitting the E above high C, when I became pure sound. My body was shimmering like the strings of a violin."

Miriam was kneeling on an Afghan carpet in the middle of her living room as she told her story. Chris poured himself a glass of the red wine, closed his eyes, and made himself comfortable on some overstuffed pillows near the picture window.

"I left the conservatory the very next day," Miriam said, "and walked over to the National Gallery where my brother Clayton was having a one-man exhibition. One of his pieces was called *I Never Wanted to Wake Up.* As I studied it, my mother approached me from behind and said she was receiving sonic impulses from Saturn." Miriam still thought this was pretty funny, and laughed for Chris.

"She told me she was allergic to everything on earth, and that Clayton and I were second-generation aliens from Mother Saturn. She said that if I rode the subways, enveloping myself in the pure whine of the trains, I could learn to sing three notes at once."

After a few months of train-riding, Miriam's singing career was in ruins. She could no longer get even one note she wanted. "And unlike Clayton, with his paintings and sculptures, I couldn't just pack up my art and head for Sydney. My voice had just disappeared in the whining of the trains."

So Miriam turned to religion. She told Chris that she'd become a disciple of Ma Chik Lap Dron, from the Tibetan province of Kham. "For me she was the primordial Buddha," she said. "I'll never forget the clicking of the beads of her *mala,* her Buddhist rosary, as she whispered her prayers."

The late afternoon sun was beaming through the picture window, and the red wine was making Chris drowsy. He listened as word-fragments wafted from the melodious voice of Miriam Slade - words like the Dreamtime and the I-Ching, the Myth of the Dragon and the Void, Carl Jung and UFOs. He heard Miriam say she'd been transported by great birds in the shape of human beings, through seas of blood and tendons, to a room of strange lines filled with what she was calling "pure oxygen." Chris thought he heard her say she was "entering the lines." As his head nodded into sleep, he caught himself and opened his eyes with a start. Pure sound, pure whining, pure oxygen. Entering the lines. What in the world was Miriam Slade talking about?

She smiled and took his hand. "Come with me," she said, and led Chris to her kitchen, where two large paintings by Clayton Slade hung from her green walls. The first showed a pair of airplanes, one flying high above the other, with a connecting lifeline in between. A man in the bottom plane was climbing the lifeline to a woman on top. The word "NOW" was written on each wing of the plane below.

"Clayton says his work is naïve," said Miriam. "Purposely so." Chris couldn't tell if Miriam liked Clayton's work or not.

Clayton Slade's other painting showed a simple wooden fence against a bright blue sky. Miriam explained that he'd first painted what was behind the fence, then covered it completely. "Sort of like Picasso's blue guitarist," she said. Chris wondered what was on the other side of the fence. He thought he could see little ridges of covered paint, outlining the shapes of women bearing swans.

Miriam guided Chris back to the living room and made a little place for them on the Afghan carpet. In the morning she said, "You'll have to go now. I need more oxygen." As Chris quietly gathered his things, she added, "Can't you hear the women's voices?" Chris laughed. He was fascinated by Miriam Slade and her shiny skull.

But when she became pregnant with their child, it seemed (to Chris) a transgression of the natural order, that divine laws had somehow been breached. He began to live two separate lives, one with Elspeth and the other with Miriam, and became obsessed with Oscar Wilde's dictum that he who lives more lives than one, more deaths than one must die. Josh was born, and this other life kept growing in the womb of Miriam Slade. Chris prayed that it would die, boy or girl, that his own child would die inside its Mother from Saturn.

He bumbled along with the minutiae of his dominant life. He and Elspeth bought an old hotel in the Melbourne suburb of Williamstown, where Confederate soldiers once stayed, incredibly, all the way over here in Australia during the American Civil War. Chris would walk around his enormous home late at night, looking into the tall ceilings, stroking the hessian wall-paper with his fingertips, talking to southern ghosts or perhaps to God, but no one was listening.

He caught the train into Melbourne each morning, walked home from the station each night, strolled down to the bay to watch the seagulls and the pelicans. He walked hand-in-hand with Sean to the docks and the rail yards and the botanical gardens, Josh strapped to Chris's chest in a snuggly like a joey, Elspeth at their side. And the baby grew in Miriam Slade, and the baby was born.

Miriam chose the name Jeshel after Chris's honorary Indian name, bestowed on him by Chief Frank Fools Crow when he lived among the Cheyenne River Sioux. In the Lakota language, "jeshel" meant messenger. Chris got his name at a sun dance in Green Grass, South Dakota, where he stood beneath an arbor as his friend Cheeto High Bear joined the other Sioux in the dry South Dakota heat, circling the cottonwood as the drummers beat the skins. Old Fools Crow stirred a mound of burning embers with a broom handle.

Cheeto's back was pierced with pencil-sized sticks of wood above his shoulder blades. Long leather thongs connected the sticks to a string of four buffalo skulls that dragged in the dust behind Cheeto, each skull smaller than the one before. Cheeto High Bear looked like a mother duck waddling across a reservation road.

Usually one buffalo skull was enough to break a dancer's skin. Fools Crow shook his head wearily and ordered a small Lakota boy to sit on Cheeto's last skull, but still the skin wouldn't snap. But when Cheeto passed before Chris, a meadowlark flew down from the cottonwood and rested on Chris's shoulder, and at that very moment Cheeto stumbled free. The other watchers breathed a sigh of relief. Cheeto grinned, and fell into Chris's arms.

"This meadowlark is a message," said Frank Fools Crow, raising his eyes from the burning embers to silence the crowd in the arbor. "This white man is a messenger." On the spot, he gave Chris his Indian name, Jeshel, and the sun dance continued. Sadly, Fools Crow returned to Pine Ridge before Chris learned what the message was.

Not long after the birth of Jeshel, Chris drove home to Elspeth on a late summer night after a stolen hour in the servant's cottage with Miriam Slade and their secret daughter. He came around the Albert Park Lake on a curving road that had once been a Melbourne speedway. As he rounded the northern bend, near the yachts, he saw two cars upended at the side of the road, their wheels still spinning and dust and smoke rising from the ground.

Chris slowed and rolled down his window and stared. No one else was around. The only sound was the whirring of the spinning wheels. But if Chris stopped to help, he'd have to explain to Elspeth what he'd been doing, he might have to report to the police where he'd been. He wouldn't get home for hours, and Elspeth would start to wonder about him. Already she was asking why he smelled of baby when he came home from his bluegrass gigs. He was in enough trouble. There wasn't much he could do for these burning cars. He rolled up his window and drove on.

The next morning, on the train to work, he read in *The Age* newspaper that two young boys, eighteen years old, had been drag-racing late at night on the Albert Park road. One of them had apparently lost control of his car, and they'd crashed. Both were dead. Their names were Darren Lewis and Ross Eveleigh. There were photographs.

The Age reported no witnesses. For a moment, Chris looked out the train window at the dreary western suburbs and wondered if the boys had been alive when he passed them by. Then he turned to the sports pages. Chris was a foreigner, a stranger in a strange land. He didn't understand Australian Rules football, but he read the sports pages anyway, just as he'd done in Illinois. It made the time pass. Chris had spent the better part of his life memorizing useless information.

And now, fifteen years after the Albert Park crash, there was a plane to catch. The Hooker family reached O'Hare, drove to the international parking area, unloaded the Windstar, and proceeded to the Japan Airlines counter. After Kazzie and Kristen checked in, they said their goodbyes and disappeared behind security. Chris and Sean and the twins got back in the Windstar and drove five minutes to Park Ridge, where Chris's sister Carol and her family lived. The plan was for Chris and the twins to spend the night there after dropping Sean off at Union Station, where he was meeting some of his Chicago friends. The following morning, Chris and the twins would drive back home to Sand River, pack, and head for the Ozarks.

Chris hardly knew Carol. He was sixteen when she was born, off to college when she was two, and he never lived with the family again. After he left for college, the rest of them moved from Okaw City to Sand River, thirty miles up the road. His childhood was over as hers was beginning. Now she was married with a couple of kids and a husband who was so nice and prosperous and well-adjusted it made Chris nervous.

After Chris and Carol exchanged a few clumsy greetings, the twins decided they wanted their youngest cousin to go with them to downtown Chicago. Chris's twins were nine, a girl named Sharon and a boy whose real name was Leonard, after his grandfather, but whose nickname was Razor. "Because he's so sharp," Kazzie would say, but the truth was that the nickname came from the label on Josh's skateboard helmet.

Carol's youngest kid was a nine-year-old boy, Bobby, and he was a handful. Carol jumped at the chance to have a Bobby-free Saturday, so the three little kids and Sean climbed into the Windstar with Chris, and they were off for the Loop. It was a beautiful, sunny morning.

They dropped Sean off at Union Station, and as Chris watched him walk away with his red headphones and his little blue Melbourne Grammar backpack, he looked all floppy and strange, like a gangly puppet jiggling from enormous strings in the sky. It was a miracle, thought Chris, that he and his oldest son were related at all.

And the minute Sean disappeared into the hundreds of Chicagoans at Union Station, Chris felt sad and wanted to get out of the Windstar and run and find him and hug him, but that didn't happen. It was only in Chris's head. And even if it had happened, it would have been crazy and weird, and Chris would have felt even worse afterwards.

So Chris and the three little kids drove downtown. They parked near the Union League Club on Jackson, walked east to the Art Institute's lions, then north along Michigan Avenue heading for the water tower. This was a long walk, especially for kids, so they stopped often to look at toys or to have a snack.

Between stops, Razor did cartwheels block-after-block, magnificent rolling circles in perfect balance, his slim muscular body seemingly made for them. Sharon and Bobby tried to imitate Razor, but their physiques were more solid, their centers of gravity uncertain. They just looked like a couple of kids trying to cartwheel. Razor looked like a whirling dervish.

Bobby soon thought of a destination near the water tower,

a place to define this great adventure. "There's a fantastic Lego store up past the Chicago River," he said. "We've got to go there!"

The twins thought this sounded great, so they all traipsed along Michigan Avenue with a purpose. Sharon announced that she was Dorothy from Kansas, skipping along on a yellow brick road.

"Razor can be Toto," she said. "And Dad can be the Scarecrow, because he's got no brain." Sharon liked to organize everybody.

So Razor started barking and wagging his butt, and Chris kept bumping into perfect strangers to show how dumb he was. Sharon told Bobby to be the Tin Man, but he wanted to be the Wizard, and Sharon said that was ok. But he had to wait till they got to the water tower.

As they approached the Chicago River, Chris could hear the beating of drums, a reggae rhythm echoing from the Wrigley Building. Chris knew this Caribbean sound well from his two years in pre-Jonestown Guyana, where he dodged the Vietnam draft. They crossed the river and saw a group of West Indian boys, some shaved bald, some in dreads, some sitting, some standing, pounding with sticks and hands on the upturned bottoms of plastic buckets.

Chris wished with all his heart that Josh could be with him at that moment, Josh the drummer, Josh who was left behind in Australia. Josh was Chris's only friend in the world as the secrets came out and the first family fell apart, when Chris was living in St. Kilda in his car next to a Seven-Eleven on Acland Street. Josh was seventeen now. Chris hadn't seen him in three years, and didn't know when he'd see him again. Josh would have liked these drummers, these mad West Indians with their tattoos and torn clothes and flowing braids, their desperate flailings somehow uniting in rhythm and smothering all the other street noises around the Wrigley Building.

Chris and the kids listened for a while, surrounded by images of murderous pioneers and dying Indians sculpted into the pillars of the river bridge, right where Fort Dearborn

used to be. Chris gave Razor and Sharon and Bobby some
coins to toss into the West Indians' hats. Then they kept skipping and cartwheeling to the Lego shop.

To get to the Legos, you had to go through a Nordstrom's
on Michigan Avenue and up an escalator. Chris sat on an
indoor bench in the walkway reading the *Sun-Times* as the
kids looked at Legos. After about fifteen minutes, Bobby
came out with a terrific kit for building a yellow saber-toothed
tiger. It cost $39.95, and Bobby wanted it. Somehow he'd just
walked out of the shop with the box, and no alarms went off.
For Chris, this was a low-life opportunity, and he told Bobby
that of course he could have it.

"Stay here," he said. "I'll go get Razor and Sharon and
pay for it." Timing was everything. But when he got inside,
Razor and Sharon had come up with Lego boxes of their
own, which complicated things.

"Go out there and sit with Bobby," said Chris. "I'll pay for
these." He watched as the twins walked out of the shop with
their boxes, and again no buzzers or beepers went off. Chris
loitered around the shop for a few minutes, keeping an eye
on the kids, and when he felt it was safe he walked out to join
them. "Let's go," he said.

"Thanks a lot, Uncle Christian," said Bobby. "I love it."

"That's all right, Bobby," said Chris. "Glad to get it for
you." Razor and Sharon said "Thanks Dad." They worked
their way back through Nordstrom's and out to Michigan
Avenue. Chris kept looking over his shoulder, but it was ok.
They'd made it, and he started feeling really good.

They kept walking to the water tower, then circled back
past the Seventeenth Church of Christ, Scientist, for the long
hike back to the Union League Club. Chris was hoping to
take the kids to the Harry Caray baseball restaurant on
Kinzie, because Harry was a hero from the old St. Louis
Cardinals days before he got fired and became the broad-
caster for the White Sox, then the Cubs. In the 1950s, Chris
had actually spoken to Harry outside old Busch Stadium after
a Cardinals game, as Harry got into a tiny white Thunderbird

with his sidekick Jack Buck. Chris couldn't recall the conversation, but he could remember Harry's slicked-back hair and checkered pants. Harry Caray was a radio god.

The baseball restaurant was closed in the afternoon, so they crossed over Kinzie and had some catfish and gumbo at the Redfish Cajun restaurant as the kids played with their stolen Legos. They thought Chris was great.

Chris was an accomplished small-time thief, and had been for years. He'd developed a moral philosophy about it. He never stole from a small store, and he never stole from an ordinary person or someone he knew. But if he could get away with it, he'd rip off anything that wasn't nailed down from a Wal-Mart or a Nordstrom's or any big chain. His idea was that it was ok, even morally necessary. It drove Kazzie crazy.

According to Chris, those places exploited everybody every day, and they factored petty thieves like him into their pricing. If you didn't steal, he reckoned, you were just letting them make even bigger profits. And his stealing made other people happy, even Kazzie, so long as they didn't know they were receiving stolen goods. Part of Chris's credo was that he never stole anything for himself. That would bring bad luck.

The new security devices in most big-time stores had complicated Chris's life of crime. Now he had to be extra careful to avoid the cameras and alarms. But he was still pretty good, and petty theft was a big part of his understanding of who he was and why his life was worthwhile. He couldn't remember the last time he'd paid for everything from a big-time store.

He'd only been caught once, wearing a pair of ski pants out of an Eddie Bauer's in Portland, Oregon. A hidden plastic disc in the left leg made the alarms go off, but Chris talked his way out of it by slobbering and acting deranged. A young shop assistant guided him back to the men's dressing room. "Just take off the pants and leave, sir," she said.

Bobby and the twins were exhausted when they got back to Carol's place, so Chris plunked himself down on the living room couch to watch the rest of the Cardinals-Dodgers baseball game on the big-screen t.v. Albert Pujols was still pounding the ball, and the Cardinals won 3-1 to move three games behind the Astros in the National League Central. The Cards had been awful this year, and their manager Tony LaRussa, a night-school lawyer, was up to his usual tricks of thinking too much and outsmarting himself into one close loss after another. Still, the Cardinals had a great everyday line-up, with Pujols and Edmonds and Rolen and Renteria, and Chris had hopes they could make the playoffs for a fourth straight year.

He'd been following the St. Louis Cardinals since the 1940s, when he first went to the old Busch Stadium on Grand Avenue, Sportsman's Park, with his father Leonard. Stan the Man Musial put on a hitting display that afternoon, banging two doubles off the short right-field screen, but Enos "Country" Slaughter was even better, hitting for the cycle. As Enos rounded the bases after his home run, the Budweiser eagle flapped its wings and a little redbird flew across the scoreboard. Forty years later, during his long Australian exile, Chris still turned to the small boxes in *The Age* that gave the U.S. baseball line scores and standings. Even so far away, just knowing the Cardinals' won-lost record could affect his daily moods.

Kazzie could never understand Chris's interest in the St. Louis Cardinals. "It's just a bunch of men playing a stupid game for a lot of money," she'd say. "What's the point? Think of all the hours you've wasted watching and listening and reading about these dumb games."

Chris knew she was right, but the Cardinals, like thieving, were part of his persona. Chris actually believed, with no hint of irony, that he could affect the outcome of Cardinals' games by listening to the radio or watching on t.v. It didn't always work, of course, and often they lost even when he was tuned in. But they were absolutely sure to lose the minute Chris ignored them.

He tried to explain to Kazzie that he wasn't a baseball fan. "I only care about the Cardinals," he'd say. "There's a difference. I don't even like baseball." And it was true.

Carol had the twins sleep in the upstairs sitting room,

and put Chris in the guest room next door to them. A tidy little bathroom was in between. To get into his bed, Chris had to remove a dozen pastel-colored decorative pillows, a Hooker family tradition, then pull back the Amish quilt and untuck the sheets and blankets from the sides and bottom of the bed.

Once he'd settled in, he fumbled around in his backpack for a *Nation* magazine to read the editor's latest rant about how stupid George W. Bush was, which got him all stoked up instead of sleepy, so he snuck downstairs to Carol's kitchen for a secret glass of soy milk. But Chris couldn't find any *Splenda* in Carol's cupboard, and he wouldn't use her *NutraSweet* because he'd read that aspartame causes cancer, so he had to have his soy milk without a sweetener. Still, it went down ok, and made him a little drowsy.

After trudging back up the stairs, he checked to make sure the twins were fast asleep. As he passed through the connecting bathroom and into his bedroom, his eyes were drawn to two photographs on Carol's dresser. He knew them well, and they used to make him sad for reasons he couldn't explain. They were pictures of his father Leonard and his mother Alma Ruth, taken when they were seventeen and seniors at Morrisonville High School.

They looked like nice young kids, trying to please whoever they were looking at, not at all like the dead weights they became over the years, clinging and sucking Chris into their tiny lives and making him feel useless and hopeless. In these old school photos their eyes were filled with energy and innocence. They looked sweet, and brimming with life. The world was enormous, and there was so much to look forward to.

On the table next to the bed was Carol's oversized family bible. The cover was a big color picture of Jesus, with long brownish-blonde hair and bright blue eyes and looking pretty sexy. This made Chris nervous, so he quickly flipped to John 3, the story of Nicodemus and the failure to communicate, one of his favorite themes.

Poor Nicodemus, big-shot Pharisee, tries to get a straight

answer to a simple question: "Who are you?" But Jesus prattles on about being born a second time, and the wind blowing whither and thither, until Nicodemus sighs, "What in the world are you talking about?" After all, he'd taken a risk in coming to this itinerant preacher under the cover of darkness. Nicodemus was earnest and literal-minded. Like Chris, he was a teacher of the law. He deserved more than this disjointed exchange. How could he be born again?

"Am I supposed to crawl back into the womb?" he asks. In the gospel of John, Nicodemus is as thick as two bricks, with about as much imagination.

Chris closed the bible and reviewed his latest discussion with Sean, trying to spin his failure into a positive. At least they'd said *something* to each other. In the absence of confusion, human beings might have no dialogue at all. If he and Sean knew *exactly* what each other was thinking or doing, they wouldn't have much reason to talk about anything. So they circled the wagons, like Nicodemus and Jesus, searching for clues.

He took up his plastic beads, the ones from Assisi, and said the joyous mysteries of the rosary, then drifted off to a peaceful sleep under his parents' pure and youthful gaze. The boy and girl in those black-and-white portraits, so neatly dressed and so exuberant, had no inkling of the fifty-seven-year-old criminal who would be their eldest son.

SUNDAY: GLORIOUS MYSTERIES

There is a patois known by everyone
below the age of consent.
A system of shouts and postures is enough:
words would just confuse things.

Richard Powers, Operation Wandering Soul

So there you were driving back and forth every week, every
week, between Melbourne and the Wombat Forest, three
days here, four days there, and of course she got pregnant
anybody would have got pregnant because how are you going
to keep track of the goddam pill going back and forth all the
time, sleeping in different beds and keeping weird hours out
in the middle of a eucalypt forest with the koalas and kanga-
roos and wallabies and cockatoos? And the last thing you
needed was another baby because here you were in this
Family Court custody thing over Sean and Josh with little
Jeshel ticking away in the background like a time bomb wait-
ing to explode in Elspeth's head, but you got all new agey
and soft and told Kazzie that if she wanted the baby it was ok
with you, but then she didn't want the baby anyway because
why would she want a baby with you when you were so
much older and already had kids with this woman and that
woman and none of the women ever stayed put with you
because why would they, and besides Kazzie had a baby of
her own to look after and she didn't need any more. So that

was that, and you would go along with whatever decision she made you big shot new age kind of soft guy but it was just a cop-out.

And the big day came and you and Kazzie drove to the clinic in East Melbourne where you waited your turn outside in the Volkswagen listening to Glenn Gould play the Goldberg Variations on the car's cassette player, and while you were waiting this Polynesian woman fat and sad walked up the footpath and behind her was this wormy white guy covered in tattoos and first she went in the red clinic door and then he followed after, and you watched them and Kazzie said she couldn't go through with this it was too awful what they were going to do in there in those rooms, and you started the car and drove down to St. Kilda to celebrate with a couple of cappuccinos at the Galleon Café where you'd first met, and there was this woman there at one of the laminex tables, a ballerina woman in her fifties wearing these baggy overalls and sandals, and you shared her table and told her what you'd just done and she was happy for you both and said so. And then three months later the baby turned out to be twins growing inside and they became Razor and Sharon and now they meant more to you than your own stupid life and you would die for them in an instant if you had to as you would for any of the kids, at least you thought you would, you told yourself you would.

* * * * * * * *

Chris and the twins woke up at nine a.m. Carol had already fixed some pancakes and omelettes, but Chris passed on the pancakes because of his self-styled Atkins diet.

It took some doing to combine Atkins with vegetarianism. Chris compromised by overdosing on eggs and fish, but his cognitive ethology made no sense. Fish had nervous systems too, just like cows. His rationale was that he needed fish and eggs to stay healthy. "So much protein," he said to Carol as he enjoyed her omelette. "So few carbs."

Over breakfast, he read the *Chicago Tribune,* and in the
Metro section found a report of the previous day's accident
near Ashkum. It was even worse than they'd thought:

> A packed charter van carrying family members of
> Illinois inmates to downstate prisons overturned
> on Interstate 57 early Saturday, ejecting 16 of the
> 18 passengers and leaving two young boys dead.

For forty dollars per adult and twenty-five dollars per
child, inmate relatives bought round-trip tickets from Chicago
to the Big Muddy Correctional Center. The van was only
designed for fifteen people, but there were nineteen on board
including the driver, Douglas King. Apparently he'd lost control because of the carrying weight.

According to survivors, the van flipped eight times and
struck a green "Exit" sign that sheared off the roof as it rolled
through a ditch and onto a frontage road. This all happened a
moment or two before the Windstar had come along.

The dead boys' names were Zeus Limonez, three, and
Desmond Brown Jr., eight months old. Desmond's mother,
Mayra Hernandez, was injured in the crash. She found little
Desmond on the side of the road.

"I was looking for my babies," she said. "Desmond was
bleeding from the head. He died in my arms. He looked at
me. I closed my eyes." Her two year old daughter Destiny
suffered head injuries and was airlifted to the University of
Chicago Hospital, where she was in intensive care. There was
a photo of Mayra Hernandez in a wheelchair, wearing a
white hospital uniform and an identification bracelet. She had
a bruise above her left eye. Mud was caked to her palms and
hair.

Mayra Hernandez, her mother-in-law, and the two children, Desmond and Destiny, had been the last ones to board,
paying $130.00 to the driver in a McDonald's parking lot.
She squeezed into a seat in the back, holding Desmond in her
lap. Destiny sat in the front next to her grandmother.

Nine of the passengers were in critical condition. One of the injured women underwent an emergency Cesarean section at St. Mary's Hospital in Kankakee, and her newborn child was airlifted to Children's Memorial Hospital in Chicago, in critical condition.

"Some crash," said Chris, passing the Metro section to Carol. He and the twins finished their breakfasts, said their goodbyes, and got in the Windstar. As they were backing out the driveway, Carol called out, "Oh Chris, thank you so much for Bobby's Lego. You didn't have to do that." Chris gave a little smile and waved.

On their way back to Sand River, Chris told the twins to be on the lookout for the scene of yesterday's accident. After passing through Kankakee, they all kept their eyes open, and before long Chris came to the outskirts of Ashkum, where he pulled over.

There wasn't much left. A few skid marks, the shattered green sign, a few empty beer bottles, a shoe, a plastic toy of one of the Seven Dwarves, Dopey, wearing a floppy hat with his tongue hanging out. Chris picked up the shoe, tossed it back in the ditch. He grabbed Dopey and plunked him on the dashboard. "Let's go, kids," he said. "Dopey can be our mascot." Sharon was happy to get back on the road, but Razor was disappointed. He'd filled his hands with bits of rubber and broken chrome.

"Can I keep these treasures?" he asked.

"No Razor," said Chris. "That's just junk, and it's dirty. Put it down. You might cut yourself." Razor opened his hands very dramatically and let his treasures fall back into the culvert.

"We can keep the Dwarf," said Chris. "That's enough." Razor got back in the Windstar, but he wasn't very happy about it. He stuck out his tongue at Dopey. Sharon rolled her eyes, and Razor kicked her in the leg.

When they got back home to Sand River, they were just in time for the midday mass at St. Anthony's, where Chris quietly said a little prayer about how truly sorry he was for not stopping for the burning van, explaining that he hadn't known what to do because of Kazzie's plane flight, and he didn't know what he could have done anyway that would have made any difference.

The weekly bulletin called this the "Sixteenth Sunday in Ordinary Time" in the liturgical year, which meant that the scriptural readings were from Wisdom 12:13, Romans 8:26-27, and Matthew 13:24-43. God's might was the source of justice, said Wisdom, and those who are just must be kind. In his letter to the Romans, Paul said that "the spirit comes to the aid of our weakness; for we do not know how to pray as we ought, but the spirit himself intercedes with inexpressible groanings." Chris groaned in his pew, audibly, hoping this was a better prayer than his last effort.

The final reading, from Matthew, told the parable of the kingdom of heaven being like a mustard seed. Razor thought this was pretty funny and laughed out loud. He whispered to Sharon, "I *hate* mustard." Chris pointed his finger at Razor and lip-synched for him to be quiet.

Chris thought these passages from scripture had the makings of a pretty good homily. He fantasized about being the priest, inspiring the St. Anthony congregation with his perceptive unification of the three readings, and then some. He would start by describing the Holy Spirit as the Cinderella of the Trinity. A nice feminist touch, he fancied.

"She was there before Jesus and she *still* is there, even where Jesus has never been," he would say. This was one of Chris's pet ideas, that the Holy Spirit was the female branch of the deity, softening the macho edges of scripture and sneaking through time with love divine, even for those who'd never heard the Vatican spiel. He would tell the congregation about the Aboriginal hand-paintings he'd seen on the walls of remote Australian caves. "She was there," he'd say. "She's still there."

The more he sat in his pew itching to be a preacher, the more excited Chris got. His Jesus would be a sixties radical, an iconoclast, a destroyer of piety and comfort. "The love of

God," he'd declare, "is a harsh and dangerous love." The first
thing his Jesus would do at St. Anthony's was turn over a few
tables in the foyer.

"Jesus was the great leveler!" Christian Leonard Hooker
would shout. "The great egalitarian! The scourge of the patri-
archs!" He would invoke his favorite passage from scripture,
Galatians 3:28. "In Cinderella's ballroom there is neither Jew
nor Greek, slave nor free, male nor female."

Then he would soften his voice to take the congregation
back down, for a learned discourse on the Syro-Phoenician
woman. "She was an outcast, a Greek," he'd whisper from the
pulpit. "But she taught Jesus a thing or two about humility.
And he was man enough to admit it." He made a mental note
to assign a working title to this developing sermon: "The
Manhood of the Master."

For his final crescendo, a rallying-cry for his brothers and
sisters at St. Anthony's, Chris would beseech them to forget
their measly sins and concentrate on social justice. "Your
God is a god at *work!*" he'd exclaim, thumbing through his
New Testament for an underlined passage. He'd find it at
John 5:17. "My father worketh even until now, and I work!"
Chris's eyes would scan the audience.

In quick staccato fashion he'd bark out snappy closing
sentences: "Jesus already died, you fools! You already killed
him! His death is your liberation! You have nothing to lose
but your chains!" He'd hang onto that final "S" like a coiled
serpent.

And then he'd finish with a huge cry, tossing his head
back like Mel Gibson in *Braveheart*, drawn and quartered:
"Freeeeeee-dom!" Chris was exhausted just thinking about it,
and sweat gathered on his brow.

But old Monsignor Reilly gave his usual boring diatribe
about the pope's authority and how you committed the sin of
pride if you had any ideas of your own. He compared the
mustard seed to a fetus, and said "this smallest of seeds
becomes a large *bush*, and the birds of the sky come and
dwell in its branches."

"George Bush is a mustard seed," whispered Razor.

"He has bird nests in his hair!" said Sharon. They were having a lot of fun.

"Be quiet," said Chris in a loud whisper, putting on a little show of discipline for the fellow worshipers in the surrounding pews, who were becoming visibly annoyed.

As he did every Sunday at St. Anthony's, Chris found himself longing for his favorite Australian cleric, Con McGrady from St. Philomena's. Con was a holy fool, fat and bald and red-faced, blaspheming from the pulpit like a madman. Chris hadn't been inside a church for twenty years when he started going to Father Con's, out of desperation in the insanity of his break-up from Elspeth. He'd been beaten to a pulp in the Australia Family Court, and he took comfort in Con's authority-bashing theatrics. Con loathed any hierarchy, especially the cardinals and the bishops who were "the pillows of the church."

On Chris's very first visit to St. Philomena's, Con set a teddy bear next to a crucifix and auctioned them both, one for Aboriginal land rights and the other for Filipino refugees. The following week, he started picking on Imelda Marcos as a Catholic elitist. "She put her husband in a fridge!" he declared, waving both arms in big circles like windmills. "Ferdinand Marcos was one of God's frozen people!" Con liked puns.

At St. Philomena's, Chris could pretend to have friends for a couple of hours each week, sharing coffee after mass with immigrants and intellectuals, gay couples and fallen nuns, movie stars and ex-convicts. The high point of his week came when Con invited everybody to offer each other the sign of peace, which meant shaking hands with a few people around you. Someone would always give Chris a great big hug and say "Peace be with you." Chris took it personally, and he would say it right back, as if he really meant it.

After Reilly's homage to ecclesiastical power, Chris joined the St. Anthony's queue for communion. He knew the drill - the open palms, the bow of the head, the delicate swallow - but it was just another dagger in his heart. He made the sign of the cross, and asked Jesus again to please forgive him for everything, please.

When the mass was over, Chris mowed his front lawn, put chemicals in the pool, fed the cats, and changed the fish bowl. Sean would be home from Chicago tomorrow to look after the animals and the pool while they were away.

Chris and the twins packed a tent and three sleeping bags, a mandolin, some toiletries and sunscreen, a first aid kit, a flashlight, the camera, a little food, a Swiss army knife, matches, towels, some changes of clothes, drawing paper, and a pair of binoculars. For reading materials, Chris threw in some old *Mother Jones* and *Nation* magazines, his Penguin pocket book of saints, and a legal brief he'd received from Boynkin & Sneed, an Australian law firm representing Yolanda Possum Kamara and the Aboriginal Child Care Agency.

Yolanda's son Cuffy had been removed from his home in Alice Springs at the age of nine. Now twenty-six, he was in a Florida prison cell awaiting execution for the murder of an elderly white woman. Boynkin & Sneed wanted Chris to help get the death sentence commuted and have Cuffy serve out his time in Australia. They hoped he'd do it on a *pro bono* basis because he'd been friends with Cuffy's dead father Russell, and he'd once represented Yolanda before the Victorian Equal Opportunity Commission. Chris promised to look over the brief and get back to them.

The Windstar had a small DVD player, the kind that plugs into a cigarette lighter, with two screens for the back seats. Before leaving town, Chris and the twins stopped off at Blockbuster to pick up some DVDs for their long trip. Chris was surprised to find Blockbuster closed in the middle of the day, and the overnight drop-off chute clogged up. Dozens of DVDs had been left on the sidewalk in front of the store. Nobody was around, so Chris sorted through the stack and found twenty great titles that he chucked in the Windstar.

"Isn't that dishonest, Dad?" said Sharon. She was thinking about becoming a nun, but she wasn't sure which religion she preferred, let alone which order.

"No, no," Chris assured her. "I'll return them when we get back from the Ozarks." He selected *Ace Ventura, Pet Detective* from the stack and slotted it into the DVD player. "If I don't pick them off the ground, somebody might come along and steal them." Razor was pretty happy with this explanation, and even Sharon seemed relieved from a moral dilemma.

So the twins were off to a good start. The plan now was to make it to Meramec Caverns in Missouri before nightfall, where they could camp out in a tent next to the Meramec River. Each DVD screen had its own set of headphones, so Razor and Sharon could watch *Ace Ventura* and other mind-numbers as Chris tooled down the highway listening to music on his car stereo or to the Cardinals on KMOX.

At the edge of Sand River, they got onto Highway 72 and headed for Decatur, where they took a fifty-mile shortcut down Illinois 48. Chris turned his head to the back seat and said, "This is the beginning of the hillbilly highway, kids," but Razor and Sharon couldn't hear him through their headphones. They both smiled at Chris, and Sharon gave a little wave.

Chris was wanting to explain to them that the hillbilly highway started at his birthplace in Decatur, soy-bean capital of the world and gothic city of the prairie, and finished at the tiny hamlet of Raymond where Chris's father Leonard was born. Once you got to Raymond, you could swing onto Interstate 55, and you would have saved about half an hour by not going at right angles in and out of Springfield, the Illinois state capital. Every town between Decatur and Raymond echoed with the mystic chords of Hooker memory, and Chris wished he could impart this knowledge to his youngest children.

Most of all he wanted to tell them that the single advantage of growing up in the desolate flatlands of central Illinois, the payoff for the absence of beauty, was that no matter which way you looked there were no obstacles in your way. You could walk in any direction you wanted, as far as the eye could see, and sooner or later you probably would. But how could he compete with *Ace Ventura?*

Illinois 48 wasn't really a hillbilly highway, of course, because there weren't any real hillbillies in central Illinois. You couldn't have hillbillies without hills. Genuine hillbillies came from Tennessee and West Virginia and Kentucky and the Deep South, the kind of people Steve Earle sang about. What Illinois had was hayseeds, but "hayseed highway" didn't seem right for the Hooker ancestral homeland.

After Decatur, the first little town was Boody. It only had eighty houses and a couple of grain elevators, but it connected some Hooker dots from Central Illinois all the way to Australia. Chris pulled the DVD plug out of the cigarette lighter so he could tell a little story, and Razor and Sharon were furious.

"Da-a-ad," they whined in unison, managing three distinct syllables.

"I wanted you to have a look at Boody," said Chris. He started rambling on about a woman he knew with the unlikely name of Memory Pistorius. Razor and Sharon scrunched down in their seats, folded their arms, and stuck out their lower lips.

"Look over there," he said, pointing south of the highway as they came to the outskirts of Boody. "I can see a few Pistorius names on those tombstones." He told the twins how he'd met Memory Pistorius on his very first day in Australia, back in 1976, and by a remarkable coincidence she'd been born in the same hospital, St. Mary's in Decatur, on the very same day as Chris.

"She was an artist," he said. "Isn't that amazing? It's as if we were twins."

"Amazing, Dad," said Sharon. "Now will you *please* plug the DVD back in?"

Chris had so much more to say about Memory Pistorius and the role of destiny in his life, but he gave in and reconnected the cord. Razor grumbled because now they had to start all over and fast-forward to where *Ace Ventura* had been, but soon the twins were happy again, laughing along with Jim Carrey and the funny animals on their screens.

The Cardinals' baseball game was due to start in fifteen minutes, so Chris decided to listen for a while to an old Ricky Skaggs CD. "Bury me beneath the willow," he sang along as Boody disappeared in his rearview mirror.

The next town was called Blue Mound, population 1200, but it wasn't blue and there wasn't a mound in sight. A road-sign on the outskirts boasted that a local girl named Alissa had won the state shot put title for seventh graders.

In the 1930s, this little place was known for its dance halls. Right there on a Main Street dance floor, Chris's young parents, the same boy and girl in those innocent photographs in Carol's house, cooked up the idea of having a child. They even gave him a name, Christian Leonard Hooker if he were a boy, Jolene Alice if it turned out to be a girl. Chris liked to think he was immaculately conceived in that Blue Mound dance hall, even if the messy details took place when Leonard came back from the war.

This being a Sunday, all the Blue Mound shops were closed, but a window sign in Old English script caught Chris's eye: "McFarland Law Office."

Chris *knew* Tim McFarland. They'd been best friends in law school, back-row boys all three years, taking turns catnapping as the other took notes. McFarland still held the law school's pre-Atkins flatus decibel record, executed in Lecture Hall A and heroically ignored by Professor Emeritus Irving Stone. And now McFarland had settled into small-town respectability, beating traffic tickets and drafting wills for farmers. Chris had heard he was a millionaire several times over.

When Chris reached the village of Stonington, population 960, latitude 39.64 north, longitude -89.192 west, he began a stretch of hillbilly highway known (to him) as the vale of dead grandmothers. Leonard's mother lived the last years of her life here, and died. Down the road in Taylorville, Alma Ruth's mother did the same. Chris pulled the plug on the DVD again, and turned off Ricky Skaggs.

"My grandmother used to live in that house," he said, pointing across the tracks as Razor and Sharon scowled. The little grey house was darkened by the enormous shadows of the Stonington Cooperative Grain Company's elevators. Razor and Sharon knew nothing of their great-grandparents. Leonard and Alma Ruth were as far back in time as they cared to go, their Adam and Eve, and Chris was either Abel or Cain, depending on their moods. Sharon braced herself for another boring family story, and decided her best strategy was to play along.

"Which grandmother, dad?" she asked. Razor just sat there. This time would pass, if only he waited. He was used to Sharon taking over for them at times like this, from as far back as he could remember. When they first started talking, neither Razor nor Sharon had figured out that they were actually two different people. Sharon used to introduce herself to strangers as SharonandRazor.

"Alice Bloom Hooker," said Chris. "My dad's mother. If it wasn't for her, you two wouldn't be going to St. Anthony's." This was true. Alice was the only papist in the family tree. Take away Alice, and you took away Leonard's sly deals with the Tireless Watcher. Take away Alice, and you took away Chris's beads.

Chris pulled over to the side of the road and told the twins how the Blooms worked their way from Boston to the rich farmlands of central Illinois, where little Alice suffered a bad fall from a horse in nearby Morrisonville. She was nursed back to health by a local farm boy named Phineas Quimby Hooker, a magnetic healer and Christian Scientist who became her first husband. And P.Q. begat Leonard, and Leonard begat Chris.

"P.Q. was your great-grandfather," said Chris. "The last time I saw Alice was thirty years ago, on my way to Australia. Your grandpa was driving me to the St. Louis airport. Alice took me to that little café right across the street for a piece of cherry pie." Razor and Sharon looked across the highway at the Christian County Diner. "She gave me a beautiful picture book of monarch butterflies."

Chris had finished his law degree a month before that first trip to Australia, and Leonard's transportation to St. Louis had come with a price. He wanted Chris to use his new skills to settle a few scores on his way out of town.

Poor Alice had shrunk to five feet tall, and wore her hair in a nervous blue Afro. Her second husband Bottomley, Leonard's stepfather, had died a month earlier, and Leonard wanted his due out of Bottomley's estate. His plan was to hold a family conference in Alice's little grey Stonington house, with his sister Sarah and his brother Jack. His hidden agenda was to put Alice in a clean little home as her three kids divided up her loot. As the eldest son, Leonard planned on getting the lion's share, to make up for everything he'd missed throughout his life.

Jack didn't like the sound of this and said so. "She's standing right there in the kitchen!" he shouted at Leonard. "How can you talk like that about your own mother?" But Leonard was on a roll. He wanted his cut, and he wanted Chris to get it for him.

During a break in the negotiations he whispered to Chris, "You're my lawyer now." He showed Chris a piece of paper listing shares of stock in Santos, an Australian oil company. "This may be worth a fortune," he said.

Chris started to get the shakes, so Alice took him across Highway 48 to the Christian County Diner for the cherry pie. As she handed him the butterfly book, she said, "Here Chris, you can look at this on the plane." Chris remembered picking at his cherry pie with a white plastic fork as Alice told him about the journey of the monarchs.

"They start up by the Great Lakes," she said, "as tiny caterpillars. In late summer, after they've become butterflies, they fly south for thousands of miles to a place they've never seen, coming to rest in the Oyamel fir trees in the forests of Mexico." Those were the last words Alice ever said to Chris. He thumbed through the book as Alice finished her pie. Scientists had been studying the monarchs' flight, trying to figure out how they could find their way to a Mexican forest when none of their ancestors had lived long enough to tell them.

Nothing came of Leonard's conniving. He was out-voted by Jack, Sarah, and Alice, as Chris sat uselessly in the living room watching Walter Cronkite on TV. Leonard pouted all the way to St. Louis, but Chris found a great southern Illinois radio station playing non-stop Stanley Brothers.

A couple of months later, in his office at the Melbourne University Law School, Chris got a telegram from Leonard saying Alice had up and died. At last Leonard would get his one-third share of Bottomley's property, and maybe more. Chris re-opened Alice's book on the monarchs, read how they ate their old skin each time they molted, how after the final molt they formed a jade-green chrysalis studded with gold, where they stayed perfectly still inside as they morphed into butterflies for their mysterious flight to the fir trees of Mexico. Alice Bloom Hooker's funeral was the first of many Chris didn't attend.

Razor was getting restless in the back seat, so Chris tapped his turn-signal and got back onto 48. As he glanced again at the Christian County Diner, he remembered another white plastic fork, a long time ago, in Cincinnati, Ohio. Chris was seventeen years old. There he was, with Leonard in an Italian restaurant with red spaghetti sauce splattered all over the white stucco walls. Chris wondered if it was blood. Why were they there? They ate their pasta with white plastic forks, over a green-and-white checkerboard tablecloth.

Leonard said they were in Cincinnati so they could get to know each other a little better. That afternoon they went to old Crosley Field for a Reds-Dodgers game, which made no sense because neither of them cared about the Reds or the Dodgers.

"Can you plug the DVD back in, Dad?" said Razor. He was a good boy. He wanted to watch his movie.

"Sure," said Chris.

After that Reds-Dodgers game, Leonard took Chris to visit a wrinkled old lady, Leonard's Aunt Thelma, in a sad little Cincinnati apartment. Chris remembered dark original paintings in golden frames, overstuffed loveseats and polished wooden tables. Thelma wore a long black dress and lots of heavy jewelry. Chris imagined this was what the inside of an upmarket brothel looked like, with really old guys for clients. As the Windstar passed a sign that read "Now leaving Stonington - please come again," Chris's white plastic forks connected. Leonard had been working old Thelma for her Cincinnati millions, another one of his schemes to make everything right. Young Chris was just along as a prop. Why hadn't he thought of this before?

Up the road was Taylorville, the half-way point on the hillbilly highway. As they came to the edge of town, Razor said, "I'll bet you've got some more dumb stories, Dad." He was trying to be sarcastic, but he wasn't very good at it yet. Chris just laughed, and this time he didn't make the twins take off their headphones.

He took a little detour off 48 to drive past the final home of Fairy Belle Fanke, Alma Ruth's mother. There was a young kid sitting on the front porch with an electric guitar plugged into a Pignose amp. He waved, and Chris waved back, then circled around to the rear alley where the monkey used to be, in the cage outside the tavern where Chris would go in the back door to buy Fairy Belle's Camel cigarettes.

As he continued past her old back yard, he was pretty sure he could still find the treasure of Mexican coins he'd buried under the swing-set, but he wasn't about to start digging in some stranger's yard. Whoever owned the property now had the treasure. He pictured the inside of Fairy Belle's house, the kitchen where she made her chicken dumplings, the living room where she earned her money looking after the ancient invalid Marcella Gottlieb.

Back in Sand River, Chris had an accordion file containing every letter Alma Ruth had ever written to him. His favorite was an aerogram she'd sent to Australia exactly two months after the death of Alice Bloom Hooker, announcing that Fairy Belle Fanke had joined Alice in heaven. Alma Ruth had written a title next to the address on the aerogram - "A Little Sad News":

Mama had a stroke on her birthday, May 9th, as I walked into her room at the lodge. Leonard and Jeff and Carol came on Saturday evening. She knew them and was happy to see them. Jeff and Carol went back to Sand River in my car on Sunday, and Leonard and I went back later. I made arrangements for a substitute teacher to take my place, and I returned to the lodge on Monday. Mama was not able to speak, but could nod yes and no to my questions. I stayed with her, fed her, combed her hair, but at 5:00 Monday she closed her eyes and they remained closed. I left the lodge around 8:00.

Tuesday I went back. It was sad to look at her - no speech, eyes closed, and left side paralyzed. The doctor came in and said to me that she was very bad. He put her on oxygen and glucose. We had the agreement that life would not be prolonged by artificial means, as Mama talked to me many times about that. Her breathing was so labored.

Wednesday she was the same. I talked to her, as the nurses were sure she was aware I was there. They say hearing becomes very acute with stroke patients.

Thursday the doctor said it was only a matter of time. The glucose was removed from her vein and she received nourishment through her foot instead.

Friday I was with her all day. Talked over old times. I know she heard me as her eyelids flickered when I said different things. On Friday the glucose was removed altogether and I nearly died but I didn't let Mama know I cried. Friday afternoon the

most peaceful look came upon her face. I kept
cloths on her forehead as her temperature was
high, and I put make-up on her and combed her
hair and she was beautiful. Friday evening with
one quick gasp she was gone. So peaceful and no
more laboring to exist. She did look lovely.

Chris read this aerogram in his law school office at
Melbourne University, then tucked it in a drawer and prepared for torts class. What else could he do?

On his way out of Taylorville, Chris drove around the
town square, past the old movie theater where he'd worn his
James Dean jacket to the grand opening of *Love Me Tender.*
He'd screamed with the other kids as Elvis appeared in the
corner of the screen, pushing a plow behind a mule.

Next came the village of Palmer, where Alma Ruth taught
kindergarten in 1943 as Leonard ducked kamikazes in the
South Pacific. Chris was about to stop the DVD again so the
twins could look at her old brick schoolhouse, but it was torn
down. Razor and Sharon were so relieved.

The Hooker Mecca of Morrisonville was minutes away,
where all four of Chris's grandparents, and Leonard and Alma
Ruth, were alive and well in the first half of the twentieth century. Chris concocted a fantasy that they were all Indians, a
confederated tribe of Hookers and Fankes, Quimbys and
Bekyeshovas, and it wasn't too late to get Razor and Sharon
enrolled. But just as this childish thought was flashing through
his mind, at an intersection surrounded by fields of July corn,
Chris came upon *another* upturned car with its wheels spinning, the same clouds of dust, the same eerie silence. He did a
quick calculation. There was no plane to catch, no wife to
keep secrets from. The Cardinals and Dodgers were scoreless
on the radio. Chris and the twins didn't have to be at the
Meramec Caverns campsite until dusk.

Razor and Sharon took off their headphones and gawked
at the wreck. "Look Dad!" said Razor. "Another one!" They
were wondering what Chris was going to do.

In his hurried calculus, Chris figured this must be something more than a mere car crash. "This is for you," the Tireless Watcher seemed to be saying, "pontificating about the Holy Spirit and Cinderella and burning vans and your pathetic soul. Well, here's another test." In his confusion, Chris thought he actually *heard* these words, and he looked at Dopey the Dwarf to see if his lips were moving. Maybe this car crash *was* a sign. Chris sighed, pulled the Windstar over to the shoulder, patted Dopey on the head for good luck, and ran across the median.

He was first on the scene, just ahead of two other drivers who'd pulled over. A very large woman was trapped beneath her car, coughing up blood, with a little girl about nine years old moaning next to her. The only thing saving the little girl from being squashed was her mother's fat. Another woman, blonde and slightly less chubby, was sprawled out face-down on the highway with a second little girl. Chris had to step over these two to get to the car.

Chris and the other guys did a one-two-three and heave-hoed the car off the fat lady. She screamed and tried to sit up, but Chris told her to lie still. She rested with her elbow on the pavement, blood pouring from her nose and head. "Where are my babies," she gurgled.

"They're ok," said Chris. The blonde woman got up and started walking around, saying over and over, "Why didn't he stop?" The little girl who'd been under the car seemed to have a broken arm and leg, but the other one was all right. She just sat there in a Buddha position on the highway, chanting "Ommmmm."

Chris went to the Windstar for a couple of blankets, and had the twins come back with him to the crash site. He put one of the blankets under the fat woman's elbow, and another around the broken girl. "Just lie still," he said.

He had Razor and Sharon talk to the young ones. "That's good," he said. "Keep them talking. Ask them about their school." Razor started waffling on about indoor soccer and how he once made thirteen goals in a single game, and

Sharon made up a story about a Japanese dancer named Rose who got a big splinter in her foot and had to miss a school performance.

One of the other drivers called 911 on a cell phone. Chris walked over to the intersection, where a boy was sitting in the passenger seat of a banged-up white Chevy. "Where's the driver?" Chris asked. The boy pointed to the corn. "He ran in there after the accident," he said, "and then across that field." Behind the cornfields was a fence-sign advertising the open area as the "Mid-America Sky Jump."

Chris heard sirens coming from the west, and walked back to the wreck. The broken girl was telling Razor her name was Sydney ("just like O.J. Simpson's daughter," said Razor) and she was eight years old and went to Memorial school in Taylorville. Her little sister Marigold was six.

Chris hung around for a while as the paramedics loaded the fat lady onto a stretcher and into the ambulance. It took six of them. They were worried that she had internal injuries, which got Chris to thinking about Princess Diana and the crash in France. He'd heard the news on the radio as he drove through the Wombat Forest on his way home from the Ballarat courthouse. Chris was all upset that day even before he heard about Diana, because Kazzie was in Melbourne and Chris had taken Razor with him to court, a bad idea, and Razor had screwed up the combination lock on Chris's briefcase and Chris couldn't get it to open. He had to ask the magistrate for an adjournment, and lost his $400 fee. Then on the way out of the courthouse, Razor slipped his little fingers behind the fire alarm's glass cover and pressed the button, causing the courtroom and the police station to be evacuated. Judges and police and lawyers and criminals were standing on the street talking buddy-buddy as fire trucks and emergency vehicles screeched around the corner. Chris called Kazzie on his cell phone, and held it high above his head in the chilly Ballarat air.

"Listen to what your son has done," he said, as the sirens wailed and firefighters scrambled into the courthouse with axes and ladders. Kazzie was impressed with Razor's power.

"Just think," she said, "he's only four years old."

Another paramedic was putting inflatable splints on Sydney's arm and leg as Razor provided her with a detailed summary of the relationship between Vincent Van Gogh and Paul Gauguin. The police were combing the cornfields looking for the runaway driver.

"He must have been on drugs," Chris heard one of them say. A cop took Chris's statement, which didn't amount to much. Chris started feeling useless, so he and the twins hopped across the median and back into the Windstar. As soon as he got the go-ahead, they moved west again towards the Ozarks.

When they finally got to Morrisonville, Chris pulled into a Casey's gas station for some snacks. The kids loaded up on nuts and juices and a couple of *Archie* comics. Chris found some Atkins chocolate peanut butter bars and bought a whole box for $29.00.

"Big wreck up the road," he said to the cashier.

"Yeah," she said, "we saw the police cars go by. Anybody dead?"

"Not yet," said Chris, "but there's a lady and a little girl in pretty bad shape."

The cashier gave Chris the once-over. "Don't I know you?" she said.

"I don't think so," said Chris. "I'm not from around here."

She kept eyeballing him. "You look like a Hooker," she said. "There's lots of Hookers around Morrisonville."

Chris thought he heard a cock crow, and said "Well, I'm not one of them."

Razor tugged at Chris's sleeve and whispered, "That's a lie, Dad. We're all Hookers." The cashier laughed.

"I thought so," she said. "You look just like Leonard. I bet he's your dad."

"No way," said Chris. He scooped up his change from the counter and started to grab his Atkins bars.

"Paper or plastic, Mr. Hooker?" said the cashier.

"Paper," said Chris grimly.

"Your dad was quite an athlete," she said. "Everybody around here remembers Leonard. You should be proud."

As Chris walked out the door, he saw a young guy pumping gas, a spitting image of his cousin David Meisenheimer, except that was impossible because David was sixty years old now. Chris hadn't seen him in four decades. But there he was, pumping gas at Casey's, and he hadn't aged a day. Jesus, thought Chris, must be a grandson, still hanging around Morrisonville. The circularity of life was circling Chris's wagons, and the only escape was the road. "Grab your food, kids," he said, and they hurried back to the Windstar.

Mike Shannon was still on KMOX, telling Chris that the Cardinals were up on the Dodgers 7 to 4, and Albert Pujols had hit his one hundredth career home run. Woody Williams was on the mound going for win number thirteen, so Chris felt pretty good. A victory today would move the Cards back within three games of the Astros. As bad as they'd been this season, they might still win the National League Central. He turned off the radio and asked the twins if they wanted a guided tour of Mecca.

"There's nothing here, Dad," said Sharon, but she knew it was hopeless.

"Except for the grain elevators," said Razor. "They're really exciting."

Chris ignored them and started pretending to be a tour guide. He drove past the house where Alma Ruth and her parents used to live, a two-storey place with a porch swing and a storm cellar and a big oak tree in the front yard. A block away was Leonard's childhood home, where P.Q. showed up drunk night after night as Leonard and Jack and Sarah lay in their bedrooms making deals with Jesus if only P.Q. would please stop shouting, please.

Chris circled back to the Loaded Dog Tavern, still standing, where P.Q. bought drinks with money the Hookers didn't have, and the old Quimby mansion on the edge of town, surrounded by thousands of acres of Illinois corn.

"Wow, look at that place," said Razor, impressed. "It's like a castle." Sharon wasn't sure she liked it, because it might be haunted. And in a way it was, because it used to belong to the widow Margaret Quimby, P.Q.'s mother. She decided to cut P.Q.'s kids out of her will because Alice Bloom had turned them into papists. Poor old Leonard - if it hadn't been for Margaret Quimby, he could have been a millionaire.

Chris drove out to the Morrisonville cemetery so the twins could see "Hooker" on some old tombstones. It was a nice spot, on a little hill with lots of trees. If you were alive, you could see for miles.

All the Blooms, including Alice, were on the Catholic side. P.Q. was all by himself except for a gaggle of Quimbys and Hookers and other Christian Scientists. The Fankes and Bekyeshovas were mixed in together with miscellaneous Protestants. Razor and Sharon had a lot of DNA in that graveyard.

Razor climbed to the top of the tombstone of one Henry Gowin Hooker, 1878 - 1937, and threatened to leap, which was ironic because old Henry had jumped off the roof of the Allerton Hotel in Chicago, holding hands with his girlfriend Roma all the way down to Michigan Avenue. Razor didn't know that, but he soared off Henry's tombstone anyway and lay there on the ground pretending to be dead.

Sharon was next door to Henry, wondering why Catherine Bekyeshova, 1889 - 1921, was only thirty-two when she died.

"She had a fiance named Hector Prinn, a cornet player," Chris told her. "When he jilted her, Catherine swallowed a jar full of acid. It burned a hole right through her neck."

Sharon put her hands up to her throat and stepped back from the grave. "Yuck. Why would she do something like that?" She was horrified.

Chris passed along the family legend that Catherine went deaf after her engagement, and Hector Prinn didn't want a dummy for a wife.

"Her little brother Grigori found her lying on her bed. He

was my grandfather. That's him right over there." Razor came back to life and joined Chris and Sharon, holding hands at the foot of Grigori Bekyeshova's grave.

Fairy Belle Fanke was lying next door to Grigori even though they were divorced and hated each other for the last fifty years of their lives. Fairy Belle's tombstone had the year of her death, but not a birth year, and Razor wanted to know why.

"She didn't want anyone to know how old she was," Chris sighed, and it was true.

Alma Ruth's parents were in a jazz band until Grigori went deaf like Catherine and all the other Bekyeshovas. He tried to make a living cutting hair, but being married to the town barber wasn't the life for Fairy Belle. Now they just looked like a happy couple spending eternity together.

Sharon went back to the car to get a few slices of bread, which she broke into sacramental crumbs and sprinkled over her great-grandparents.

"What in the hell are you doing, Sharon Mae?" said Chris.

Sharon said Alma Ruth had told her to bring some bread crumbs whenever she visited these graves, because Fairy Belle liked birds. And sure enough, a flock of sparrows came out of the oaks right on cue and ate the Bekyeshovas' crumbs.

As they got back in the Windstar, Chris noticed something new in the Morrisonville Cemetery. Leonard and Alma Ruth had pre-purchased their tombstones, right across the lane from Grigori and Fairy Belle. Leonard had spent a few extra bucks to have a bat and ball etched above his name; Alma Ruth had a deck of cards. Their headstones were waiting for them, with a gap on each for the death-year to be chiseled in.

That was enough of Morrisonville. The twins were itching to get to their new DVD, *Happy Gilmore,* and Razor already had *Happy* in the machine. Chris drove on to Harvel and Raymond, young Leonard's home towns before moving to Morrisonville. They passed the Harvel baseball diamond where Leonard once hit a fastball over the top of the giant burr oak behind the cyclone fence in center field. According to Leonard, it was the longest ball ever hit in Montgomery County, and Chris believed him.

As a boy, Leonard would ride Shank's mare along the train tracks from Harvel to Raymond just to play weekend ball games. There were elms every fifty feet or so on both sides of the hillbilly highway in those days, but they'd all been killed off by the Dutch elm disease. For reasons he couldn't explain, the empty places where the elms used to be made Chris feel like weeping. He came to the end of the hillbilly highway and turned onto Interstate 55 to St. Louis, with Mike Shannon still on the radio and *Happy Gilmore* rolling along merrily on the DVD. But Chris didn't weep. He hadn't shed a tear in years.

A KMOX news bulletin at the top of the hour reported four tornadoes in southern Nebraska and northern Kansas. One man had died in the wreckage of a flattened workshop in Deshler, Nebraska. Seven others were injured, and four homes were flattened. A hailstone that fell in Aurora, near Grand Island, Nebraska, was the size of a cantaloupe, measuring six and one-half inches in diameter. This was a new Nebraska record, and nearly broke the national record of six and five-eighths inches, set in Coffeyville, Kansas, in 1970. The storm system was moving east, according to the radio.

"Right at us," said Chris, but no one was listening.

On the outskirts of St. Louis they passed the Cahokia Mounds, off to the left of 55. "That used to be the City of the Sun-God," said Chris. Razor thought he said "Son of God," and got his wires crossed. "Jesus never came to America, Dad," he said.

Chris sighed. Too much Catholic education. "Sun, son. The sun in the sky. Around a thousand years ago, twenty thousand Indians lived over there. This was a big city, set up in rows around open plazas, kind of like Assisi."

This made sense to Razor and Sharon, because Chris and Kazzie had taken them on a trip to Assisi the year before, although Chris didn't call it a "trip." He called it a pilgrimage. Chris told Kazzie he felt "drawn" to Assisi, because he'd once attended St. Francis grade school in Quincy, Illinois.

The images of Francis in his sandals and brown robes had been etched deeply into Chris's impressionable mind. Kazzie was more interested in Rome and Florence, but she agreed to humor Chris with Assisi, on one condition: "Just promise me," she said, "that you won't take off your clothes in the Piazza del Comune." She'd seen the paintings of Francis handing his stylish apparel to the bishop. Chris agreed, and kept his promise.

For the most part, he behaved himself throughout Italy, although he insisted that they visit as many stigmatic shrines as possible. "Francis wasn't the only one," he said to Kazzie on the train back to Rome. He had everyone go with him to the National Gallery in Siena to see Beccafumi's painting of St. Catherine receiving the wounds of the crucifixion, then on the day before their flight home he made the whole family sit out in the summer sun in St. Peter's Square for the canonization of Padre Pio of Pietrelcina, another stigmatic. The kids were so bored, and the metal folding chairs were so hot and uncomfortable. In the Sistine Chapel afterwards, all Kazzie wanted to do was lie on her back and gaze at Michelangelo, but Chris kept pestering her to look at a couple of reddish spots on his palms.

"No Chris," she said patiently. "You don't have it." And sure enough, the marks disappeared before they got to the airport.

Sharon and Razor were so taken with Cahokia Mounds that they'd turned off the DVD player, which gave Chris a chance to parent. "These were the flood plains of the Mississippi," he said with authority, "with lots of plant and animal life. The Indians even cultivated crops outside the city."

This was all true. Chris had been an Indian history buff since his years on the Cheyenne River Sioux Reservation in South Dakota. Now he was teaching "Indigenous People and the Law" at Sand River College, a survey course comparing the native peoples of Australia, Canada, and the USA. It was a frustrating subject for his students, because none of the ancient laws was written down. So every year someone would challenge Chris in the first class.

"Those are just customs, not laws," they'd say, usually with a knowing smirk. And every year Chris would reply with the same *non sequiter* on the difference between being and gaining, lumping Marxism and capitalism together in the European tradition of de-spiritualizing the universe.

"Gaining is a material act," he'd say slowly, so they could take notes. "Being is a spiritual proposition." The students wrote down everything Chris said, in case it might show up on a test.

"What happened to the Indians?" Sharon wanted to know, looking out the back window at the Cahokia Mounds. Chris was about to answer when Razor shouted "There's the Arch!"

The St. Louis Arch, "the Gateway to the West," had become a Hooker family landmark. Chris and the twins had ridden to the top in the tiny elevator cars when they first arrived from Australia. Razor and Sharon had peeked out the little windows, across the Mississippi and back into Illinois, clinging to Chris because they could feel the Arch swaying in the wind.

"Look," said Chris, "there's a couple more." He pointed to the golden arches of a McDonald's hamburger joint, and a sign saying three zillion sold.

"Ha, ha," said Sharon. Chris made this same stupid joke every time they came to this spot on the outskirts of St. Louis. "Really, Dad, what happened to the Indians?"

"Nobody knows," said Chris. "They just disappeared around five hundred years ago." He told the twins the Cahokia Indians were sun-worshippers. Sun calendars had been unearthed at the City of the Sun, and if you stood in the central plaza at sunrise, as Chris did once as a kid, the street alignments would mark astronomical changes, just like the concentric circles at Stonehenge.

"Cool," said Sharon, as she thought about this. She'd been calling herself a Buddhist all through the third grade, like her big sister Jeshel, but sun-worship became an attractive option.

Sharon's interest in eastern religions started during the family's stopover in Kyoto on their flight from Australia. Chris took her photograph in front of the Golden Temple, Kinkaku-ji, catching both Sharon and her glowing reflection in the ripples of Kyo-ko Pond. He was so excited he reached for his Japanese phrase book to tell an elderly couple, "Look, she's the golden princess from the golden temple," but he got on the wrong page and said "Kurejit-to kado tskae-mass ka," which meant "do you take credit cards?" The old folks shuffled along sadly without a reply.

Razor was more literal-minded than Sharon, and wasn't impressed with sun-worship. "This is stupid," he said. "The sun's not god. It's just the sun." His idea of fun in Kyoto was break-dancing in the subways with the Japanese skaterboys, their boom-boxes echoing off the concrete walls as they spun on their heads in cheap football helmets. They wanted to adopt little Razor and keep him for a pet.

Chris and the kids crossed over the Mississippi River on the Poplar Street Bridge. "Careful," said Chris. "Make sure your seatbelts are on. We might slip off the side of the bridge." They were still young enough to fall for this stuff, over and over. West of the Arch was an empty Busch Stadium, scheduled for destruction in 2005. The Cardinals' broadcast was beaming in from Los Angeles, and as Highway 55 merged into 44 West, the Cardinals led the Dodgers 6-3 in the fifth.

By the time they got to the Meramec campground, the Cardinals had won 10-7, and both teams had combined for a Chavez Ravine record of nine home runs. Chris found a campsite and put up the tent while Razor and Sharon waded in the Meramec River. He started a fire, then walked down to join them. The shore was covered with smooth flat stones perfect for skipping, so they counted skips from one side of the Meramec to the other as daylight faded and the stars came out. Razor made one stone skip seventeen times, a Hooker family record.

After cooking dinner and toasting marshmallows around the fire, they cleaned up at a water tap, then crawled into the tent for some stories and drawing. It was good to get in there, because the mosquitoes had started to bite. Chris fancied that being in the tent was like being in a womb with his own children. He felt like a triplet.

They wanted to hear stories about the days before they were born, so he started with the little white house with the green roof. There was his dead rabbit, frozen stiff in the garage one winter morning, and little Chris hiding under his bed until Leonard talked him out in time for school. There was the turtle he bought for fifty cents from some older boys at the softball diamond across the street, until Alma Ruth found out about it and made him give it back. There were the soldiers camped in the vacant lot next to the softball diamond, and Chris riding his bicycle through their neat little rows of tents and jabbering in make-believe army-talk. And there was the rubber-tipped arrow he lost in the bushes while shooting at clouds in the sky.

Razor and Sharon had heard all these stories before, but they never got enough of them. They had some primitive need to be programmed with all things Hooker, no matter how mundane. Next they wanted to hear again about their home in the forest, and the kangaroos and cockatoos. Chris told them about the fat wallabies swimming across their pond, and the four-foot tiger snake Kazzie killed with an axe, and the koalas' mating growls as they changed eucalypts during the night; about dancing like savages around the crackling winter bonfires, deep in their Wombat Forest, as thousands of sparks shot high into the ghostly gums against the black southern sky.

He told them a new story about Leonard's visit to Australia, and how Leonard had peed out his name in the dirt of the forest under the basketball hoop, in the light of a full moon. They liked this last story best of all, and for the rest of the trip Razor peed outdoors every chance he got, sketching more elaborate designs with each effort. Sharon complained because it was hard for a girl to spell her name with pee. Whenever she tried, she looked like a hula dancer.

"I didn't even know grandpa came to Australia," she said. She and Razor were only a few months old at the time. Leonard and Alma Ruth had flown over to see their two new illegitimate grandchildren, and Chris was a nervous wreck for the whole two weeks. It started even before they arrived. Chris kept winding the kitchen clock until the springs were so tight they almost broke. His theory was that it would be bad luck for the clock to stop while his parents were there.

He did the right thing and picked them up in his jeep at the Tullamarine Airport. Except for Leonard's two years in the South Pacific, neither he nor Alma Ruth had been out of America. Just driving on the left side of the narrow two-lane roads was enough to make them crazy.

Chris stopped at a milk bar in Woodend, and the shop-keeper asked where they were from. "Sand River," said Leonard. "And Morrisonville before that," said Alma Ruth. Chris hurried them along as the shopkeeper grinned.

Somewhere in the middle of the Wombat Forest, Chris suddenly announced that they were home, but there were still two miles of gravel driveway to go. Leonard had no idea about Australian fauna other than kangaroos, so he kept a watchful eye out for lions and tigers. What in the world had become of his son?

They passed Chris's twenty-thousand gallon water tank, and the house appeared in the valley below. Seventy-two squares of mud-brick and timber, solar panels, a composting toilet, no heat except for wood-burning stoves, no drinks except rain-water. A goddam hippie commune, thought Leonard. My, oh my.

It didn't help when Kazzie came out to greet them in her wood-chopping clothes, holding a breast-feeding twin in each arm. Chee-soo and Oscar, the visitors from Korea and Finland, started jabbering away, and Leonard and Alma Ruth couldn't understand a word anyone was saying. An anorexic homeless man named Scott Free worked a hoe in the organic garden north of the house. Jennifer Juniper, a Grateful Dead groupie from California, was in the kitchen staying warm by the cast-iron stove, making hemp necklaces and marijuana cookies. She sang along to Bob Dylan's *Foot of Pride,* which was playing on the solar-powered stereo: "Say one more stupid thing to me before the final nail is driven in."

Leonard and Alma Ruth tried to be big about it. All Leonard wanted to do anyway was play golf and go to daily mass, which he could have done much more easily back in Sand River. All Alma Ruth wanted to do was clean the house and get the twins to sleep. If they finally dozed off after six hours of Bye-O-Baby-Bunting, she said to Kazzie, "Oh my, they're such good babies."

Chris kept dragging himself out of bed every morning before sunrise to take Leonard to the Trentham golf course. Par was only 69, and Leonard figured he could score in the mid-seventies to accomplish one of his last remaining goals in life, shooting his age.

Chris hated golf, and hated male-bonding even more. He and Leonard would trot around the course in about two hours, Leonard in the low eighties and Chris in the high nineties with his wooden-shafted clubs, and then they would go to morning mass.

The local priest, Father Marvic, took a shine to Leonard, as did all the priests back home in Illinois. Leonard was on the parish council at St. Anthony's, making sure the new age Catholics and their historical Jesus didn't take over the school curriculum.

Leonard's god was active, interventionist, and politically conservative. Ever since childhood, Leonard and the Tireless Watcher had been negotiating everything from basic survival to baseball games. Their deals worked, but not always exactly the way Leonard expected, and the rules of engagement were tough. You had to follow the R.O.E., or the whole thing could collapse.

Their latest arrangement concerned little Ricky, the youngest son of Chris's sister Rachel. During his first year, Ricky needed a breathing monitor just to stay alive, so Leonard prayed day and night and Ricky survived. There was cause and effect here, to Leonard's way of thinking, and he took credit for saving Ricky's life. No one could get within an arm's length of the little guy when Leonard was around.

Day after day Leonard and Chris stuck to their pattern, up at dawn, off to Trentham for eighteen holes, mass with Marvic, back home. Then Chris would go to work at the Ballarat courthouse, tired and grumpy. At night he and Kazzie would gossip about Leonard and Alma Ruth. The house smelled funny with all that American after-shave and perfume and hairspray and cheap Qantas soap. Alma Ruth and Leonard didn't like Kazzie's liberal parenting. They didn't like it that Chris made them pee on a gum tree instead of in the composting toilet. Chris tried to explain that the composting process wouldn't work if the tank was full of liquid, but this was hard for them to appreciate. And the smell. Good God.

They didn't like the solar-powered washing machine with its brown dam-water, where Chris cleaned the twins' dirty diapers. They worried that little specks of baby-poo would get on their pastel-colored Illinois clothes, so they took them to the laundromat in Daylesford.

Alma Ruth kept cleaning. At the beginning of the second week, she saw a mouse run across the floor and nearly fainted. That same afternoon Leonard found a cockroach in the sink.

"Kazzie," he said softly, "there's a roach in the sink."

Kazzie was feeling wicked and asked him "What kind of roach, Leonard?" just to see if he'd say cockroach, but he wouldn't. He just said "roach" again.

After they'd gone, Chris was sure his parents, or at least Leonard, had put a curse on the place. It had to do with their next-to-last day, which was a Sunday. Chris had decided he'd had enough mass to last the next thirty years or so, so he went to play tennis with Josh at Little Hampton. He and Josh ducked out of the house a half-hour before mass time, and it was left to Kazzie to get Leonard and Alma Ruth to church. They wouldn't drive, especially after Leonard tried the jeep on the way back from the Daylesford laundromat and took out two young gum trees, a wooden road marker and a blue-tongue lizard. There was now a big long scratch along the side of Chris's jeep, and a tail-light was broken, so Chris didn't really want Leonard to drive again. The feeling was mutual.

Kazzie loaded the twins and Kristen and Leonard and Alma Ruth into the van for what was a very big deal, this last mass in Australia. Leonard and Alma Ruth had gone overboard with the cologne and perfume for the occasion. They were wearing their Sunday-best pastel suits, and Leonard had spit-shined their shoes.

The ride to Marvic's church in Trentham took twenty minutes, and passed by the Little Hampton tennis courts. Everybody waved from the van, but Chris was trying to teach Josh how to overhead slam from mid-court, so he didn't pay any attention.

When Kazzie got to Trentham the church was closed, because Marvic traveled a circuit on Sundays from Trentham to Blackwood and Chris had misread the times. There was nothing to do but turn back.

On the way home, they passed Chris and Josh again, still practicing slams. This time, Chris flagged them down. "What's the matter?"

"We missed mass," said Leonard in a very solemn voice. "You got the times wrong." Alma Ruth was pale in the back seat, sensing a replay of some ancient Hooker ritual. Chris morphed into a twelve-year-old right before Kazzie's eyes.

When they got home, Leonard and Alma Ruth changed clothes and waited for Chris and Josh, but Chris took his time. About two hours later, he rolled up in the jeep. He'd stolen a bunch of cement pavers from the Little Hampton school, but that wasn't obvious to anyone but Kazzie. Leonard helped him unload, but he had a martyr's look on his face, and his body language told everyone that he'd been terribly wounded but was toughing it out.

"It wasn't my fault," Chris finally said.

"I don't want to talk about it," said Leonard. "Just forget

it." Alma Ruth lurked near a stack of mud-bricks in the shadows of the verandah, like a frightened animal.

"It was *your* fault," said Chris. "You're the one who wanted to go to mass. You should have checked the schedules." He pronounced it "shed-yules," like an Australian, which made Leonard even madder. He let one of the stolen pavers slip from his hands, and it shattered into three big pieces. Leonard looked at Chris with a whole lot of hatred.

"I haven't missed Sunday Mass in fifty years," he said. "All you had to do was tell me the right time, and I would have crawled to get there." He sat down and began rubbing his thighs back and forth, back and forth. He looked at Chris out of the corner of his eye like one of those nasty seagulls in Melbourne's Botanical Gardens, staking out its territory for a breadcrumb.

Nothing more was said. Chris went into the house and packed his bag, and he and Josh drove to Melbourne for the night. Alma Ruth ran up to the jeep as it passed under the basketball hoop and said, "I'm sorry we spoiled your summer." She was crying. This was the last Chris saw of his parents on their Australian vacation.

The next day Kazzie took Leonard and Alma Ruth to Tullamarine for their flight back to Illinois. Alma Ruth kept looking around for Chris, but he didn't show. Leonard just had to get to the airport McDonald's for a cup of coffee and two Big Macs to satisfy his two-week hunger for caffeine and red meat.

"You know, Kazzie," he said, "they have McDonald's all over the world now." For a moment it looked as if he would cry, either from pride in McDonald's or something else. He was wearing the black Daylesford Returned Servicemen's League shirt Chris had bought for him. He and Alma Ruth exchanged a few *sotto voce* insults that Kazzie couldn't catch.

Leonard was nervous that they might miss their plane, so he wanted to go through security about two hours ahead of time. Alma Ruth protested a little, because she wanted to stay with the twins until the last minute, but she gave in and they walked to the international boarding area. Kazzie waved goodbye.

A few weeks later, as Chris tried to type a legal memorandum on his Smith-Corona, the A key kept getting stuck. Chris decided that Leonard had left a curse. He made Kazzie come in to look at the electric typewriter. This sticking A key was just an example.

"See," he said. "I type any word with an A, and the A's run right across the page." He showed Kazzie. She could see that it was true. Chris pried underneath the keys with his index fingernail, but nothing helped. Kazzie tried to explain that the Smith-Corona was old, and if they just got a few more solar panels they could run a computer, but she was missing the point. Finally Chris gave up on the A key and sat back in his chair.

"There was this Russian archbishop," he said, wadding up a sheet of paper full of A's. "I read his book. When he was about my age, in 1927, Jesus came and sat across the table from him. He said he never had any doubts about the resurrection after that." Kazzie was wondering what this had to do with anything, and wishing that Jesus would visit Chris and fix his stupid typewriter.

There in the tent at the Meramec campground, Razor and Sharon fell asleep somewhere between the Tullamarine airport and the archbishop. As Chris drifted off next to them, saying the glorious mysteries of the rosary, it occurred to him that this Sunday had been one of the happiest days of his life.

MONDAY: MORE JOYFUL MYSTERIES

*Among all my patients in the second half of life, that
is to say over thirty-five, there has not been one
whose problem in the last resort was not that of finding
a religious outlook on life. It is safe to say that every one
of them fell ill because he had lost that which the religions
of every age have given to their followers, and none
of them has been really healed who did not regain his
religious outlook.*

Carl Jung, *Modern Man in Search of a Soul*

*If you had to you could go right back to Okaw City to the
west side of the tracks and walk right through your old paper
route again and not miss a house. Only 35 subscribers,
because the Chicago Daily News wasn't all that popular
because people liked the Sand River papers better because
they had more local area news and sports, or the Tribune
because it was more conservative. In the winter old Grigori
Bekyeshova your deaf grandfather would drive you around
the route in his 1953 Chevy with all of his advertising wares
in the back seat, pencils and matchbooks and combs and calendars. He'd pull up before the houses and stop, and you'd
jump out and throw the paper on the porches, but once in a
while your aim was bad and you broke a couple of windows,
and once you hit the side of a mobile home thunk and the
man came out and yelled at you and you deserved it because
of your rotten aim.*

*And Grigori lived with your family in this little room
where he kept his stuff because he had no other family who
could take him in and he and Leonard fought all the time*

because of Alma Ruth and who was she most loyal to and there was always tension in the house and you were in the middle of it pulled three ways, but at night you'd tune into WLS radio from way up in Chicago and you'd listen to Dick Biondi and he would make you laugh and play the best songs and once he even read a poem you'd sent in about a duck and it was broadcast for thousands of miles your poem. And Grigori who couldn't hear a word would cut your hair every month or so just like he used to do for a living in Morrisonville when Alma Ruth was small but you never liked his haircuts because he cut it old man style like Harry Truman and made you look stupid and you got made fun of at school, so you always got upset with him as he swept your hair from the floor and brushed the back of your neck with a soft-bristled handbroom. One summer day he called you into his room and said "Most of life is just plain sad," and you got mad at him for that because what was the point of thinking things were sad why not just be happy? And you got your baseball glove and bat and ball and went off to Halloway Park to play all day long with the other boys from the north end and when you got thirsty you'd cup your hands under the tap and the cool Okaw City water would come into your palms like a sacrament and make you feel like nothing could ever be this good again.

* * * * * * * *

In the morning Chris stirred the campfire and cooked up some breakfast. He and the kids walked along the river to the Meramec Caverns. They joined the first Monday morning tour, led by a guide whose nameplate read "Sheila Crosley." Even though the Meramec Caverns were privately-owned, Sheila wore a Smoky the Bear outfit to look official.

"Look Dad," said Razor, "Jesse James." He pointed to an assortment of outlaw posters in the gift shop. Jesse James and his gang used to hide out between robberies in the Meramec Caverns. "Maybe we can find some old bones or buried treasure."

They followed Sheila and the other tourists into the grand ballroom. Sheila said this used to be a popular dance venue before the Second World War. Razor started annoying everybody by shining a pocket laser light off the stalactites to see if he could make them sparkle. Chris and Sharon loved it, but the rest of the tourists growled to Sheila that it was spoiling the serenity of the cave, so she took the laser away from Razor. Immediately, he started doing fantastic cartwheels up and down the path, which perturbed everyone even more, so Sheila gave him back the laser just to keep him quiet.

The "climax" of the tour, according to Sheila, was the Stage Curtain. "It's seventy million years old," she said, "and the largest single cave formation in the world!" Sheila invited the tourists to be seated on the wooden benches as she dimmed the cave's electric lights and switched on a recording of Kate Smith singing "God Bless America." Red, white and blue strobe lights darted over enormous stalactites and stalagmites. Sheila asked the tourists to bow their heads in memory of all those who had died in the September 11th terrorist attacks. A couple of NASCAR dads actually stood up in this dumb cave and put their hands over their hearts, but Razor spoiled the show by shining his laser at their privates. Sharon sang louder than anyone, doing a melodramatic Kate Smith imitation and going down on one knee with her arms outstretched as she belted out "my home, sweet hooooooomc." Chris applauded loudly at the end, but nobody else did.

When the tour was over, they walked back to the campsite and packed up their tent and sleeping bags. On the short drive through the trees and back to the highway, Chris spotted a grotty hitch-hiker who'd been set up next to them during the night. He had an Australian flag on his backpack, so Chris stopped to offer him a ride. He helped the guy with his pack, and invited him to sit in the front of the Windstar.

"I'm Ian McCallum," said the Australian, thrusting out his right hand like a Bowie knife. Chris offered his usual limp-wristed handshake, and Ian squeezed till it hurt. In Australia, firm handshakes were a sign of character, especially for men. Chris actually heard some of his fingers crackle in Ian's grasp.

"Christian Hooker," said Chris, grimacing. "Quite a grip there, Ian. Where you from?"

Ian McCallum was from Tasmania, just bumming around America looking for adventure. "It's winter back home," he said. "Nice to be someplace warm." Chris detected the smell of marijuana coming from his Nirvana-style shirt.

"I know," Chris nodded. "My wife and three of our kids are in Australia right now." They talked Australian politics for a while, finding common ground in their loathing for Australian prime minister John Howard.

"A real drongo," said Ian. "A fuckwit."

"He's right up Bush's ass," said Chris, hissing out the S to sound macho. "What in the world is Australia doing support-ing Bush? All they're doing is making themselves a soft target for Indonesian terrorists." They went on like this for half an hour, seeing who could say the most spiteful things about George W. Bush and John Howard.

When they reached the Rolla turnoff, Ian said he was meeting some Cambodian friends at the University of Missouri campus, so Chris dropped him off at a Starbucks.

"Look after yourself," said Chris, keeping his sore hand to himself. "It's not very safe hitch-hiking in America. Too many nuts around."

Ian smiled and said he knew that. He reached under his shirt and pulled out a silver-and-black Walther PPK, outfitted with a metal coathanger that held it in his pants. He handed it to Chris with both hands, like a peace pipe. Razor and Sharon took off their headphones and gaped over the front seats at the gun.

Chris held the Walther between his right thumb and index finger and kept his left hand on the steering wheel. "Interarms, Alexandria, Virginia" was written on the barrel, and Chris wondered if it was loaded. He passed it back to Ian, trying to look impressed in a manly sort of way. "Some gun," he said.

Ian slipped the Walther behind his zipper, patting the front of his jeans when it was back where it belonged. It made a nice bulge. "I'm ready for them," grinned Ian McCallum, and with a little wave he walked into Starbucks.

After he disappeared, Chris gave a big sigh of relief. "I never should have picked him up," he told the twins. "I never pick up hitch-hikers." Ian McCallum's gun had unnerved him.

"He was nice," said Sharon. "I like Australians."

"Yeah, Dad," said Razor. "He wasn't going to hurt us."

"You never know," said Chris. "It's dangerous picking up hitch-hikers. I only picked him up because of his Australian flag, and I shouldn't have."

He turned and made Razor and Sharon look at him. "Don't ever do it," he said. "Promise me."

"We promise, Dad," they said in unison. Then they smiled at each other the way they always did whenever Chris gave advice.

The last time Chris had picked up a hitch-hiker was twenty years ago, in his old Ford pick-up on Highway 212 crossing the Cheyenne River Sioux Reservation, somewhere between Eagle Butte and Dupree. A Lakota woman he'd seen before at the Eagle Butte bowling alley had her thumb pointed west.

Chris stopped for not altogether altruistic reasons. He tried to strike up a conversation, but she was not in a talkative mood. Chris bided his time with a Steely Dan cassette, *Gaucho*, singing along from Faith to Howes, where he turned onto Highway 34 for the Black Hills. As they passed an inactive volcano in the shape of a sleeping bear, Chris started to point out a big herd of buffalo. The Lakota woman pulled an ice-pick from her handbag and rested it on her lap.

"I just want a ride," she said. Her face was covered with pancake make-up and heavy eye shadow. Her hair was long and straight and black. She wore a choker made of bone and pipestone, and twin half-moons dangled from her earlobes. Chris tried for a moment to make eye contact, but felt his face shake, his jaw twitch. He took one hand from the steering wheel and pressed a closed fist against his chin to steady himself.

"Hey," he said, "that's all I want to give you." This may not have been true a few minutes before, but it was now. The ice-pick had a chilling effect.

But this exchange of monosyllables seemed to open her up, and as they drove through Sturgis she began to tell Chris about her recent experience in a sweat lodge, where she astral-projected as little specks of electric light darted around her in the darkness.

"Those specks of light were spirits," she said. "Spirits of my ancestors." She settled back against the car seat, and Chris could tell he was in for a long story, which was ok because it would make the time pass.

"I left my body and floated to the top of the sweat lodge, and when I came back down someone had killed a cow. So I cooked it and sorted its remains into three plastic bags. I went home and put the bags in a trunk, and buried it beneath the floorboards. Then I hid, but I don't know why. My mother came out of her bedroom wearing jeans and a wine-colored shirt under a fur coat. It was so cold. The windows were frosted and our breath turned to mist in the air." She let the back of her hand fall on Chris's knee. He noticed an uneven scar scrawled across her left wrist.

"I thought I heard a buzzing of bees. Above the fireplace, on the mantle, was a glass ball with a human fetus inside, a female. She cursed at me and said, 'How can I ever be born if no one will help me?' She pushed her tiny wrinkled hands against the sides of the glass ball, and it fell to the floor. I covered my ears, expecting the glass to shatter, but instead the ball bounced back to the mantle. Green tears fell from the fetus's eyes." By this time, Chris was keeping his own blue eyes straight ahead on Highway 34.

The Lakota woman put the ice-pick back in her handbag and started getting flirtatious. "I like Steely Dan," she said, resting her head on Chris's shoulder. "Hey Nineteen," she laughed. "Good choice, white man."

"Bodacious cowboys," he said, trying to be a good sport. He was also trying to remember the name of that Michael Douglas movie where Sharon Stone keeps a pick under her bed. Every two-word title he could think of mixed sex with death.

The Lakota woman started to sing along with Steely Dan. "Here come those Santa Ana winds again." She said her name was Brenda Which Woman and her boyfriend was Evan Chasing Hawk.

"I know Evan," said Chris, happy to change the subject. "We used to play pool at the bowling alley." This was true. Evan Chasing Hawk was about six-four and weighed three hundred pounds. Chris had stopped playing pool with him when Evan got mad after a game of eight-ball and yanked out Chris's left earring. Chris's earlobe had never closed up properly after that. Now it looked like a map of Botany Bay.

Brenda started talking in Lakota. Chris wasn't sure whether she meant for him to understand. He could pick out "Wakan Tanka," the Great Mystery, and "catkuta iyaya yo." He knew she was saying something about a white man, or maybe a black white man. He reckoned her subject matter was the spirituality of sex, that she was recounting pleasant memories along those lines. Other than that, he just listened politely and kept his eyes on the road. She asked Chris, in English, if he believed in God.

"I try to," said Chris. No eye contact.

"Do you pray?" asked Brenda Which Woman.

"I try," said Chris, "but I'm not very good at it." Brenda was clearly whacko.

She laughed. "We Lakota pray all the time, for courage and strength," said Brenda Which Woman. "We pray to the buffalo and to the eagle. We pray for a good hunt." She leaned forward so she could look Chris in the eye. "Whenever we Lakota pray," she said, "we assume we may not come out alive." She was getting pretty creepy.

Chris thought he knew a thing or two about the Lakota after three years on the reservation. "I read somewhere that

Sioux words don't mean things the same way English words do," he said. "Is that right?" Cheeto High Bear had told him that a Lakota word for an object described the object in motion, the object in being.

Brenda looked impressed. "Not bad, white man," she said. She explained that the Lakota word for "house" meant the house being built and the house standing and the house falling into ruins.

"And sex is never, ever, a noun," she purred, letting her long black hair fall across Chris's chest. The pick-up veered to the side of the road as Chris tried to put the ice-pick out of his mind. He struggled to regain control, and he guessed that death was never a noun either.

When they got to Spearfish, Brenda Which Woman directed Chris to her grandfather's house at the edge of town, just as Steely Dan was wrapping up "Third World Man," *Gaucho's* last track. Her grandfather lived in a little stone cottage with a grassless front yard. Tumbleweeds and grasshoppers were everywhere. A little shrub at the side was decorated like a Christmas tree with packs of cigarettes and brightly-colored ribbons and beads.

After shutting the pick-up door behind her, Brenda poked her head back inside the window and said, "When I asked you if you believe in God, you said you try to. That was a yes."

She seemed perturbed, and tossed her mane like a young colt on the South Dakota prairie. "That's what the Great Mystery is, white man. The closest we can ever get is trying."

Chris breathed a sigh of relief as he watched her traipse into her grandfather's house, and swore he'd never pick up another hitch-hiker. And he never did until Ian McCallum. And now he never would again.

Before leaving Rolla, Chris and the kids found a little fish joint for lunch. Then they continued down 44 to Springfield, where they exited onto 65 for Branson. Chris had been hearing this word "Branson" for awhile, and wanted to see what it was like before going to their houseboat on Table Rock Lake.

Leonard and Alma Ruth had been going to Branson every couple of years for World War II reunions. They loved it.

Branson was Chris's idea of hell. There were roller coasters and magic shows and wax museums and go-carts and WWII amphibious ducks and SUVs full of really dumb American tourists stuck in small-town traffic jams and gawking at billboards. God-awful country music pounded from all sides of the main drag. If Chris had been so inclined, he could have heard live performances by Moe Bandy or Mickey Gilley or Bobby Vinton or the Osmonds; he could have taken the kids to the American Presidential Museum, or the Veterans Memorial.

Instead, they drove over to the old section of Branson, where it was quieter in fake down-home 1950s style. They got some ice cream at a place that called itself a "shoppe," and bought a couple more Archie comics at the Extreme Discount Bookstore ("nothing over five dollars"). The bookstore had a little back room behind a cotton curtain, and Razor wondered what went on in there. "Just bookkeeping," said Chris.

They found an IGA Thriftway grocery and loaded up with supplies for their houseboat on Table Rock Lake: eggs, milk, mustard, canned pear halves, grape juice, a bag of pistachios, Italian bread, cucumbers, another box of Atkins bars, granny smith apples, watermelon, blueberries, peanut butter, catfish nuggets, strawberries, cheese sticks, vegetarian hamburgers, a six-pack of Michelob Ultra low-carb beer, and vegetarian bacon. Then they got out of Branson lickity-split.

They arrived at Tri-Lakes Houseboat Rentals in Kimberling City around three o'clock. Chris inspected the boat, a six-sleeper PlayCraft on pontoons, and laid down $744 in cash for two nights. The boat had a kitchen, a small refrigerator, a radio, and a barbecue on the front deck. It also had a water slide coming off the roof, which had Razor and Sharon hollering and high-fiving.

A sun-baked Adonis with rippling muscles gave Chris some basic houseboat instructions. Don't start the engine when swimmers are in the water, he said. Head for a cove at night and aim the boat straight into shore. Never beach sideways against the shore. This can result in punctures to the pontoons, because only the fronts of the pontoons are reinforced for beaching. Remember Missouri's weather can change quickly. Tie up at night with two ropes to two different trees, spread wide apart. Stretch the ropes in a V-shape from the boat to the trees. Use square knots or half-hitches or bowlines. No fireworks. And enjoy your stay.

Chris nodded at all this, and made as much eye contact as he could, but he only took in half of it. It was a beautiful sunny afternoon, and there wasn't a whole lot of time left for fun. They moved the Windstar to the parking lot and left Dopey the Dwarf in charge, then unloaded their supplies, including the DVD player and a few of the stolen DVDs. The houseboat had a top speed of eight miles per hour, and they had to find a sleepy cove before dark.

Chris reversed out of the dock and wove around the buoys at marker No. 7. Razor and Sharon wanted to waterslide right away, so he found a spot out in the middle of the lake. At first he made them wear their life jackets, because when they went into the murky water they disappeared for a few seconds and Chris's heart pounded until they bobbed up like ascending ghosts, but he got more confident as they surfaced time after time, laughing their heads off. Razor and Sharon were excellent swimmers.

Chris found a good place to dock for the night, called "Little Cow Cove" on the map. It was calm and peaceful, and there wasn't another boat or house in sight. Chris steered straight toward land, as he'd been told to do by Adonis. There were big rocks and tree stumps along the shore, so he had to steer carefully. He imagined himself as the captain of the Titanic, dodging icebergs in the North Atlantic, responsible for the lives of thousands of souls.

He stopped the houseboat about twenty feet out, and he and the kids jumped into the shallow water to tie the ropes to a couple of trees. Chris wasn't very good at knots, having been kicked out of cub scouts for turning his paper maché boat into a hat, but he looped a rope around one of the trees and felt like a real woodsman.

"That should do it," he said. He let Razor and Sharon tie the other rope.

They cooked up dinner on the barbecue as Chris played some of his old bluegrass songs on the mandolin, with Sharon singing harmony. She knew all the words to every one of his songs. Razor kept zooming off the back of the slide into the shallow water until the sun went down. After he got sick of that, they watched *The Perfect Storm* on the DVD, where George Clooney goes fishing in the North Atlantic with a crew of really dopey men who think they're heroic because they manage to sink the boat and kill themselves, and Mark Wahlberg gets the idea that swordfish are more attractive than Diane Lane. Everybody was yawning by the end of the movie. Chris took the double bed at the rear, Razor chose a bunk, and Sharon slept on the fold-out in the kitchen.

A real drawback of the houseboat trip, Chris discovered, was that he couldn't get the Cardinals on the boat radio. They were playing the Padres in San Diego this Monday night, and the game started at nine o'clock Central time. Chris fiddled with the dial for a while but got nothing but static and crackles that sounded like a distant storm. He wondered how the Cards would go without him. Their ace right-hander, Matt Morris, was on the mound, and the Cardinals always did well against the Padres. Still, without Chris, anything could happen. The only thing keeping this evening from being perfect was the poor reception.

Disappointed but not discouraged, Chris said the joyful mysteries of the rosary, glanced over Boynkin & Sneed's Cuffy Kamara brief, and drifted off to sleep. It had been another great day. Two in a row. A modern-day Hooker record.

But it wasn't quite over. Around midnight Chris woke up with a swaying motion, feeling like he was rolling around on a waterbed. He stumbled to his feet, all groggy and disoriented, and went out on deck to pee into the lake. The houseboat was listing badly, first one way and then the other, and

Chris's pee was going everywhere, but it was totally dark and he couldn't see a thing. The wind was fierce and thick streaks of lightning pierced the black sky. Deafening claps of thunder followed the lightning in a matter of seconds. Whatever this was, they were in the middle of it.

Suddenly Chris heard Sharon cry out from the darkness, "Dad, we've come loose from the shore!"

Chris inched his way down to her end of the boat and tried to see where they were. When the lightning flashed he could see around the boat for a split second, but there was nothing but lake in front of him. The trees and the shore had disappeared.

Chris felt something close to panic. As the thunder cracked, he blinked and remembered lying in his bed in the little white house with the green roof, six years old, wondering what it would be like to be in a tiny coffin in the cold ground. A pack of wild dogs ran past the little house, yelping and snarling. His Aunt Teresa heard him crying, and came in to check on him.

"What's the matter, Chris?"

"Nothing," he said, trying to sound tough. He didn't want to tell her about the coffin. "I just heard the doggies bark." Aunt Teresa tucked him in and went back to the living room to listen to *Gangbusters* on the radio. She left the door open so Chris could hear, and the story put him to sleep.

Now Chris felt his way to Razor's bunk to check if he was still there. He patted around on the sheets and blankets and finally felt Razor's little feet. He was sleeping right through this squall, which was just as well. Chris had no idea where they were, how far they'd drifted, what the condition of the boat was, or what to do. He told Sharon to lie back down in her bed and he'd take care of everything.

"Are we going to die?" she asked. It was a reasonable question.

"No way," said Chris. "I just have to tie us back down."

So Sharon climbed back into bed, but kept watching Chris to see if he was scared. Chris tried the cabin lights, and they were working, but they didn't help him see outside. He fumbled around in his backpack for the flashlight. The boat was bobbing up and down on gigantic waves, and rotating in slow semi-circles, first one way then the other. Chris heard horrible creaking noises coming from the pontoons below. They were scraping on rocks or tree roots somewhere under the water.

Chris went out on deck with the flashlight, holding tightly to the railing. He walked around the boat, shining the light on the lake. For some reason, when he got to the *back* of the boat, he was able to see trees in the distance, but he had no explanation for this. He'd tied the *front* of the boat to the shoreline. Had they drifted in this storm for miles, winding up rear-ended in some new cove or smashed into an island? Chris had no idea.

Then he saw something in a flash of lightning that confused him even more. A straight line ran from the stern to some of the trees in the distance. It took him a while to figure out this was one of the ropes. He groped around on deck and found where it was attached. It was taut and stretched above the water to the trees, like a tightrope. Still Chris couldn't figure out what it meant. The ropes were supposed to be in the front. He was almost delirious from lack of sleep and the howling wind and the strobes of lightning. He sat down at the helm just to gather his thoughts.

"What is it, Dad?" said Sharon, poking her head from under her covers.

"I don't know," said Chris. "I'm trying to figure out where we are."

"I'm scared, Dad," said Sharon. "Are we going to drown?"

"Of course not," said Chris. But he was already making plans for swimming in the darkness with Razor and Sharon clinging to him in these cold raging waters, and wondering what they would do if they got somewhere. He had no idea whether the houseboat would stay afloat for long, or how deep the waters were.

Finally he came up with a theory about what had happened. One of the ropes had slipped away from its tree, but

the other knot had miraculously held. The houseboat had
swung around on its single-rope axis, still tied to the original
shore, but back-end first and a few dozen yards south. The
rope had wound around the cabin. They were now a boat's-
length closer to the shore, scraping against rocks and roots.

He checked this by holding the taut rope in his hands and
walking to where it was tied at the front. His hands were
bleeding badly when he completed his test, but at least he
was able to confirm what had happened.

Still, the pontoons were making those terrible groans.
Chris couldn't just go to bed now that he knew where they
were. The remaining knot might not hold, and the pontoons
might split. The houseboat could still sink, and little Razor
would never know what hit him.

At last Sharon had gone back to sleep, but the lightning
and wind were as bad as ever. Chris was alone now to focus
on their predicament. His first idea was to start the engine and
go slowly forward, hoping the boat would be pulled around
on its axis and right itself toward the trees. He turned the key
and pushed the throttle forward, but the boat didn't move, and
Chris started to realize this was a really dumb idea. All he was
going to do was snap the remaining rope. So he shut off the
motor and started thinking again. It wasn't easy with the wind
howling and the boat rocking from side to side.

There was only one thing to do, Chris decided, and that
was to get into the swirling waters and find the untied rope,
wrap it around a tree, then walk along the shore to the taut
rope and re-knot it to make sure it was secure. The boat could
stay backwards for the night.

Before getting out of his pajamas, Chris munched on an
Atkins bar and mulled this over. There was a chance he could
drown, he reckoned, which was no big deal, but if he died in
the water, Razor and Sharon would be in a tight spot. He had
to make sure he was doing the right thing. Finally he decided
there was no real option, so he'd try it.

He tug-of-warred a few feet of the loose rope from the
water and gripped it in his bleeding hands. He slipped naked

into the water, but lost his footing and fell against a big slimy rock, spraining his ankle, smashing his elbow against the hull, and pinning his forearm between the rock and the boat. He had to wait until the boat bobbed again before he was able to slip his arm out. Blood ran down Chris's arm and into the water, and he thought of *Jaws*. He managed to hold onto the rope with his good hand, and waded across the rocks and into the trees. He looped the rope around a trunk and tied a rough bowline knot. His den mother would have been proud. Then he groped his way through the trees and re-tied the other knot. He waded back to the houseboat, wrapped a towel around his arm, and fell into the double bed to wait for the storm to stop.

For no particular reason, he thought of his mother and his sister Lauren, walking with them from the little white house with the green roof to the swings in the park, swinging as high as he could against the autumn sky until it was time to go home. "Let the cat die down," Alma Ruth would say, and Chris and Lauren would stop kicking as their swings looped lower and lower. He lay on his bed in the houseboat wondering what could this mean? "Let the cat die down?"

After a couple more hours, the winds slowed and the lightning was off in the distance, like heat lightning at the end of a summer day. The rocking became gentle, like a cradle, and Chris drifted off to sleep. He dreamed of his father, standing on the sidewalk as Chris walked home from cub scouts wearing his little blue uniform and yellow scarf. Something was wrong, Chris could tell, and he might be in trouble.

"Skeeter's dead," said Leonard. Skeeter was Chris's puppy, a brown and white fox terrier. "A car hit him."

Leonard took Chris to the back yard behind their apartment, where he'd already dug a tiny grave.

"Go ahead and bury him, son," Leonard would always say in this recurring dream.

"But he's not dead," Chris would say. "He's still shaking." This is what Chris always said.

"He's dead," Leonard would say. "It's just nerves." And Chris would dutifully take his warm little dog in his arms and lower him into the shallow grave and cover him with earth.

TUESDAY: SORROWFUL MYSTERIES

Say, maiden, wilt thou go with me
Through this sad non-identity,
Where parents live and are forgot
And sisters live and know us not?

John Clare, *1793-1864*

*You lived in this little hut on stilts in New Amsterdam, near
the Berbice River, and you'd painted comic book figures all
over the inside walls and "Stop the War" all over the outside,
so much that your mail actually came addressed to Hooker at
Stop the War and it always got through. "Which war?" they'd
ask sometimes, and you'd say "Any war, stop them all, stop
all the wars." You were the only white man in town, Mr.
Socket they called you because of the magic tricks you'd do
for the little kids in their school uniforms who circled round
your bicycle, Mr. Socket. "Oh that man Socket," the elders
would say.*

*And next door to Stop the War was Lily Jaundoo and her
thieving son Tony who figured he had a right to anything you
left in your jeans pockets and that was ok with you. You and
Lily would talk about it as you sat in your respective outhouse
toilets beneath your houses, and she would say that Tony's a
good boy and you would always agree as the barefoot kids
played cricket in the dirt outside using your briefcase as the
wicket, and afterwards you'd meditate on the front steps with*

your eyes closed trying to be conscious of every single sound all at once and sometimes it worked.

And one day you took the ferry across the Berbice River and caught a taxi to Georgetown and then flew to Trinidad, and there was this girl at the airport sort of cute and very young and you were young too, and you talked because in those days you could talk and then you got seats right next to each other for the flight to Caracas. And she was going to Maracaibo to see her fiancé Roberto and her name was Beryl a name you didn't hear in central Illinois and this was exotic. So you arrived in Caracas and she traveled on and you stayed alone in a place called the Cazador until you hitched a ride to the boats to take you to the island of Margarita to hunt for pearls and as you walked down the streets of the island the people actually came out of their huts to watch you because they'd never seen a white man with long hair and a long beard like this and real hippie clothes too this was only 1969.

And you didn't get any pearls so you went back to Caracas for the flight back to Trinidad and there was Beryl by complete coincidence in the airport waiting for the same plane and while you were talking to each other you missed the boarding call and the next plane didn't leave for three days. So you stayed together in the Cazador and walked through the park and the young Venezuelan boys call her "puta" because she was with a pimp-shirt white man but you didn't care and neither did she. And you got back to Trinidad and decided to get married so you did and the steel band played "Let It Be" and "Bridge Over Troubled Waters" at the wedding. And you went back to New Amsterdam and moved into the house across the street from Stop the War and it used to be a whorehouse but you didn't know that, and every now and then a carload of Indian guys from upriver would come knocking on the door and you'd tell them the women didn't live here any more, and one time a guy came after you with a machete but your bicycle was too fast for him.

* * * * * * * *

Next morning, Chris sat up in bed and looked out the houseboat windows. He felt silly, as if he'd exaggerated the whole thing. It was a calm and peaceful morning, except for a few broken trees floating in the water. His arm hurt, and his elbow was swollen to twice its normal size. Even more distressing, when he moved to get out of bed he discovered his back had gone again. This hadn't happened in three years. Whenever it did, Chris's movements were restricted for a couple of days until the pain went away.

Before his seven-year exile in the Wombat Forest, he'd always prided himself on a strong back. He could move anything - a couch, a fridge, a piano, an adolescent. That changed one day when he drove his jeep past one of the dams and spotted something organic poking out of the water. He investigated, and found that the visible bit was the tip-of-an-iceberg of a dead wallaby.

No big deal. Chris waded into the dam and dragged the stinking carcass to the water's edge. But when he went to pull it out, he learned that a waterlogged wallaby weighs about four million pounds. Still, he couldn't leave it in the dam, because that was where the family's dishwater and shower-water came from. So he grunted and groaned and lifted it into a wheelbarrow, then rolled it deep into the forest for the crows to enjoy.

Next day his back was gone and would never be the same. "Wallaby's Revenge," Kazzie called it, whenever his back gave out.

Hunched over, Chris fixed up some breakfast and roused the kids from their beds. Sharon told Razor all about the storm, and he was furious that he'd slept through it.

"Why didn't you wake me up?" he said to Chris. He pouted and said he wouldn't eat his cereal.

Chris still had to get the boat untied, turned around, and out onto the lake. He wasn't sure if the pontoons had been damaged. He and the twins waded over to the trees, loosened the knots, and rolled up the ropes. Then Chris started the motor and eased the houseboat across the tops of the rocks to the middle of Little Cow Cove. Everything seemed ok, but Chris wanted to be sure.

"Let's go find a marina," he said. "I want to get on land for a little while." The kids thought that was a good idea. They wanted some junk food. Razor grabbed the map of the lake and handed it to Chris. Chris took a right, heading for Indian Point. It didn't look far on the map, but it took about an hour.

When they got to the Tonka Bay Marina at Indian Point, Chris docked and filled up with fuel. He and the kids went into the bait shop, where Chris bought a Kansas City *News-Leader.* They sat at an outside table and ordered some drinks, a cappuccino for Chris and hot chocolates for the kids. The news from San Diego was terrible. Not only had the Cardinals lost to the Padres 4-3 in ten innings, but Matt Morris had been hit on his pitching hand by a line drive in the first inning and was expected to miss 4-6 weeks with a broken index finger. "It's just another speed bump in the road," said Morris.

Chris turned to the front pages to read about last night's storm. It had been a monster. "A violent wave of thunderstorms passed through southern and central Missouri," the *News-Leader* reported. The winds were described as "hurricane force," up to 100 miles per hour with powerful lightning and heavy rains. A quarter of a million people in Missouri were without power.

Chris showed the kids some photographs of capsized sailboats on the Lake of the Ozarks. This made Razor even madder. "I can't believe you let me miss it," he said. Now he wouldn't drink his hot chocolate.

Chris's back was killing him when they got back on the boat, plus he was on the verge of diarrhea from eating way too many Atkins bars loaded with lecithin and other crap. He motored out of the marina and horse-shoed around Coombs Ferry point, but he needed to lie down. The kids didn't mind, because they were hankering for a chance to take the helm. Sharon went first as Chris lay on the fold-out bed. She flipped the radio to a Branson pop station and was thrilled to get a song by the Black Eyed Peas, her favorite group. She spun the wheel any way she felt like, and sang along with the radio.

Table Rock Lake got pretty wide after Coombs Ferry, so Chris wasn't too concerned about letting the kids play captain. They couldn't hit anything if they stayed away from the shoreline, and they were only moving at walking speed. It was mid-week, so there weren't too many people on the lake.

"Just keep to the middle and don't go near anybody," said Chris.

"Aye, aye," said Sharon. She managed to look smug and thrilled at the same time. Razor was busy with his English-edition Yu-Gi-Oh cards, teaching himself how to shuffle. He said he wanted to be a flapjack dealer when he grew up.

The houseboat puttered along at seven or eight miles an hour, stopping every now and then for water-sliding. When Razor took over, he steered over to Moonshine Beach, where somebody with a lot of money had bought up a coastline and trucked in a small desert's worth of sand. A tourist's galleon was leaving Moonshine Beach, which prompted Razor to start playing pirate.

"Shiver me timbers," he'd say. "Ahoy matey."

Sharon got into the spirit and started singing "a pirate's life for me" to the tune of "row row row your boat." Chris grabbed the mandolin and played along.

The kids decided to christen the houseboat "Andrea Gail" after the fishing boat in *The Perfect Storm*. There were some great hurricane scenes in last night's DVD, and Razor and Sharon thought they must have lived through the same thing on Table Rock Lake. Razor took a permanent black marker when Chris wasn't looking and wrote "Andrea Gail" upside down all over the bow and the stern, with little drawings of pirates and pirate ships. Chris was not pleased. "We'll have to pay for that," he said as he confiscated the marker from Razor.

Whenever Razor or Sharon passed near another boat or a water-skier, everybody waved as if they were each other's long lost friends. Chris kept looking around through his binoculars, and spotted a couple of topless girls sunbathing in their yachts.

"Whatcha looking at, Dad?" said Sharon.

"Oh, nothing," said Chris. "Just those beautiful houses off in the distance. Look at that one with the three green points." And there *were* magnificent houses all around them on the shore, owned by people with more money than Christian Leonard Hooker would ever have. But he didn't care. The Quimbys could keep their treasure and their Morrisonville cornfields. Chris just lay there in this crappy houseboat pretending to be Huckleberry Finn, thinking this was as close to heaven as he'd ever get.

But whenever Chris had thoughts of heaven, his built-in eschatology detector would remind him he was a heartbeat from hell. When Sean was four years old, Chris asked him about heaven and hell. Chris wanted to know what a four-year-old thought about the end things, before the world corrupted him into seeing everything in his own image.

Heaven, according to Sean, was when everybody you loved was with you forever and ever. This included pets. Hell was when you died and it was just as if you had never been born. Nobody remembered you, and nobody cared. Chris wrote Sean's thoughts in his diary, for Sean to see when he grew older. At the bottom of the page, he wrote a reminder to himself: "it is important to be remembered through your children."

For Chris to think he was in heaven, even for a minute or two on a houseboat in the Ozarks, he had to shut out a lot of uncomfortable realities. Where was his son Josh? Where was his daughter Jeshel? What were they doing right then, ten thousand miles away in some Melbourne suburb? And why wasn't he with them?

His last memories of Josh and Jeshel went back three years, and they were fading. They'd gone to the seaside village of Lorne and booked a room above a fish and chips shop, with an ocean view. All three knew Chris was saying goodbye as best he could, but nobody knew for how long.

For no particular reason, Chris overdressed on that last day in Lorne for a stroll along the esplanade, wearing his dark blue suit, white shirt and silk arabesque tie. Josh was in his frayed-bottom jeans, untied Converse sneakers, and a t-shirt with a rainbow-fish hologram. Jeshel clomped along in high-topped Doc Martins and brightly-striped stockings, a snug cotton skirt and a delicate mauve blouse that showed her bra. Her hair was blowing in the ocean breeze, and she looked a lot older than twelve.

A car pulled up alongside them, a dark station wagon with tinted windows. A young man with spiked blond hair, wearing a sleeveless Hellboy t-shirt, poked his head out the window and said to Jeshel, "You look good enough to eat."

Jeshel stifled a laugh, enjoying the smell of testosterone. Hellboy waggled his tongue obscenely between two fingers. Chris glared, and motioned for Josh and Jeshel to keep walking along the esplanade.

Hellboy got out of his car and strutted towards Chris. His arms were tattooed with musical instruments, and he wore tight moleskins with a big Harley belt buckle.

"C'mon, Dad," said Josh the peacemaker. Jeshel shook her head sadly as Chris stood his ground, arms akimbo. When Hellboy got into Chris's body space, Chris grabbed him by both wrists and said, in a low whisper just loud enough for Josh and Jeshel to hear, "Do you want trouble? If you want trouble, you can have it."

Hellboy grinned and said nothing, peering over Chris's shoulder at Jeshel. He was missing one of his front teeth. Chris let go of his wrists and walked slowly to Josh and Jeshel, back-of-hands first like a South Dakota cowboy. He figured they'd be impressed, but he was on another planet, and very uncool. Josh and Jeshel were embarrassed. People on the esplanade were staring.

"He wasn't going to *do* anything, Dad," said Jeshel. Actually, Chris had been hoping that Hellboy might have a switchblade in his back pocket, that he would plunge it deep into Chris's cowboy back so he could die a hero's death defending the honor of his love child. But no such luck.

And here on his idylic houseboat in the Ozarks, alone with his twins, Chris closed his eyes and wondered what had become of little Zig Shulman, the nine-year-old boy who'd come up to him in Melbourne, at the Forty Martyrs Grammar School, after his mother was murdered, and said, "Just you wait till I'm bigger!" Little Sean just wanted to be Ziggy's friend, and couldn't understand why Zig was snarling at his dad in the playground. Even now, every time a white boy Sean's age knocked at the front door of their home in Sand River, Chris wondered if it might be Ziggy, all grown up and come at last from Australia to take his revenge.

Zig's wall-eyed father Baruch, a Russian immigrant to Australia, was eventually tried and acquitted of murdering his wife Jillian, a well-known fashion model. He'd died of stomach cancer last May, but not before Chris testified via satellite video at the Melbourne murder trial. Chris wore his best double-breasted suit to a Sand River studio, and spoke in detached professorial tones about his brief affair with Jillian Daley Shulman. It hadn't been much. A couple of tosses in the back of Chris's van, once at the end of Acland Street and a couple of weeks later in a parking bay in the Melbourne Botanical Gardens. A few lunches on the fourteenth floor of BHP House on William Street, two blocks down from Chris's barrister's rooms.

At lunch one day, Chris asked Jillian what would happen if Baruch ever found out. She laughed.

"He'll kill you," she said. Then she didn't laugh, and said "he'll kill you" again. So Chris proposed a pact. If anyone ever asked, especially Baruch, they'd deny everything, no matter how much evidence there was to the contrary.

Jillian clapped her hands together. "What a marvelous idea," she said. "No one could prove anything. No one *knows* what we do. No one *sees* us."

She wanted to leave Baruch anyway, and take Ziggy and his little sisters with her. She'd been offered a job as a hairdresser in a Toorak salon called "Curl Up and Dye." It was a big step down from modeling, but it was freedom. Her lawyer told her that if she slept in a separate bedroom for twelve months, she could get a divorce under the user-friendly Australia Family Law Act. Then she'd get at least half of Baruch's money for her new life as a hairdresser - and custody of the children would almost certainly go to their mother.

Chris's fatal mistake was to give Jillian one of his bluegrass band's cassettes after the Acland Street rendezvous. When Baruch found the tape hidden in Jillian's underwear drawer, he hired a private investigator to follow her. Chris started getting murderous messages on his car phone.

"You're dead meat," the voice would say in a thick Russian accent. "I know what you did." Whenever Chris managed to get a word in to deny everything, the voice would just laugh. "I've got a bullet, and your name's on it."

Chris reported the calls to the Victorian police, and they ran a check on Baruch Shulman. No criminal record, but he owned a lot of guns that he kept on his country property. The police told Chris they couldn't do anything until Baruch committed a crime, so Chris went about his daily life peeking behind every bush and into every parked car for the hit man who was bound to come.

He thought of John Lennon at the arched entranceway of the Dakota Building in New York City, across from Central Park, signing a final autograph for Mark David Chapman before getting plugged with four bullets from Chapman's Charter Arms .38. Someone, somewhere in Australia, was reading *Catcher in the Rye* all over again, as thousands of children played at the edge of a crazy cliff. If Christian Leonard Hooker couldn't catch them all before they fell over the cliff, he'd be dead meat too. Imagine.

Chris broke off the affair. "Too risky," he told Jillian Daley Shulman.

The voice on the phone continued. "Ever had a gun in your Yankee mouth?" it said. "Up your Yankee arse?"

Two weeks later, Jillian telephoned Chris at his barrister's rooms. "Don't bother lying anymore," she said. "Baruch's got photographs of us in the Botanical Gardens. He's got an affidavit from your banjo player. He's got your cassette."

In mid-winter, Detective Senior Sergeant Tony Colangelo stopped by Chris's rooms to tell him that Jillian Daley Shulman was missing, presumed dead. He asked Chris to come to the police headquarters on St. Kilda Road for an interview. Christian Leonard Hooker - foreign barrister, divorced father, and serial monogamist - was a prime suspect for a few days, until the police verified his alibi that he'd been camping on the island of Tasmania with Sean and Josh.

Twelve years later, Chris found himself seated alone at a conference table in Sand River, Illinois, staring at a television set. A couple of technicians had adjusted the sound levels and left the room. Chris could see the Melbourne courtroom on the screen. Baruch Shulman, the defendant, was on the right with his barrister. He'd lost a lot of weight, and his hair was white and stringy. Ziggy sat next to him, a grown-up university student just like Sean.

Chris testified about the affair, and the phone calls, and cowering in a Seven-Eleven as Baruch tapped on the window of Chris's van with the barrel of a shotgun. He told the court how Baruch took Elspeth to a coffee shop in Toorak to suggest that they have a little affair of their own. "They've got it coming," he told her. "Fair's fair." Elspeth phoned Chris afterwards to tell him how much she hated him. "It was so humiliating," she said.

Baruch's defense lawyer put his face right into the camera and asked Chris a bunch of snotty questions to show the judge what a slimeball he was. "You had affairs with half the mothers at Forty Martyrs Grammar, didn't you, Mr. Hooker?" Chris denied it was half. After all these years, with a satellite transmitting his double-breasted suit into a courtroom on the other side of the planet, this seemed like a bad soap opera from Neptune.

"I didn't kill her," Chris wanted to say to Ziggy that day in the schoolyard. In the Sand River studio, he still wanted to say it to the grown-up Zig who sat there in an Australian courtroom. "I didn't kill her. Your father killed her. Hate him." But Chris was an easy target for poor Zig. As a nine-year-old boy, he'd watched on television as the police divers dragged nasty hooks along the bottoms of the Shulmans' country ponds, hoping to snag the body of Ziggy's model mother. Now his father was all he had left. And his father was dying of cancer.

After the trial and Baruch's acquittal, *The Age* ran a series of unkind stories suggesting that justice had not been done. Baruch Shulman was portrayed as Old World eye-for-an-eye. Jillian was described as a prominent socialite and long-suffering victim of her own indiscretions and her husband's brutality, forced into the arms of Christian Leonard Hooker by her marital loneliness. And, according to *The Age*, Chris was the Svengali who spanned the chasm in their lives.

Little Zig Shulman was quoted in *The Age* as saying the wrong man was tried for his mother's murder. "Hooker killed her," he said. "My dad told me." Chris's photograph appeared with the story, over the words "Dead Model's American Lover." Zig's photo was there too - walking away from the courthouse, back to the camera, looking tiny against the cold stone buildings of William Street.

Chris didn't allow himself to reflect on these things very often. But he was having a field day of remorse there on the Andrea Gail, mulling over the fact that he didn't have a friend in Australia or South Dakota or Illinois or the Caribbean, or anywhere else he'd ever lived in the world. He lay there wondering why he didn't care - not in a chip on the shoulder way, he just didn't care. Maybe he'd moved around too much. Maybe he'd left too much of himself behind. Maybe there wasn't enough of him left.

The closest he came to a grown-up friendship, other than Kazzie, was his old high school pal Finbar Studge, now an author and occasional e-mail correspondent living in Florida. Studge had written a novel called *Groin Damage* with a central character named "Hooker," drawn from Studge's recollections of a youthful Chris. The portrayal wasn't very flattering. Studge's anti-hero was self-obsessed, flamboyantly sexist, a professional failure, and a destructive person to have for a friend.

'

Groin Damage begins in the streets of Louisville, Kentucky, where two skinny dogs are coupling in an alley. The female dog dies in the middle of the act, and the male is unable to disengage himself because of *penis captivus.* He runs through the streets of Louisville, yelping and dragging the female carcass behind him. Hooker hears the racket from the lobby of the Galt Hotel, where he has booked a room for sex with a suicidal nun. His long hair is tied back with an elastic band cut from an old pair of Jockey underpants. He steps into the street with great bravado, sensing a chance to be a savior, and follows the dogs down to the Ohio River, where he liberates the male with a scrap of two-by-four.

Studge's unflattering symbolism was obvious, but Chris didn't mind. He was thrilled to be the most talked-about character in a published novel. On one visit back to Sand River from Australia, he learned that Studge had just flown in and out of town for a book-signing at the Pages for All Ages bookstore, and they'd missed each other by a few days. Studge's handsome photograph had been on the front page of the local newspaper, the *Courier-Review.* So Chris swaggered into the *Courier-Review* office, looking very wild and woolly, and announced: "I am Hooker." He demanded that his photograph be taken and published with the headline, "The Real Hooker Returns."

A reporter pretended to take careful notes, nodding her head and making eye-contact. Chris had a one-liner for her that he thought would help the story: "A life that is lived in full outshines a life that is only imagined," he declared with rhetorical flourish. "And you can quote me." The reporter ushered him out as soon as it was safe to do so. Then she turned to the photographer and said, "What an asshole."

For Chris's fifty-sixth birthday, Studge e-mailed a poem from a critically-acclaimed collection of "unholy sonnets" by Studge's writer buddy, Mark Jarman. In the e-mail address box marked "Subject," Studge wrote "For CLH." Chris committed the last six lines of Jarman's poem to memory:

There is, as doctors say about some pain,
Discomfort knowing that despite your prayers,
Your listening and rejoicing, your small part
In this communal stab at coming clean,
There is one stubborn remnant of your cares
Intact. There is still murder in your heart.

Chris rolled over on the Andrea Gail's fold-out bed to get his back into a less painful position. He closed his eyes and tried not to think, picturing some Hemingway hero diving brain-dead into the chill waters of San Sebastian. Deep he would go, weightless, nothing but feeling, holding his breath until he passed out and floated unconscious to the surface.

Razor was still at the helm of the houseboat, reveling at his power over ten tons of vessel-in-motion, with no brakes. In this second afternoon on the Andrea Gail, the kids were going feral. Sharon looked like a Rastafarian, and Razor had become a scaled-down barfly.

Their crazy faces brought a smile to Chris. He'd seen a black and white photograph, years ago, of a young Italian woman with wild eyes like these. It was in a Chicago shop window, and only for a passing moment as Chris walked along State Street. Slender and spirited, her auburn hair held high by a plastic comb but falling in loose strands across her neck, she threw her arms around the blue-jeaned hips of a farm boy. She would never let go, you could tell by her eyes. Chris knew better, even then. She'd let go, all right, sooner or later, this Italian girl. But it didn't matter. He lived for moments like these, still-life photographs of strangers or kin, and kept them in his mind forever.

As he surfaced from his brainless musings in the icy waters of San Sebastian, Chris remembered standing in the hot shower of his Melbourne home, across the street from the Caulfield race track, enjoying another conversation with himself, another moral dilemma. Should he be honest and tell Elspeth about Miriam and Jeshel? Or would that just be a self-indulgent power play, unburdening his turgid soul but wreaking havoc on everyone around him?

He'd asked his psychiatrist, the Panda, who uselessly told Chris it was his own decision to make. There in the shower, lathered in soap and shampoo and swarmed by fallen angels, Christian Leonard Hooker let slip another defining moment, as he always did. What good was a neurosis if you didn't protect it?

The Panda was slightly more interested in an enormous gap in Chris's memory. Chris could remember sitting in the back seat of a 1949 Ford holding his new-born sister Rachel, the second of three, in his lap. He could see Rachel's full head of hair, her thick black curls. Then twenty-five years passed, and Chris came back to Illinois from South America. He visited Rachel in her college dorm, and realized while she was chattering away that he could not recall a single thing about her since that moment in the Ford.

"How can that be?" Chris asked the Panda. "How can you live with someone every day for so long, and not have a single memory of her?" Chris's psychiatrist had dark eyes, white hair, bushy black eyebrows, and a chubby little body. He really did look like a panda.

The Panda shifted his weight in his overstuffed armchair and glanced at the small traveler's clock just over Chris's left shoulder. Mercifully, this interminable session with Mr. Hooker was almost over.

"Maybe you just have a selective memory," the Panda suggested. He wasn't even trying.

Despite the Panda's disinterest, he'd made a perceptive observation. Chris remembered what he wanted, and threw away the rest. He remembered Leonard with a spoon on a sunny weekend morning in the little white house with the green roof, flipping mashed potatoes across the kitchen table into Alma Ruth's face. Chris thought it must be a funny game, and laughed as Alma Ruth scraped away the white goo. "Oh my," she said. Chris stopped laughing when Leonard told her she'd wind up in a puddle of blood.

His selective memory fast-forwarded to Leonard chasing Alma Ruth into the bathroom of the apartment above the Quincy bookstore, Alma Ruth locking the wooden door, Leonard pounding to break it down, a scene from *The Shining,* Alma Ruth screaming for Chris to help, Chris too little and too scared and hiding under his blankets pretending to be asleep. He remembered Alma Ruth pulling up her blouse to show her bruises to Fairy Belle Fanke. But he couldn't remember the rest. Maybe it hadn't happened.

"There are two sides to every story," Kazzie liked to say. She and Leonard got along well, and she could understand how Alma Ruth could drive anybody crazy, always cleaning and saying stupid things.

But Lauren and Rachel remembered. "Once it started, it never stopped," said Rachel. "I don't want to talk about it," said Lauren.

Chris started to tell the Panda millions of details covering half a century, about his wooden house on stilts in Guyana, about Jillian Daley Shulman and her psychopath husband, about Russell Kamara's suicide in Alice Springs. But the Panda gently tapped his wrist watch. Time was up. The Panda was strict with his patients. Discipline was helpful. Maybe next week.

Chris opened his eyes and watched as Razor guided the Andrea Gail past Moonshine Beach to the Table Rock Dam, built by the Corps of Engineers, and on to the outskirts of a tiny island in the middle of the lake. The kids wanted to explore the island and claim it for their gang of pirates, so Chris took the wheel and steered the Andrea Gail headfirst to the shore, where they tied the ropes to a couple of trees.

This was a cool little island, shaped like Tasmania and about the size of the Little Prince's planet. You could walk its circumference in about fifteen minutes, even if you were nine years old or had an aching back. Or you could hide away among the trees and bushes and fantasize that you were Huck and Jim on Jackson's Island in the middle of the mighty Mississip.

Obviously some folks had enjoyed a few fantasies here before. There were charred remains of campfires, old beer bottles, and dozens of condoms filled with stuff Chris didn't want to think about.

"Don't touch those," Chris told the kids. Sharon was getting ready to blow up a few balloons.

Razor got the mandolin off the boat for Chris, and they all made up pirate songs, sitting on some big rocks near a dead campfire. Razor and Sharon had an idea to build a hut on the island, buy a row boat, and live there forever. "We could get supplies at the marina, Dad," said Sharon. "Why not?"

Razor wanted to christen the island with a noble name. Sharon suggested "Little Tasmania," because the real Tasmania was her favorite island, but Razor said that was too boring. "From now until the end of time," he declared, standing the way he thought a grizzled explorer should stand, "she shall be known as . . . Hookermania." He saluted to no one in particular, and Sharon and Chris did the same.

Chris didn't discourage the kids from their game. It was fun to think about, living here on Hookermania, and not unlike the first five years of their lives, in the middle of the Wombat Forest with their nearest neighbor five miles away. All that was missing out there in the eucalypts was a moat. Chris's favorite people were the six kids and Kazzie, and if he could cut off the rest of the sorry world except for brief cameo appearances in some town for supplies, that was ok by him.

Since moving back to Illinois, his life wasn't really all that different. He stayed home and minded his own business, ventured out to play with the earnest young minds at the law school for the sole purpose of getting some money, improvised on his Yamaha upright piano, read his biographies of politicians and adventurers, helped the twins with their grade school homework, slept on the right side of the double bed, went to one church or another on Sundays, tinkered in the yard, took long walks at Allerton Park, swam in the backyard pool in summer, rode the Schwinn exercise bike through the winter, wrote crank letters to the *Courier-*

Review comparing George W. Bush to Beelzebub, and generally had a great old time.

"How are you?" Kazzie would ask each day as Chris crossed the moat after squandering a few more brain cells at the law school. This had become a family ritual over the years. Kazzie even managed to sound sincere, no matter how many times she played the game.

"Couldn't be better," Chris said day after day, his line in the drill, and he delivered it well. The law school gig wasn't that bad. You could come and go as you pleased except for a couple hours of classes each week, and Chris had the highest student ratings of any of the professors because he made self-deprecating jokes with one common theme, that lawyers were assholes.

Each semester he'd quote Charles Hamilton Houston, the old dean of the Howard University Law School, that lawyers were either social engineers or they were parasites. "If you're lucky, you'll be both," Chris would always say in his best Atticus Finch impersonation, and the students would smile warmly. "I've been both," he'd say, removing his wire-rimmed glasses. "And I wasn't very good at either one."

"Ha ha," went the students, semester after semester. Good old Professor Hooker. Chris could count on their response. For the rest of the semester, his class preparation would be a model of economy. He'd learn his lines, stay ahead of his students by a day or two, and deliver his lectures Australian-style, where it was a great crime to take yourself seriously.

And here on the island of Hookermania, Chris and the kids were having so much fun they decided to settle in for the rest of the afternoon and night. They planned an early barbecue supper, lots of water-sliding, an Adam Sandler DVD, some more songs and stories, and a good night's sleep with the Andrea Gail's ropes tied in killer knots. Chris even got into water-sliding himself, aching back and all. After supper and the movie, Razor had the great idea to pull the sleeping bags out of the tent and sleep under the stars. Chris said ok, but he grabbed a mattress from the houseboat - he didn't want to take any chances on Wallaby's Revenge.

As Venus and then the stars started coming out above Hookermania, Chris pointed to Orion, with his twinkling belt and dangling sword. "In Australia, he's upside down," he said. This was true. Out there in the Wombat Forest, Orion looked like he was lying on his back with a huge erection.

Chris gave a little astronomy lecture about the southern hemisphere's Magellenic clouds, and how the kids could go about finding the Southern Cross if they ever got lost in an Australian forest, and about the pulsing northern lights he'd seen on the Cheyenne River Sioux Reservation, and the gray-and-black rainbow that appeared to him and Elspeth one misty night under a full moon on the Southern Ocean.

This idea of a nighttime rainbow got Razor all agitated. "It couldn't have been a real rainbow," he said. "A real rainbow has lots of colors."

"This one had black and gray," said Chris. "Those are colors."

Razor and Sharon started searching the sky above Hookermania, hoping to find a nighttime rainbow, or maybe the northern lights, or at least one of Magellen's fuzzy spots. But there was no mist to prism the moonlight, and they were way too far south for the northern lights, and way too far north for the Magellenic clouds. They gave up after a while, and everybody was quiet, looking at the heavens as a soft summer breeze blew across their island.

Razor had an idea. "I know," he said. "The rainbow you saw *did* have colors, but you just couldn't see them." This had the makings of a pretty good epistemological argument. Chris was impressed, but played devil's advocate.

"If you can't see the colors, they aren't there," he said in his most annoying professorial voice. "Colors don't exist if you can't see them."

This made Razor so mad he scrambled out of his sleeping bag and stood up in the middle of his island and screamed at the top of his voice. He pounced on Chris and started pummeling him until Chris struck back with sneak-attack tickles that left Razor in a fetal position screeching for mercy.

This went on and on until Sharon finally shouted, "Shut up, guys." Sharon could be pretty bossy, and everything was quiet again.

Razor crawled back in his sleeping bag and caught his breath. He said it was strange to think of Josh and Jeshel living way over there on the other side of the world, and all of the family floating on this same big ball in space, and how tiny they all were.

"And mom and Kristen are over there too," said Sharon. "Like little ants."

After the kids fell asleep, Chris said the sorrowful mysteries of the rosary. They were his favorites. They started in the garden at Gethsemane, where Jesus asks God to let this cup pass from him. That's just what I would have done, thought Chris. Let the cup pass. But then Jesus says "Thy will be done," and Chris knew he was outmatched. He could never say those words and mean them. They were the scariest words he could think of, "Thy will be done." At a minimum, Chris needed to pretend he had some control. His fingers moved along the beads to the scourging at the pillar, then the crown of thorns, then the carrying of the cross, then the death on Golgotha, the place of the skull.

Chris came close to reverence as he said this last sorrowful mystery. He came very close to love. With the twins asleep, he felt all alone out here on this little island in the middle of Table Rock Lake. He was missing Kazzie.

His back was killing him, and even though he was exhausted he couldn't get to sleep out there on his mattress on Hookermania under all those stars. Some paternal instinct had him full of nervous energy after the drama of the previous night's storm. He waded out to the Andrea Gail to read the Cuffy Kamara brief, hoping that Boynkin & Sneed's soporific legalese would put him to sleep.

Cuffy was in a whole lot of trouble. He'd all but confessed to the murder of eighty-seven year old Enola Somerville, but blamed it on crack cocaine. The Florida jury took twenty minutes to return a guilty verdict.

In the sentencing phase his court-appointed lawyer, Rufus Collins, had done a pretty good job, touching all the bases. After Russell Kamara's suicide and Yolanda Possum Kamara's nervous breakdown, Cuffy was adopted by a white American preacher named Johnny Bob Harrell who promptly changed his exotic son's name to Cuffy Harrell and removed him from Alice Springs to Tupelo, Mississippi.

There wasn't another Aboriginal kid for thousands of miles, and Cuffy was ridiculed mercilessly by whites and blacks alike for his funny accent, protruding lips, and prominent brow. Rufus Collins produced a heartbreaking high school essay written by Cuffy in tortured English, about "the man in the middle, the man in-between" who had nothing. "I had no sense of where I could call home," wrote Cuffy. "No sense of being wanted, all traces of my family disappeared." Cuffy described himself as a "half-caste" who had fallen by life's wayside. "I must say that every human being has to have these basic elements," he wrote. "A sense of belonging to someone, some identifiable area you can call home. Once you have got these things you know that love is there. They make life for a human being worth living."

After dropping out of high school at the age of 19, Cuffy left the Harrells and drifted across the South, ingesting various cocktails of illegal drugs, and dealing to stay alive. On the night of Enola Somerville's death, Cuffy was out of his mind on crack. He couldn't even remember killing her, but his fingerprints and DNA left no doubt.

The Florida jury listened politely to Rufus Collins, then recommended death by 2,000 volts of electricity in "Old Sparky," Florida's famous electric chair. Part of Boynkin & Sneed's appellate argument was that Old Sparky was cruel and unusual. They cited the botched execution in 1997 of one Pedro Medina, where flames shot out of his head, and his body continued to jolt for a few minutes after the electricity was turned off. Boynkin & Sneed's brief had covered cruel and unusual pretty well. Chris's role in Cuffy's appeal, if he wanted one, was to play the Aboriginal card and write an *amicus curiae* brief about Cuffy's horrific childhood being an inevitable consequence of Australia's misguided policy of removing Aboriginal kids from their parents.

Chris scribbled some preliminary thoughts on a yellow legal pad at the kitchen table in the Andrea Gail. Russell Kamara, Cuffy's father, had been a student of Chris's at the Melbourne University Law School. They even lived together for a few months in Chris's apartment above an old fire station on Swanston Street. Russell would come back to the fire station night after night, drunk and carrying a loaded shotgun, claiming he'd been looking for "white bastards" to blow away. Chris would listen patiently then tuck him into bed, exempted from Russell's wrath because he wasn't Australian.

But Russell never hurt anybody. His anger was aimed deep inside, at the white rapist's blood that flowed through his black veins. Chris went with him one day to the Melbourne Museum, where Russell pulled the Aboriginal skeletons out of their display cases and sat on the floor caressing them until the police arrived.

Purely by chance, Chris was in Alice Springs on the day of Russell's suicide. He'd taken the Old Gahn from Adelaide to Alice to perform at the national folk festival, and dropped by to see Russell and Yolanda at their home in The Gap. But he was too late. Russell's father-in-law, Alec Possum, told Chris that Russell had shot himself in the early morning hours after an argument with Yolanda over car keys. Chris watched little Cuffy dart between the ghost gums in the dusty front yard, wearing a Superman cape.

Chris stayed around after the folk festival for the funeral, joining the wailing Aboriginal relatives tossing handfuls of ochre earth over the red, black and yellow flag that draped Russell's coffin. If he decided to write an *amicus* brief, Chris would have a lot to say.

But he wasn't a hundred percent sure he *should* do it. Of all the lawyers in the world, he probably carried the most baggage that could come back to haunt Cuffy if the American press ever got hold of it. Cuffy's appeal was a delicate mixture of law and public relations. Chris could do the law bit. The P.R. made him nervous.

Chris drew a vertical black line down the middle of the legal pad. At the top of one column, he wrote "For," and at the top of the other column he wrote "Against."

"For" was easy. Chris wrote two things: "because it's the right thing to do," and "because I know more about it than anyone else."

But Chris's scrawlings under "Against" soon had the makings of a stream-of-consciousness novella. On page after yellow page, Chris sketched his remembrances of Yolanda Possum Kamara after the death of her husband Russell. When Cuffy was taken to Mississippi by Johnny Bob Harrell, Yolanda worked her way from Alice Springs down to Victoria and landed one afternoon on Chris's doorstep at the fire station. Chris took her in, fed her, bought her some clothes, and soon they became an item of sorts. What a sight they were, wandering around Carlton's university district, Chris in his hippie gear and his headband cut from Jockey underpants, with his woe-begotten Aboriginal sidekick.

Night after night, Yolanda cried herself to sleep in Chris's arms, telling him how much she missed little Cuffy. "I miss him more than Russell," she'd say. "It's harder when someone's still alive." At least Russell was all right now and no one could hurt him any more. He was safe in the Dreaming.

According to Yolanda Possum Kamara, Russell's maternal great-grandfather was named Djankawu, and his spirit had come from Tjukurpa, the eternal Time of the Dreaming. Chris had no idea what to make of this, but he listened anyway because Yolanda was the best storyteller he'd ever met. She didn't just tell a story - she acted it out at the foot of their fire station bed.

"Djankawu's spirit was carried around inside a Rainbow Serpent," said Yolanda. "He assumed the form of a crocodile with kangaroo ears and the tail of a platypus." She bared her teeth wide like a crocodile's, and waggled her hands at the side of her head like giant make-believe ears.

"The Serpent traveled underground, teaching Djankawu where to look for food and water, and how to conduct the ceremonies." Her voice became very soft and low, and she stood in the center of the bedroom making sweeping gestures with her long arms.

"One day a kookaburra, who had been a man in the Time of the Dreaming, speared the Rainbow Serpent in her side!" Yolanda was so excited! "And as she lay dying, she *vomited* her spirit as a seed of grass!" Yolanda brought her face close to Chris's, and for a moment he could see his own reflection in her dark pupils.

"Djankawu's father was hunting, and he heard a crying sound coming from the grass. So he called to Djankawu's mother and said that her son had already been born. Djankawu lived a long life, and when he died, his spirit went to a secret cave near the Olgas to rest in a dreaming stone until Russell was born." Yolanda sat at the edge of the bed and smiled at the thought of Russell as a child.

And she smiled again at the memory of his death. "Because at that moment," she said, "the dreaming stone was destroyed by a flash of lightning, which was the forked tongue of the Rainbow Serpent." Somehow this made perfect sense to Yolanda Possum Kamara, so she mourned no more for Russell.

But her grief for Cuffy was a different matter, and each day it went deeper and deeper inside. To bring her back, Chris sought the assistance of his pals at the law school in landing her a job with Victoria's Minister of Aboriginal Affairs, Billy Shears. Yolanda was to be Victoria's public face for the upcoming government white paper on the "stolen generations" of kidnapped Aboriginal children. Her big smile was all over Victoria's television and billboards. She didn't have to say anything. Her face said what Billy Shears wished he could say but couldn't: after all you've done to us, we are still here, and still smiling.

But one day Yolanda came back to the fire station and her smile was gone. Chris had a devil of a time finding out what had happened, and it was this: Billy Shears wanted his way with her, and if he couldn't have it, she could look for another line of work. "Just a little piece of black velvet," said Yolanda Possum Kamara. "Billy said that's all he wanted."

Chris filed a claim with the Equal Opportunity Commission on Yolanda's behalf, against the government of Victoria for sexual harassment. State Premier Judith Kennan went into damage control, and Equal Opportunity Commissioner Moira Mutimer, a Kennan appointee, ordered *in camera* proceedings. Chris wheeled and dealed with the Attorney General, reaching a final agreement that provided for a private letter of apology from the government, the relegating of Billy Shears to the back benches of parliament, and a $200,000.00 secret payout. The only catch was that Chris and Yolanda had to sign a confidentiality agreement.

This was fine until the following week, when Yolanda spilled her guts to *The Age* and the details of her payout appeared on the front page. "Hush money," it was called. An *Age* editorial demanded the resignation of Judith Kennan and her Attorney General. At first Kennan denied that any payment had been made at all. Then ABC television phoned Chris to ask him to confirm or deny *The Age's* story, and he confirmed. Chris's tell-all was the lead item for every network and newspaper in Australia.

Moira Mutimer promptly filed a complaint with the Victoria Law Institute, asking that Chris be barred from practicing or teaching law because of his unethical breach of the confidentiality agreement. Chris sued Judith Kennan for labeling him a liar. Kennan and Mutimer sued the ABC for defamation. All hell was breaking loose, and the government was on the ropes, ready to fall.

At that very moment, a waste disposal plant on Coode Island blew up, killing four workers and polluting half the State of Victoria. Kennan put on a yellow hard hat and walked heroically through Coode Island's sprawling wasteland as the cameras captured the dramatic story. She promised to avenge the death of the workers with the toughest environmental laws in Australia. Chris's litigation moved to page three of *The Age*, then to page seven, then to no page at all. Finally the government settled his lawsuit quietly, giving him enough money to disappear into the Wombat Forest with Kazzie. Christian Leonard Hooker was yesterday's news. Christian Leonard Hooker was nobody.

Chris stopped daydreaming and rested his pen on the Andrea Gail's kitchen table. Clearly he did not come with clean hands to the defense of Cuffy Kamara. If he was going to jump in on this appeal, he had to be sure he wouldn't do more harm than good. He sighed and put the Kamara brief back in its case.

Despite their best efforts, Boynkin & Sneed hadn't succeeded in putting Chris to sleep on the Andrea Gail. In fact, even though it was well past midnight, he was more awake now then ever. He decided to try watching a movie on the DVD player, and found *The Bridges of Madison County* in his stolen pile, starring Meryl Streep and Clint Eastwood. Chris had never read Robert James Waller's book, and was sure he wouldn't like it if he tried. He'd read somewhere that *The Bridges of Madison County* was a favorite of Bill Clinton's, which worried him for reasons he couldn't explain.

Chris made himself comfortable on the kitchen's fold-out bed. It was weird watching this DVD alone in the middle of Table Rock Lake, little lights flickering from the shore all around him as his twins slept beneath the constellations.

In the movie, an Italian woman, Meryl Streep doing one of her accents, marries an American soldier after WWII. He's kind, but a bit boring. Actually, quite a bit boring. They have two children, a boy and a girl. When the kids are approaching early adolescence, Dad takes them off to the State Fair for four days in the summertime. Meryl stays home to look after the farm.

A handsome and soft-spoken National Geographic photographer, Clint Eastwood, pulls up the driveway in a pick-up truck on Day One. He's shooting the covered bridges of Madison County for the magazine, which is no real surprise

given the title. He's lost. Meryl helps him find his way. They
feel a distant stirring, especially when Meryl learns that Clint
has been to her little home town in Italy. He's been all over
the world, and naturally he's divorced with no family ties.

Meryl asks Clint to dinner, and he says ok. Clint and
Meryl eat in the kitchen, where the floor is covered with
linoleum. They talk, but he doesn't stay the night. Chris put
the DVD on pause as he made some microwave popcorn and
opened a Michelob Ultra low-carb beer. He started to wonder what Kazzie was doing in Australia. Hmm.

Meryl and Clint meet at a bridge on Day Two, a covered
one. They smoke cigarettes and drink beer. Later, they dance
on the linoleum floor. And this time, at the end of the day,
they hop in bed together.

For some reason, Meryl is peeved the next morning. She
and Clint argue in the kitchen, on the linoleum. She doesn't
want to be just another one of his girls in every port. She
wants it to mean something.

So Clint tells her it does. He says it means more than anything, so she's happy. They talk about running away together,
but she can't really do that because of her family in Iowa. So
Clint leaves, and the family comes home, and thirty years
later Clint is dead and Meryl is dead and her boring husband
is dead. Meryl's grown-up children, who now have children
of their own, open their mother's box of Special Things and
learn what she was up to while they were at the State Fair.

The grown-up children come to a greater understanding
of the complexities of love, and start *right now* to put their
own houses in order. Life is short. They scatter their mother's
ashes from one of the covered bridges, the same one where
Clint's ashes were scattered. Together at last, just like Grigori
Bekyeshova and Fairy Belle Fanke. Chris finished off his popcorn and took the last swig of low-carb beer.

The Bridges of Madison County was just what he needed,
because it made him really exhausted. He waded back out to
his mattress on Hookermania, dried his feet, and crawled
under a sleeping bag to think himself to sleep.

What was he supposed to make of this movie? What if Meryl had been having her period when Clint pulled up in his pick-up? Would he have minded? Would she? What if she'd stepped onto the porch on Day Two and slipped and cracked her head against the porch-swing, getting a big cut? Would Clint have driven her to the hospital for stitches? Would they have got so worked up on the linoleum after that? What if it had been the middle of an Iowa winter, not summer, and Meryl couldn't have stood on the porch opening her bathrobe to let the cool evening breeze blow over her parts?

Chris wondered just what it was they *did* over those three days, and what Kazzie was doing *right now.* The movie only showed a few candles around a bathtub, a few gropes and kisses. There must have been more, and it must have been pretty good. In one scene, Clint slid down the bed and disappeared from the screen, leaving the top half of Meryl all alone with the camera. Where had Clint gone? Chris wondered. And why was Meryl moaning? He was getting *really* drowsy now. Orion had moved halfway across the Table Rock sky. His thoughts were becoming a jumbled mess.

What if they *had* run off together, Meryl and Clint? At one point, Meryl's bags were packed and ready to go. Then after her husband got back home, she had her hand on the door handle of his truck, ready to jump out and run after Clint in the pouring rain! What would have happened then? Would she have gone with Clint to live in his apartment back east? Would she have met his cousins and nephews and nieces? Who would have done the shopping? Would Clint have helped with the cooking, or just chopped an occasional carrot?

Would Meryl have found a job, or stayed home looking after the apartment? Would Clint have kept trotting around the globe taking photographs while she waited for his return, or would she have tagged along like Anne Morrow Lindbergh?

Would she have written to her children? Would she have had visitation rights? Would her husband have filed for a nasty divorce, with a smarmy Iowa lawyer? Would Clint's and Meryl's love have grown, or just become bogged down, or settled into cruise control? Would she have tried to get Clint to stop smoking? Would he have been unsettled by her bathroom noises? Would they have had kids of their own? Would Clint have been a good dad, helping to change the diapers, driving the kids off to gymnastics classes when they got older, helping them with their homework? If they did have kids, would poor Meryl have thought, "This is a nightmare. If only I'd stayed in Iowa, I'd have been finished with the kids in *seven years*. Now I won't be through until I'm *fifty-six!*"

What in the world *did* they do to each other over those three days, wondered Chris, in and out of sleep now. What wisdom was this movie trying to impart? That if you put your love in a bottle like a pickled fetus, that's better than the mess of letting it spill out all over the place, as Chris had done over and over again?

Maybe you should just sit there and admire your little love-fetus for the rest of your days, never changing, always perfect, always on the edge of becoming. Chris's last conscious thoughts for this Tuesday night were that he bet Bill Clinton's ashes would never be scattered over the Potomac with Monica Lewinsky's, and he wondered one more time just what Kazzie was up to.

WEDNESDAY:
MORE GLORIOUS MYSTERIES

I hold a beast, an angel and a madman in me,
and my enquiry is as to their working,
and my problem is their subjugation and victory,
downthrow and upheaval,
and my effort is their self-expression

Dylan Marlais Thomas

You wondered why you couldn't just be nice. What was the matter with you? Why couldn't you go to a dinner party with your wife and just talk to people? Why couldn't you stand to be in the same room with either of your ancient parents, or both of them? They were so old now, in their eighties, with only a few more years to live. They would be dead, and then what would it have meant that they'd been alive? What in the hell was the matter with you? You were in your fifties, for Christ's sake. What in the hell was the matter with you? You should have fixed this up a long, long time ago. Instead you got as far away as you could get, in mind and in body, you pretended you were remaking yourself when all you were really doing was spinning your wheels. Even now you were hiding in rooms until they all left, until you could tell by the sounds coming through the walls that they were gone, your sisters or your brother or your wife's friends. How pathetic was that?

Studge came pretty close to getting it right, in his short story "Southern Cross," where he turned himself into one of his own characters and flew himself all the way to Australia to visit his old Okaw City pal Hooker, his own creation, right there at the law school where Hooker was teaching, where Hooker had this reputation as a wild man in a rock band running marathons and serial-dating his own students, and Studge got Hooker all hung up between personae, trapped in a double-bind between law school cool and Okaw City nobody, in no-man's-land between axon and dendrite. Remember? You saw that same thing later with Sean, after the split with Elspeth, when he became a sorrowful boy with darting eyes whenever he had to sit in the same room or in a car with his father and his mother, all torn up because he was one way with her and another way with you and the two Seans could never be reconciled.

And there at the law school in Melbourne Studge had his Hooker fall in a heap in the commons, people staring at him, faculty and students, he lay there in a heap, a great big heap, just the way you'd done that night when Studge's father was killed in that car crash. Sort of twitching there on the ground in neuron disconnect or synapse overload until finally the students and faculty got bored watching him and moved along.

And now in real life you were doing the same thing, still doing the same thing, here in Sand River, in your fifties for Christ's sake. You would sit there in rooms, at tables, and not talk. You would sit there in driveways and not come inside. You would find a hidden room, a garage, at family gatherings and stay there until it was time to go. You couldn't think of anything to say. You didn't want to make them uncomfortable you told yourself, but you couldn't think of anything to say. So you'd hide until it was safe, or go out to a book shop or a coffee house to sit alone at a table reading your newspapers or left-wing magazines, people would know who you were because you were there so often sitting at your tables, but you'd never spoken to a soul.

After all, you'd gone all the way to Australia to get away from them and from Illinois and from yourself, and to the *reservation, and to South America, and finally to the forest, and now you were back (home?) in Illinois and when you were in the same room with them it was as if you'd never been away at all, as if twenty years of your life, thirty years, forty years, had passed and nothing had ever changed and nothing had happened except that you were incommunicado. He could be pretty perceptive, that Studge, he really could.*

* * * * * * * * *

On Wednesday morning, Chris's goal in life was to get the Andrea Gail back to Tri-Lakes by noon so he wouldn't have to pay the late fee. The rental form said "late returns will be charged $100.00 per hour or any part of an hour. To avoid late charge, your boat should be refilled with gasoline and unloaded no later than noon." It was bad enough that he was going to have to talk his way out of paying for Razor's graffiti.

Their island of Hookermania was at least four location markers from Tri-Lakes, and Chris reckoned that translated to about three hours' travel. He didn't want to rush, because that missed the whole point of lazing around on a houseboat with the kids. So he fixed up a little breakfast on the grill, untied the ropes from the island, and reversed to the middle of the lake. Sharon took the helm.

"Stone the crows," she shouted. Chris had no idea what she meant.

Chris's back was feeling a whole lot better, but not great. His elbow was still swollen, but the cuts on his arm were healing nicely. He propped himself up on a pillow and enjoyed the ride. Razor was spying on other boats with the binoculars. Then he'd turn them around and look through the big end to make everybody tiny. Then he'd mess with the focus so everybody got fuzzy. Then he used just one lens to make it a telescope, which was more pirate-like. Chris hadn't known there were so many ways to be amused with a pair of binoculars. He'd bought this pair in Fiji almost thirty years ago, on his first trip to Australia. Since then, he'd used them at

Australian Rules football games, but hardly anything else. If he kept them long enough, they'd be collector's items.

After a couple of hours, Razor took the wheel and Chris looked through the binoculars for a location marker. Table Rock Lake winds around a lot, and it's so wide in places it's hard to see the markers. In the hills before them, Chris could see three little green spikes, like half a crown, sticking up from the trees. Through the binoculars, Chris saw that the spikes were the top of somebody's idea of a cool lakefront house, a triple A-frame tucked away in the hills.

"Look there, Razor," he said. "Didn't we pass those green things yesterday, going the other way?"

Razor didn't know. Sharon thought she remembered some green towers. Chris was totally disoriented. He looked to the sun to try to get some bearings, but it was too close to noon to be of any help.

"I think we're going the wrong way," said Chris. He considered his two options. The hundred dollar fine was a growing possibility.

"Let's turn the boat around," he said. "We've got to make up some lost time."

"Hey, Dad," said Razor in mid-turn, "this is just like George Clooney."

Here on Table Rock Lake, the sky was clear and the waters were calm, but Razor made-believe he was in *The Perfect Storm*, crashing trough monstrous waves and turning the Andrea Gail against all odds, a precise maneuver by the skilled captain of a ten-ton fishing boat.

Chris was getting worried, and kept multiplying the hundred dollar fee times the number of hours he figured they'd be late. He took over the wheel, as if that could somehow make the Andrea Gail go faster. He told Razor and Sharon to keep a lookout for markers, but they had better things to do with Razor's Yu-Gi-Oh cards.

Forty-five minutes later, Chris saw something that made him rub his eyes. He pulled the throttle back to neutral. There in the distance, high in the trees, were three green towers rising from the hills. What could this mean? Had he been going in circles? Had Razor screwed up the turn while Chris wasn't paying attention? Chris had no idea which direction would take him to the Holy Grail of the Tri-Lakes dock. There were no markers to be seen, and the sun beat down from the midday sky. He got very grumpy, and just sat there for a few minutes at the wheel with the houseboat motor idling away. Worse, his gasoline was getting low, and he didn't know how far he was from a marina. Sharon finally figured out the obvious.

"There must be two pointy houses," she said. "I remember we saw one yesterday near Moonshine Beach."

Chris mulled this over. It made sense. The green towers ahead of them must be yesterday's. He'd been going in the *right* direction when he saw the ones that were now behind them. Some rich Branson architect probably sold these green triple A-frames by the dozen.

"We've got to turn around again," said Chris, but he still wasn't sure he had it right. "Keep looking for markers."

"Good one, Dad," said Razor as Chris started his turn. He and Sharon tried not to laugh. They were happy to stay on the Andrea Gail all day long. Chris growled to himself. If only there'd been a foot accelerator on the Andrea Gail instead of this stupid hand throttle, Chris could have put the pedal to the metal and had them home in no time. But they were crawling along at eight miles an hour. And even at that walking speed, Chris had the Andrea Gail groaning like the *Orca*, Quince's fishing boat in *Jaws*, on its smoky last legs as the great shark circles and Richard Dreyfuss and Roy Scheider have simultaneous heart attacks.

Chris thought of JFK Jr. on his fatal flight to Martha's Vineyard. Chris had no bearings out here on Table Rock Lake. If he'd been John-John flying a plane at night, with no stars or lights to guide him, he wouldn't have known whether he was going up or down, left or right, and he would have crashed straight into the sea, killing himself and Carolyn and her sister. Chris could be a real drama queen.

Finally, around one o'clock, Chris saw the marker near Tonka Point, where they'd stopped yesterday at the Indian Point Marina. He was elated, and let out a little whoop. He docked the Andrea Gail to fill up with gasoline, then quickly got her back on the lake for the last stretch. Even as he was exiting around Tonka Point, though, he double-checked to make sure he was headed in the right direction. All these coves and A-frames had him mistrusting his judgment.

Finally they started to recognize familiar landmarks. Sharon saw Little Cow Cove, where they'd docked the first night and nearly drowned in the hurricane. Then came the buoys they'd passed before they became pirates. At last the Tri-Lakes sign came into view.

Chris hadn't noticed on the way out, but Tri-Lakes was part of a big complex called "What's Up Dock." The twins thought that was pretty funny, and started doing Bugs Bunny imitations, crossing their legs, tilting their heads and putting make-believe carrots to their mouths. "What's up, Doc," they'd say. They didn't sound much like pirates anymore.

"Where should I park?" Chris shouted to Adonis, still shirtless, the same guy who'd given the houseboat instructions two days before. Chris realized he shouldn't have said "park," but it was too late. Adonis was smirking. He had Chris toss him a rope, and he pulled the houseboat in.

"What's this Andrea Gail crap?" he asked, pointing to Razor's graffiti all over the hull.

"Don't worry," said Chris. "It'll come off. The kids were just having a little fun."

Adonis wasn't impressed. He rubbed his finger across one of Razor's indelible pirate ships.

"My boss'll have to charge you fifty bucks for that," he said. "It's in the contract."

Chris pulled out his "Rental Confirmation" documents. On the first page, right under "late returns," were the words "a cleaning charge of $50.00 will be made on boats returned unclean."

"But this boat's not unclean," said Chris. Except for the graffiti, this was true. He and the kids had the Andrea Gail spic & span, and Razor and Sharon were unloading their belongings onto the dock. Adonis ignored him and walked over to the Tri-Lakes office. His boss, a stern-looking woman wearing a Jimmy Buffet T-shirt, came out a few minutes later with a piece of paper.

"Have a good time, Mr. Hooker?" she asked.

"Great," said Chris, "except for that hurricane the first night."

"That's southern Missouri for you," she said. "If you don't like the weather, wait five minutes." Chris could tell she thought this was a pretty funny line, one that had drawn chuckles from hundreds of happy houseboaters in the past. Chris chuckled too, hoping it might save him a few bucks. She told Chris she'd almost sent a rescue boat out to look for them, but "it was too dangerous."

"I understand," said Chris. He was being very polite. Sharon and Razor were amused.

She handed him the piece of paper. "I'll only charge you an extra three-fifty," she said. "Three hours' late fee, and fifty bucks for cleaning off that graffiti."

Chris looked at his watch. He was only a couple hours late, but he didn't feel like arguing. He pulled the cash out of his wallet and settled up on the spot. Razor and Sharon were surprised to see their dad give up money without a fight. This was most unlike the Chris they knew.

"Thank you for your business, Mr. Hooker," said the Jimmy Buffet lady. "We hope to see you again next summer." She gave him a dirty little wink: "Bring your wife along next time."

Chris could tell she was fishing for information, trying to find out if Chris was divorced or a widower or some guy who was kidnapping his kids. "So long," he said, and loaded up the Windstar. Dopey was still sitting on the dashboard, faithfully tending his post.

They took Highway 160 up to Springfield, then got on 13 to take them all the way to Interstate 70 and Independence, which boasted that it was the home town of President Harry S

Truman. More importantly for the Hookers, it was now the home town of Chris's sister Lauren and her husband Brian. They lived not far from the old Truman house, and they'd agreed to put Chris and the kids up for a couple of nights.

"We'd love to have you," Lauren said on the phone, and it sounded to Chris like she really meant it, although he was never quite sure with Lauren because she was always nice to everybody and especially to Chris.

They stopped for gasoline and lunch at Smith's Restaurant in the little town of Collins, Missouri. Chris bought a St. Louis *Post-Dispatch* to check on the Cardinals and anything else that was happening. While Chris was neglecting them on Tuesday, fooling around counting condoms and constellations on Hookermania, the Cards lost 3-2 to the Padres, falling four games behind the Astros in the National League Central. Jeff Fassero and Garrett Stephenson had combined their bush-league pitching skills for the loss.

There was a full-page column about the Cardinals' close losses. They were 5-18 for the year in one-run games, including the last two losses while Chris was on the houseboat. This was the worst close-games record in the major leagues. Even the Detroit Tigers, the season's lousiest team, were 11-12 in one-run games.

"No team will win a division title or go deeper into the playoffs with a close-games mark like that," wrote the columnist. A photograph of a glum Brett Tomko accompanied the article. Chris didn't like the way Tomko wore his Cardinals hat. He made Chris think of some European tourist trying to ingratiate himself with Americans. Tomko's bill had no shape, and the sides sat down too far, touching his ears. The hat made Tomko look like a giant elf, not a big-league pitcher.

A waitress with big hair walked over to the Hooker booth and said, "Good afternoon, my name is Della Lu. I'll be your waitress today." Chris forced a smile and asked for glasses of water all round. He could tell Della Lu wasn't impressed with the big spender. "With lots of ice," he said.

The booth had a little coin-operated t.v. set, so Chris and Razor went to the men's room while Sharon watched a local program. Chris and Razor shared the same urinal, and Razor wanted to make an X with their pee, so Chris pointed left while Razor pointed right, except Razor's aim wasn't so good and he splashed Chris's shoes.

"Sorry Dad," he said. "The room was shaking."

Chris noticed the bathroom *was* swaying back and forth.

"Did you feel it?" asked Razor.

"Yeah," said Chris. "It's like the whole room's moving. Must be a Missouri earthquake."

But when they went back to their booth, everybody was acting normal, as if nothing had happened. Chris asked Della Lu if there'd been an earthquake. She looked at him like he was crazy and said in an official voice, "No sir, I don't believe so." She sucked in her fat little cheeks. Chris watched her go behind the counter and whisper something in another waitress's ear. They both giggled.

"I felt something when I first came in," said Sharon. "But it stopped."

Chris decided to phone Sand River to check with Sean on the pets and the pool. He walked over to Smith's pay phone, still feeling a bit wobbly. Sean was home, and seemed to be in good spirits, although he sounded like he was talking far away in a tunnel. He'd had a good time in Chicago, and caught the City of New Orleans back to Sand River on the same Sunday Chris and the kids had left. He said the weather was good, the pool was fine, and the pets were doing well except the big cat, Merlin, had disappeared.

"Don't worry, Dad," he said. "He does that every time Kazzie goes away. He'll be back." Chris told Sean he missed him.

"Huh?" said Sean. He wasn't sure if Chris missed him or the cat.

Frankly, Chris was a little worried about the pets back in Sand River. Kazzie would kill him if the cats disappeared, and even the death of the beta fish or the frog would cause a family feud. Chris had a disastrous history of taking care of

Hooker pets, beginning in Australia shortly after Sean was born. Chris felt terrible that, inevitably, his first child would die one day in unpleasant circumstances. For as long as possible, he vowed to keep Sean blissfully ignorant of death.

So when Sean turned two, Chris skipped the part of the Babar story where the little elephant's mother is killed by cruel hunters. And if Chris and Sean came near a dead cat on one of their Williamstown walks, Chris would have Sean chase a butterfly or blow on a dandelion, anything to avoid having to explain about the cat.

So one morning, Chris was shocked to hear Sean's little voice: "What happened to fishy, Daddy?" It was six a.m., and Chris thought he was alone. Dangling between Chris's thumb and index finger was the tail fin of Sean's pet goldfish, Bertie. Beneath Bertie's carcass, on the kitchen table, was a neatly folded piece of tissue paper. Chris released his grip and Bertie fell into her homemade casket.

"Bertie jumped out of her bowl," said Chris. Sean edged closer to the kitchen table for a better look.

"Is she dead?" he asked.

Chris realized there'd been gaps in his death-screening. He gave in to Sean's dawning of mortality.

"Yes, Bertie's dead," he said. "Shall we bury her?"

To Chris's surprise, Sean was pretty enthusiastic, and knew just what to do. He plucked the dead fish from the tissue and grabbed a teaspoon. He led Chris to the back yard and dug a little hole under the rosebush. After covering Bertie, Sean put up a little cross made of popsicle sticks.

Six months later, after Josh was born, and then the secret Jeshel, Chris tried to make up for Sean's dead goldfish by buying a pair of gray finches. But Chris didn't know that only the males have a patch of orange on their cheeks, or that two males in the same cage do not get along. After waiting a week for his male finches to start breeding, Chris was horrified one morning to find the mutilated body of the weaker male lying belly up at the bottom of the cage. Sean took it in stride, and got a couple more popsicle sticks from Elspeth.

Chris tried again. He bought a white female for the alpha male. But her eyes got red and she lost her tail-feathers. Within a week, she too was lying at the bottom of the cage with her feet in the air, dead of diarrhea.

"What a way to go," Chris whispered to the dead body. He noticed that Sean started taking a keener interest in his toilet training after that.

Chris went back to an expensive shop in downtown Melbourne, known as "Pet Paradise." He checked all the females' eyes, peeked under their tail feathers. He went for the one that was hardest to catch, with a clean little bottom and shiny black eyes. He brought her home, and was ecstatic when she mated with the male. Two tiny white eggs appeared in the nest Chris had stapled to the top of the cage. The mother and father finches took turns sitting on the eggs, and two weeks later a couple of scraggly babies, unfeathered and sightless, poked their bony little heads through the egg-shells. Sean was thrilled at the miracle of new life.

But a week later, the spring rains came to Williamstown from across the bay. "Shouldn't we bring the birdies in?" asked Sean. Elspeth agreed, although she was never very happy about having the birds in the first place. She thought it was cruel to keep creatures locked up in cages.

"Nah," said Chris. "Birds are used to rain."

He went to bed and fell asleep, cuddling the boys, mid-sentence in Sean's favorite Dr. Seuss story about Thidwick the kind-hearted moose. That night the rainfall set a new record for the State of Victoria. In the morning, Chris was first-up and found his adult finches still alive, but wet and shivering. Sadly, the babies had drowned in their nest. Chris said a little prayer and flushed them down the toilet.

The adults recovered to breed again. Chris hung their cage on the orange tree in the back yard, and brought it inside whenever he saw a drop of rain. When two more eggs appeared in the nest one morning, Chris thought nothing could go wrong. The eggs hatched. Two naked babies appeared. The parents fed them. They grew. Then one night it started to pour.

"Aha," Chris said to Sean, "I'll move them inside!"
But as he untied the cage from the outstretched limbs of
the orange tree, his smooth-soled sandals slipped on the wet
porch. Chris fell flat on his back with a thud. The bird cage
somersaulted across the porch, coming to rest awkwardly
against the back doorstep. Chris speed-crawled to the cage to
shut the wire door, but the white female had bolted.
He looked into the cage. The father bird and the babies
were fine. But the mother just darted from tree to tree in the
back yard, like a tiny haywire beacon. With one final arro-
gant cheep, she flew into the night sky never to return.
In the coming days, the stupid male had no idea how to
take care of the babies by himself, and they died. Chris
cursed his luck as Sean and Elspeth, and even baby Josh,
seemed to avoid eye contact.
A year passed before Chris was brave enough to try again.
By that time, Elspeth had left him and the boys were with her
most of the time. Chris kept the male with him in his van at
the end of Acland Street, across from the Seven-Eleven.
They'd sleep there together at night, then Chris would drive
early each morning to his office in the heart of Melbourne, in
the Owen Dixon Chambers on William Street, where there
was a grotty old shower on the top floor for homeless barris-
ters like himself. He'd leave the bird cage in his office when
he went off to court.
In these lonesome weeks before his brief affair with Jillian
Daley Shulman, Chris was badly in need of romance. He
bought another nubile white female with a firm, healthy bottom. Her eyes sparkled with devilment. She seemed attracted
to the male right from the start, but Chris kept her in a separate carrying cage for a couple of days, right next to the
male's larger cage, to whet their appetites.
When the exciting day of transfer arrived, Chris lined up
the door of the female's carrying cage precisely against the
door of the male's big cage. He checked the van's windows
one last time to make sure they were shut tight. Nothing
could go wrong. Even if the female did get loose during the

move, there was no place for her to go. Chris's nervous fingers fumbled with the cage doors.

Yes, she *did* manage to slip away, but Chris just laughed.

"Where are you going, my sweetie?" he said aloud. "There's nowhere to go. Come to Hooker."

He stretched the palm of his hand toward her. She danced around in the van, mocking him. He took a couple of playful swipes at her in mid-air, but she pirouetted away. Chris laughed again. He loved being back in the chase.

He cornered her near the foot pedal, but she bobbed and weaved like a bantamweight and flitted under his elbow. She darted to the rear of the van, where she sat at the top of the back seat, panting. Perversely, Chris felt a twinge of animal passion. To his surprise, he was turned on. The male finch, preening in his cage, cheeped encouragement. Chris leered at the female. "Gotcha now," he whispered.

He moved slowly and paused within inches of her undulating breast-feathers, ready to pounce in final assault, but she deftly side-stepped his enormous face and flew forward to the radio, slithering into a dark crack behind the dashboard. Chris had never even *seen* the crack before.

"Jesus," he said to the male. He waited and listened for about half an hour. He could hear the fluttering of her wings somewhere in there, maybe over by the electrical system now. He opened the driver's door a crack and slipped out as quickly as he could. He crawled under the van, but couldn't see any sign of her. He could just hear her flapping wings.

A homeless woman named Sirita, a Hungarian immigrant, watched this whole drama from outside the door of Thula's second-hand clothing shop. Chris knew Sirita pretty well. They often spoke with each other, and Chris bought her packets of Winston cigarettes from the Seven-Eleven whenever she needed a smoke. She spent her nights there in Thula's dooryard, all rugged up with blankets in winter, smoking her cigarettes. Most evenings, she and Chris would be the last to bid each other good night, like an old married couple, before retiring to their separate bedrooms. In halting English, Sirita told Chris that his bird would never come back.

"Don't be silly," said Chris. "Doesn't she know I won't hurt her? All I want to do is get her to mate and feed her and take care of her. Why won't she come out?"

These were rhetorical questions. Sirita just sucked on her Winston and stared away. Somehow she managed to look regal, squatting there in Thula's dooryard.

For two days Chris skipped work, fearing that if he started his engine he'd grind the female to bits. But on the third night, the sound of her wings stopped completely. Chris crawled under the van for another look, and mercifully there were no white feathers. She'd just disappeared.

In the morning, Chris drove to the Owen Dixon Chambers, splashed himself in the top-floor shower, put on his horse-hair wig and robes, and went to court. He found a home for the male finch the following day, and stayed away from pets until he moved with Kazzie to the Wombat Forest. Then he relented, and they got a couple of goats, a pony, a dozen bantams, and a Pomeranian watchdog named Bear.

All this time, as Chris was remembering his dead pets, Sean was hanging on at the other end of Smith's pay telephone.

"Are you still there Dad?" he shouted. Chris snapped out of his reverie, still a little wobbly from the undulating bathroom. Surely there must be a series of Missouri earthquakes underway.

"Yeah, I'm still here." He'd forgotten what they'd been talking about, and decided to end the conversation.

"Look after yourself. And take care of the pets," he said. Razor and Sharon said a few words to Sean until a recorded voice on the pay phone demanded more money.

Chris and the kids arrived at Lauren's home in Independence around supper time, and Lauren had a surprise for them. She'd gone all the way to Sand River and brought Alma Ruth back to Independence for a few days.

"She and Dad need to get away from each other," Lauren explained. "They were driving each other crazy."

Alma Ruth couldn't remember how to cook or drive any-more. She had trouble putting her shoes on the right feet. Leonard was trying to keep the house going and still find time for his crossword puzzles and television shows. So they weren't eating much in Sand River, and their house wasn't as clean as it used to be.

Alma Ruth started to give Chris a big hug, but Chris wasn't a very huggy guy except for Kazzie and the kids. Poor Alma Ruth. Her doctor had loaded her up with estrogen, which gave her breast cancer and got her all confused, and now she was humped over and losing her speech. Her cats were dying down.

Her new doctor said she was in the early stages of Alzheimer's, but Chris didn't believe it.

"You just have trouble with your words," he told her. "Your brain's fine."

Chris told everybody to think of her as an old Chinese woman speaking an obscure regional dialect. All they had to do was learn the meaning of her sounds and gestures.

"If they just take the time to figure you out, you're always making sense," he told her. Alma Ruth liked to hear that, but Lauren told Chris he was in denial.

Alma Ruth was in the process of giving everything away to her grown-up children. She'd brought a bunch of old scrapbooks going back eighty years or so, family histories of Hookers and Bekyeshovas and Fankes in photos and faded letters and old newspaper articles. These were for Lauren, because Chris couldn't be trusted to take care of them.

When Chris was little, he was the one most interested in Alma Ruth's scrapbooks. The photos and stories seemed so old then. But now the old times didn't seem so long ago, even though a lot more years had passed. It didn't make sense. Time was shrinking.

The scrapbooks had photos of Alma Ruth with people who could remember Lincoln and Grant and the Civil War; Razor and Sharon would live long enough to know kids who would grow old in the second half of the twenty-second century. But that huge span of three hundred years, with Christian Leonard Hooker at its epicenter, was compressing as he grew older. Now he felt closer to the people in the old photos, not farther away.

For Chris, Alma Ruth had a big suitcase full of posters, newspaper articles, and critical reviews from the American tour she'd organized for his Australian bluegrass band, the Rank Strangers, fifteen years earlier. She'd put in hundreds of hours writing letters and working the phones, negotiating gigs in Iowa and Tennessee, Kentucky and Indiana, as well as Illinois. The Rank Strangers got nice critiques from *Bluegrass Unlimited* and some overseas music journals, and Alma Ruth had laminated every one. The *BU* review of the first album was typical:

> The Rank Strangers sing songs with lyrical intrigue - some are serious, some are fun, and nearly all of them are challenging in one way or another. Lead singer and guitarist Christian Hooker wrote the ten songs on the album. Although born in Illinois, Hooker now lives in Australia - the native country for all his fellow band members.
>
> The main appeal in the Strangers' sound is in their trio singing and sensible band arrangements. The whole project is well produced. The sound quality is good and the lyrical scope and melodic substance of the Rank Strangers' original material leaves BU anxious to hear their second release, which is already on the market.

"I was so proud," said Alma Ruth. She'd traveled with the band to the International Bluegrass Music Association concert in Owensboro, Kentucky, on the banks of the Ohio River. Everybody was there - Bill Monroe, Ralph Stanley, Doyle Lawson, Peter Rowan, Jim & Jesse, Mac Wiseman.

Emmy Lou Harris had the top billing, although she wasn't really bluegrass. Little Alison Krauss had come down to Owensboro from her home in Sand River, but she was only sixteen years old and hadn't won any of her grammies yet. She wasn't even as famous as dumb old Christian Hooker, just a little schoolgirl fiddler who couldn't miss. She palled around with Chris because they were both from Sand River, and because Bob Dylan had told her to be nice to everybody on the way up - one day she might meet them coming down. She kept introducing Chris to her bluegrass buddies as "the Australian bloke."

Alison Krauss loaned Chris her dobro player for the IBMA concert, and the Rank Strangers warmed up the huge crowd with eight of Chris's songs. They got a nice hand, but they knew everybody was hanging out for Ralph and Emmy Lou.

Alma Ruth had brought some framed photographs of Chris standing with Bill Monroe and Doyle Lawson on the banks of the Ohio, all of them wearing dark blue suits. She kept taking things out of her suitcase and setting them next to Chris, but he didn't seem interested in all this stuff. He just sat there on the couch reading Boynkin & Sneed's Cuffy Kamara brief as Alma Ruth pulled the Rank Strangers out and put them back again. Finally she packed up and went into the kitchen to talk with Lauren for a while, then went to bed early.

"I'm not feeling so well," she said, climbing the stairs one-by-one. "See you in the morning." Razor and Sharon ran to the stairs to give her a goodnight kiss. "Don't let the bedbugs bite," said Sharon.

After Alma Ruth had gone upstairs, Chris re-opened her suitcase and thumbed through the bluegrass photos. He was looking for one that would have meant nothing to her, but was the only one that mattered to him. He found it in a manila folder, and motioned for Razor and Sharon to come sit next to him on the couch.

He showed them a picture of four cowboys standing on a dirt road outside an American Legion hall in Eagle Butte,

South Dakota. One of them was Chris, looking a lot different, with three guys he identified as Gerald Yellowhawk, Hobo LeBeau, and Raymond Charging Thunder. Each of them was holding an instrument - Chris had a mandolin, Gerald was on bass, Hobo had a fiddle, and Ray held a guitar. Chris's head was shaved, and he had a long brown beard. He wore a Western-style white shirt, a string tie, blue jeans with a big-buckled belt, and a pair of purple cowboy boots. Nobody was smiling.

"We called ourselves the Missouri Valley Drifters," said Chris. "Our banjo player isn't in the picture. We were playing that day at his funeral." Chris handed the photo to Razor for a closer look. "He was my best friend."

Razor and Sharon had never heard this story. They hadn't heard much at all about Chris's reservation days, and they wanted to know more. Chris told them his friend's name was Cheeto High Bear, an ex-Air Force pilot and rodeo rider who'd taught Chris how to play bluegrass.

"We played two of Cheeto's favorite songs for him that day - 'Strawberry Roan' and 'Blind Willie McTell'."

Razor shook the folder and a piece of paper dropped out. It was a memorial holy card from Cheeto's funeral mass at Eagle Butte's All Saints Catholic Church. On the front was a picture of St. Sebastian, rapt in ecstasy and pierced with a bevy of sharp arrows. On the back was a poem by the fiddler Hobo LeBeau, written specially for Cheeto's funeral. Razor handed it to Sharon, and she read it out loud:

> O Great Mystery,
> I, Cheeto High Bear, your humble servant,
> Have made my final ride here on earth.
> I know you're proud of me, 'cause I marked my
>   final score of 87.
> I dreamed of being world champ,
> But I have been called to ride a bronc for you
> In the Biggest and Best Rodeo of All,
> Where only the best can ride.

But O Great Mystery, I have one final request for you,
And that's to watch over my rodeo buddies
As they ride their stock,
And keep them from any harm.
And please don't be sad, my family and friends,
For my dreams have all come true.

"How did Cheeto High Bear die?" asked Sharon. She enjoyed the sound of his name, and how the words formed in her mouth. But Chris didn't feel like talking anymore. He put the photo back in the folder, and the folder back in the suitcase.

The kids liked hearing about the bluegrass. They were amazed at the idea of Chris standing in front of a big audience, singing and playing his mandolin or guitar. He'd stopped all this before they were born, and they couldn't imagine him doing it now. "You should start playing your guitar again," said Razor. He wanted his dad to be famous so he could impress his friends at St. Anthony's.

"Maybe some day," said Chris. His Martin D-28 hadn't been out of its case in five years. But sometimes he'd put his old songs on the Windstar's CD player when no one was with him, and sing along with himself.

Lauren and her husband Brian cooked up a late barbecue as Chris and the kids freshened up in the swimming pool. Razor and Sharon looked radiant in the underwater light after the murky waters of Table Rock Lake. When they swam over near the light, their whole bodies were luminous with shimmering halos.

When Chris got out of the pool to use the toilet, he felt *another* earthquake. "Did you feel that?" he asked Lauren when he came back to the pool.

"What are you talking about?" she said. She was used to Chris saying crazy things.

"I didn't feel a thing," said Brian, flipping over a hamburger.

"It felt like the house was moving," said Chris. He sat in one of the deck chairs like a film director. "I've been wobbly all day." He gripped the arms of the chair and watched the kids swim.

"It's the houseboat," said Brian. "A couple of days out on a lake and you'll wobble for sure."

He put a slice of catfish and some vegetables on Chris's plate, and handed him a low-carb beer. Brian and Lauren were nice about Chris's weird eating habits.

"That's it!" Razor shouted from the pool. "It was the Andrea Gail, not an earthquake!"

"Dad, you're so dumb," said Sharon. She was practicing synchronized swimming in the middle of the pool, but she couldn't get anyone to join her. It took another day or two for the three wobbly pirates to become landlubbers again.

That night Chris played his mandolin and sang to the kids in Lauren's basement, but they were restless and wouldn't go to sleep. Sharon was still badgering Chris to tell about the death of Cheeto High Bear. "Yeah, Dad," said Razor. "What's the big secret?"

Chris put down the mandolin. "All right," he said, "but you've got to promise to go to sleep after the story." Sharon and Razor agreed, and gave each other a victory thumbs-up.

"Once upon a time," said Chris, and with those four magical words the twins lay back on the fold-out bed and closed their eyes. "The Great Mystery sent a woman to the Lakota. She was wearing a buckskin dress, and appeared from the west in a white mist with her long black hair flowing in a soft breeze. The Lakota built a tepee for her, and she sang them a beautiful song. As she sang, a sweet cloud came from her mouth, smelling of roses." Sharon tried to make a cloud with her breath, but Lauren's basement was way too warm on this summer evening.

"The woman removed a bundle from her back and laid it on a bed of sage, near cotton flags of black, red, yellow and white. Inside the bundle was a pipe, which she said was for the Lakota's most solemn prayers to the Great Mystery. 'If it ever disappeared,' said the woman, 'the world would end by fire.'"

Razor opened his eyes. "Did you ever see it, Dad?" he asked.

"No," said Chris. "Only the Lakota could see the sacred pipe. And even among them, only the good people were allowed to hold it. The woman said, 'The bad shall never see it.' Then she walked away to the west, changed into a buffalo cow, and vanished over the horizon. She came to be known as the Calf Pipe Woman."

Now it was Sharon's turn to open her eyes. "What did she have to do with Cheeto High Bear?" she wanted to know. She really liked saying his name.

"I'm getting to that," said Chris. He reached over and tucked a couple of blankets around the twins, one at a time. Finally they were getting sleepy.

"After Calf Pipe Woman left, the Lakota built a little shack for the pipe in the tiny settlement of Green Grass, in the heart of the Cheyenne River Sioux Reservation. Each generation had its keeper of the pipe, and as it turned out, Cheeto High Bear became the keeper after he came back from Viet Nam.

"He did a good job, and he was still looking after the pipe when I met him. But one day a tribal policeman named Wilson Eagle Plume drove out to Green Grass and took the pipe to Eagle Butte. Cheeto tracked him down at the American Legion Hall. 'I only want the pipe for a day,' Wilson told Cheeto. He wanted to take some photographs for a Sioux Falls magazine. Cheeto told him that was a very bad thing to do. 'It doesn't matter whether it's for a day or an hour. You must never touch the pipe.'

"So that night they got in Wilson's tribal police car to take the pipe back to Green Grass. But on the way, the road became covered with a thick fog. 'I can't see more than a few feet ahead,' said Wilson. He was about to pull over to the side of the road when a deer ran in front of the police car, and there was a terrible crash. Cheeto wasn't hurt, but Wilson crunched into the steering wheel.

"Cheeto got out and dragged Wilson to the front of the car so he could see him in the headlights, but he told me the next day that Wilson's chest felt like a bag of broken eggs. He didn't make it."

Razor and Sharon had gone to sleep. Chris put an extra pillow at each side of their fold-out bed, in case they started to roll out in the night, and turned out the light. There in the darkness, he played out the rest of Cheeto's story in his mind. There was Cheeto, placing Wilson in the back seat of the police car and waiting for the fog to clear. Telling Chris the next day that Wilson had been taken away by Calf Pipe Woman, that he'd seen her there in the fog. Getting drunk and staying drunk for three days. Mumbling over and over again, "Mitakuye oyasin, mitakuye oyasin," but refusing to tell Chris what he meant.

On the third day, Cheeto High Bear was found floating face down in the Moreau River, three miles from Green Grass. His horse Little Britches lay dead by his side, bobbing in the shallow water near the bank. Cheeto's left foot was still tangled in its stirrup. A Fools Crow delegation traveled from Pine Ridge to Green Grass to return the pipe to its shack.

Chris walked back up the stairs and took a seat at Lauren's piano. As his left hand played descending arpeggios in the key of D, his right hand improvised with random notes from the scale. With each chord change, he released the sustain pedal then pressed it again. As he played, he was carried back to the high point of his parents' lives. It came and it went in his recollection, as it had in their lives, and as it was coming and going they'd had no inkling that this was the best that life would ever have to offer. It was the spring of 1954, and they were only 32 years old. Chris closed his eyes and saw them as he played his chords. They rode in the back of a shiny new convertible, perched on top of the back seat, waving to the crowd. The sun was shining, and the air was filled with confetti. They waved again, and the people cheered. The convertible rolled past the bookstore, where they all lived in the upstairs apartment. Chris was just a boy in his memory, eight years old, and he watched from the college side of the street, in front of the chapel.

As they passed, things started to fall apart, slowly at first, then settling over the years into a dull pain you could never mention. To speak of it would be to acknowledge that it had happened.

Lauren came and sat next to him on the piano bench. She listened for a few minutes, then said, "We have to have a talk."

Chris kept playing and staring at the keys. During a chord change, he said "What about?" He hated talks, especially the Hooker kind.

"That's very nice, what you're playing," said Lauren. "I just wish you had a soul."

This was about as angry as Lauren ever got. She told Chris that he couldn't have had a better mother. "She loves you more than all the rest of us combined," she said. "And she doesn't ask for much. All you have to do is talk to her."

Chris played on, finding a particularly nice groove two octaves above middle C. Lauren waited, but he wouldn't say anything.

"You'll regret this one day," she said. "She's fading fast."

Lauren walked up the stairs to bed. Chris went down to the basement to catch the end of the Cardinals-Padres game from San Diego. The Cardinals won, 8-4, to move three and a half behind the Astros. The hat-challenged Tomko was the winning pitcher. Tomorrow was a day off as the Cardinals flew back to St. Louis for a weekend series against the Pittsburgh Pirates, starting on Friday.

Before going to bed, Chris phoned Australia to talk with Kazzie. It was already early Thursday afternoon in Melbourne. Kazzie was staying at Miriam Slade's house, with Miriam and Jeshel, and she'd already picked up some of their new-age jargon.

She and Kristen were having a great time, she said. They'd been out to their old property in the Wombat Forest, and Kazzie said it had a wonderful energy.

"The new owners have done a lot with it," she said. "They've put in a flush toilet and a spa, and added lots of solar panels." She told Chris that the property prices in nearby Daylesford had skyrocketed since they left.

"Our house would be worth a million dollars now," she said. "We should have waited. Miriam always said it was bad karma to sell when we did."

Chris shrugged, but Kazzie couldn't see that. He was glad they'd moved when they did. He was sick of Australia after two decades, and this professorship at Sand River College was probably his last crack at a regular job anywhere. He was 54 when they'd left. He'd been earning income for the past seven years by driving his jeep every day from the forest to the Ballarat courthouse to skim legal aid cases from the bottom of the barrel, moonlighting with a weekly column for the Daylesford newspaper, *The Advocate.*

His columns had established quite a local following, but they were getting weirder and weirder at the end. After one particularly bizarre piece, about discovering the East Magnetic Pole in the wilds of the Wombat Forest, Kazzie was forced to write a letter to *The Advocate* explaining that Chris's perception of the universe was not the same as hers. She was worried about guilt-by-association, and pleaded with Chris's readers not to lump the two of them together. "I've got a mind of my own," she wrote. To Chris's amusement and Kazzie's embarrassment, a truckload of Daylesford tourists came out to their place the following week, asking for directions to the East Magnetic Pole.

Kazzie's entreaties didn't stop Chris from writing his crazy stuff. His very next column was about "The Wanking Angel of Warrnambool," providing *The Advocate's* readers with directions to a particular street in a seaside village where, if they stood at just the right angle northeast of a certain heroic statue, they could witness an abiding act of self-abuse. Chris compared it to Keats's Grecian Urn, fast fixed in timelessness.

Kazzie told Chris that she and Kristen had been to a Thai restaurant on Acland Street with Miriam and Jeshel and Elspeth and Josh.

"Such a strange combination," Kazzie said, "but everyone

got along fine." It occurred to Chris that he was the common denominator for this disparate group.

"I can assure you we talked about everything but the Great Denominator," she said.

Here was Chris in his sister's basement with his twins, talking with Kazzie on the other side of the globe about her dinner with his daughter and Miriam, and his son and Elspeth, and his stepdaughter Kristen, with Sean at home in Illinois. His ancient mother was sleeping somewhere in the house above, and his father was probably going to bed in Sand River after finishing his ten-millionth crossword puzzle. Little African and Indian children he'd once taught in Guyana were now in their forties, and Chris's old girlfriend from the Cheyenne River Sioux Reservation, Thelma Medicine, had just joined his pal Cheeto High Bear in Rodeo Heaven. Assisi tourists were ordering granitas at a table in the Piazza del Comune, where Chris had sat with Kazzie a few months before. He couldn't keep track of it all. Everyone was scattered. Everything was broken.

"One more thing," said Kazzie ominously.

"What's that?" said Chris. He waited in suspense.

"The Galleon's closing down," she said. There was a long silence.

The Galleon was the bohemian coffee shop in St. Kilda where they'd met. Kazzie had been sitting in a booth with a stack of books by Nietzsche and Foucault, and Chris asked if he could join her. It was his forty-fifth birthday, he said. He was wearing a blue pin-striped suit, purple anteater cowboy boots, and a white Akubra hat, his usual Rank Strangers gear.

"Sleaze," was Kazzie's first thought, and in later years she remarked that first impressions are often correct.

She sloughed him off by handing him a piece of paper with the first four digits of her seven-digit phone number. This was an old trick she used whenever anyone hit on her.

"What's the rest of it?" Chris asked, way too eagerly.

"If you're interested," Kazzie said with an insouciant air, "you only have to dial a thousand times, worst-case scenario."

She figured this would be the last she'd see of this dickhead, and returned to her Foucault. Her fondest wish was that none of her friends in the Galleon had witnessed this conversation.

So she was surprised two days later to get a call from a man introducing himself, in an American accent, as "Christian Hooker." He told her he'd just finished recording a bluegrass album at Men At Work's studio, and wanted her to hear it. For reasons Kazzie never understood, she agreed to meet him at the Water Rat Hotel for a drink and a free cassette. She didn't even like bluegrass, but at least no one she knew hung out at the Water Rat. Two years later, she was living in the Wombat Forest with Chris and their infant twins.

Over time, the Galleon had assumed legendary status for the Hookers. All the kids had spent hours there, eating pesto and spanakopita and reading the graffiti in the Galleon bathroom. Even before he met Kazzie, Chris had written most of his lyrics at the Galleon's laminex tables. Later, whenever Kazzie or Chris drove down to Melbourne from the Wombat Forest, they always went to the Galleon for a poetry reading and a cappuccino from the fifty-year-old Gaggia espresso machine. The Galleon was Chris's alternate living room for years.

And now its little sea-horse doorknobs had been dismantled, its artworks were set to adorn other walls in other rooms. The closing of the Galleon was a *memento mori*, a reminder of transience. Way over here in Independence, Missouri, Chris felt a sense of loss.

"No Galleon, no twins," he said.

"Nah," said Kazzie. "If we hadn't met at the Galleon, we'd have met somewhere else. Or you would have had twins with some other woman."

"No," said Chris, sounding like Miriam Slade. "It was all meant to be."

Kazzie didn't want to end the phone conversation on such a gloomy note. "I've got some good news," she said in a chirpy voice. "Rollie's still alive."

Rollie was their Wombat Forest pony, now around 27 years old. In horse-years, she was a lot older than Alma Ruth, and probably in a lot better shape. Chris and Kazzie had sold Rollie with the house. Chris used to bring her into the kitchen for breakfast with the rest of the family. He was glad she was still alive.

After saying goodnight to Kazzie, Chris said the glorious mysteries of the rosary, feeling far from glory. As he settled for sleep he remembered the last time he saw his deaf Grandpa Bekyeshova, Alma Ruth's father, waving from the window of his old folks' home in Sand River. Chris was holding Sean, and together they mouthed the word "goodbye" through the double-glazed window. This wasn't unusual, because Chris had been lip-synching his words to Grandpa Bekyeshova as far back as he could remember, window or not. What was it like to be deaf for half a century? he wondered. How far into yourself would you go if you couldn't even hear your own music?

For some reason, all the Hookers whispered when they mouthed their words to Grandpa, even though he couldn't hear their whispers any more than he could hear a scream. There in Independence, lying in Lauren's basement next to his twins, Chris whispered "Good night, Grandpa," and went to sleep.

THURSDAY: LUMINOUS MYSTERIES

So the sun shines on this funeral, the same as on a birth
The way it shines on everything that happens on this earth
It rolls across the western sky and back into the sea
And spends the day's last rays upon this fucked-up family

James Taylor, *Enough To Be On Your Way*

And when Leonard couldn't make any money coaching anymore because he'd been fired so many times and he had to go cap-in-hand looking for crummy jobs at crummy high schools just to put food on the family table and not have to relive what he'd been through in his own childhood, and he had to swallow all his pride and smile nervously at morons and keep his rage inside except when he took it out on his family, he moonlighted by refereeing high school basketball games for next-to-nothing throughout the great state of Illinois, and he'd drive on icy roads in the dead calm of winter to cold gymnasiums and booing fans to mete out justice in his black-and-white stripes, justice for teenage boys establishing their alpha maleness in meaningless rituals before inane cheerleaders and wannabe townsfolk. "Put 'er in, put 'er in!" the cheerleaders would shout. "Let's go!" And during those long rides after the games in his crummy car with the crummy heater Leonard would see his own breath form scentless clouds before his eyes and consider crashing his car into a tree at the side of the road so it would look like an accident but he never did it.

And it so happened that he refereed one of your stupid games, the Okaw City Purple Riders against the mighty Farmer's Grove Blue Devils, and you were the point guard but you weren't any good you could have been good and you were good when you were all alone in your driveway but you weren't any good in a real game and you knew it and everybody else knew it and it embarrassed him the same way it embarrassed him when you were playing third base in Little League and a guy slid into you with his spikes and put a hole in your thigh and you cried and he told everybody that you were ok you were just scared. And you got fouled by a Blue Devil and went to the free-throw line and the cheerleaders said "Chris, Chris, he's our man, if he can't do it nobody can" and they said "Sink it Chris" and you did, both free throws, nothing but net but those were the only points you scored the whole game, and in the second half a Blue Devil Randy Scheidler stole the ball from you and drove down the court for a lay-up but you caught up with him and hammered him across his arms and he lost his balance and tumbled head-first into the wall and Leonard blew his whistle for a technical foul and threw you out of the game, and your face got all screwed up as you tried not to cry again and you took your place at the end of the Purple Riders' bench and your coach who was an asshole anyway said "That's a terrible call Leonard" and everybody booed your dad.

And after he retired he tried to make the life he had lived mean something, to have some meaning, and he kept going back to where he'd been, back to Morrisonville for the annual picnic or to reunions of his shipmates from the war or to Quincy where some of the players who were still alive would talk about the glory days and he would ask you to go with him but you never would and all over the walls of his house were photographs, hundreds of them, Leonard with somebody or other from the old days smiling and looking good and he'd never look that good again and what did it all mean if he didn't have that he had nothing. And he just kept getting older and the only thing he knew how to do was to retrace his *steps and maybe if he just retraced them one more time it wouldn't end up the same way.*

* * * * * * * *

In the morning, Chris woke up before anybody else and went for a walk in the neighborhood. It was a nice time of day, cool and fresh and quiet. He walked for about an hour, and passed by the Christ Church High School on the way back, the same school that Lauren's kids had gone to. They were all grown up now, a doctor and a nurse and a teacher. Chris saw a kid shooting basketball all by himself on the school playground, wearing a Karl Malone jersey. Chris walked over to him and motioned for the ball. The kid flipped it to Chris, whose shot clanged off the front of the rim.

"I'm a bit rusty," said Chris. "And my legs are wobbly."

They talked a little as they exchanged shots, but stayed nameless. The kid was a starting guard for the Christ Church team. He was about to go into his senior year. He had a basketball scholarship waiting for him at Mizzou.

"One on one?" he smiled. Chris could tell he just wanted to beat up on an old guy before breakfast.

"Sure," said Chris. They set the rules: make-it take-it to eleven, each basket counting as one. Check the ball at every possession. This was fine with Chris. Eleven goals were about all he could live through.

After a flip of a coin, the kid went first and popped a fifteen-footer from the baseline. On the way back to the top of the key, he walked the walk and bounced the basketball to Chris. "Check," he said. Chris handed the ball back to him and assumed an awkward defensive position, not too low and a little flat-footed. Chris couldn't bend too far, even when his back was a hundred percent.

The kid shot another fifteen-footer from the same spot, but this time it rolled around the rim, in and out. He had no chance for the rebound, because Chris was good at blocking out and crashing the backboards. Pound for pound and inch for inch there was nobody who could out-rebound Chris. It was his only true basketball skill, because all it really required was being annoying as hell. And when he was rebounding, Chris could reduce the world for a split second to a single inanimate object, something outside himself, with no thought of right or wrong. Just go for the ball.

Chris dribbled back up the asphalt to an imaginary half-court line at the top of the key. He turned and maneuvered his way back toward the basket. When he got about five feet away the kid put an aggressive hand-check on Chris's back. It was the first time Chris had been touched by anybody in four days, except for a twin or an Australian hitchhiker.

Chris shuffled around to the left of the key, made a pump-fake with his right hand, then scooped the ball off the backboard and into the basket with his left. One to one.

Chris scored the next five points with this very same move, and the kid became quite agitated. He couldn't defend against it because Chris kept his body between the defender and the ball. You could tell the kid thought this was stupid and almost unfair, backing into the basket, pump-faking and scoring on a one-foot scoop shot. It had no style, no class. Thankfully, Chris missed on his next attempt, and the ball fell into the kid's hands as Chris breathed heavily. Six-one Chris.

Now the kid gave Chris a taste of his own medicine, backing into the key then popping a short fadeaway that Chris had no hope in hell of blocking, so he just waved at the ball as it swished through the hoop. The kid looked like he could do this all morning, and all afternoon too. On the next possession, he popped another fifteen-footer from the baseline, clearly his favorite shot, and now he trailed only 6-3. His swagger had returned. Chris was breathing pretty hard. A heart attack was not out of the question. After all, he was fifty-seven years old.

"Want more of that, Grandpa?" the kid smirked.

Chris grinned and nodded and checked the ball. He didn't dare say anything because all he could do was wheeze. The kid tried another fifteen-footer, this one from the top of the key, but lost his balance on a crack in the asphalt and missed badly. He came hard over Chris's back to try to get the rebound, knocking Chris's head into the metal support post. It made a loud noise but didn't really hurt. Chris got possession of the ball, because the kid touched it last before it went out of bounds.

Chris was so exhausted he didn't feel like doing his little back-into-the-basket shuffle any more. But he was feeling it at the check-point at the top of the key, where he didn't have to move at all. Straight in front of the basket was his favorite spot as an Okaw City Purple Rider in the 1960s, the spot most central Illinois white boys learned to shoot from in their driveways. Most of them couldn't jump, and their feet were slow, but they practiced alone when there was nothing else to do, sinking undefended jumpers and free throws by the thousands. Sometimes Chris would get this feeling, where he was absolutely certain the ball would go in.

Although he couldn't rise off the ground more than a few inches, the kid gave him a lot of room on defense, figuring this old guy couldn't even get the ball that far anyway. This was a mistake. Chris drilled five jump shots in a row, nothing but net. Eleven-three, game over.

"Let's go again," said the kid. He was really angry.

"Nah, that's enough for me," said Chris. He knew he'd get creamed next game. The kid would kill him. "Thanks for the game."

He waved goodbye and walked back to Lauren's place. The kid went back to practicing fifteen-foot jump shots from the baseline. Swish, swish, swish. He'd make a pretty good shooting guard for the Missouri Tigers.

"Where have you been?" said Lauren when Chris came in the door. She was making some Atkins diet pancakes to humor his eating habits. "You look awful."

Chris was feeling pretty awful. Light-headed and nauseous. "I went for a walk and played a little one-on-one over at Christ Church. Some kid who plays for the team."

"That's Randy Twinner," said Lauren. "He's out there every morning. His parents are good friends of ours." Chris remembered Randy's dad Harvey, though he hadn't seen him in a while. Sometimes when Chris was visiting Lauren, Harvey would bring over fresh vegetables from his garden. He'd always try to bait Chris into talking politics by quoting Rush Limbaugh's attacks on liberal activist judges. But Chris didn't want to argue with him. "Nice tomatoes," he'd say.

Chris ate Lauren's pancakes, and couldn't resist bragging that he'd outscored Randy 11-3. He was hoping to impress her, but it had the opposite effect. She'd known Randy since he was a baby.

"Why'd you want to go and do that?" she said. "Randy's a nice kid. What's in it for you to beat him up at something he loves?" She glared at Chris. "Basketball doesn't matter to you."

Lauren was madder than hell. Maybe she was just letting off steam because of Alma Ruth. She said it was just plain selfish for Chris to get his kicks by humiliating a high school kid whose whole life was basketball.

Alma Ruth came into the kitchen and joined them for pancakes. She mumbled something in a remote Chinese dialect, and Chris deciphered that she was asking him how he'd slept.

"Fine," he said.

Lauren had some leftover tickets to a place called "Oceans of Fun" over by the Kansas City Royals Stadium, and she said Chris and the twins could use them. Chris had been there once before, thanks to Lauren. He'd taken Sean and Josh about ten years ago during a visit from Australia, after the marriage to Elspeth fell apart. He had to get a special order from the Australia Family Court to get them out of the country for a couple of weeks. Elspeth was sure Chris would go underground and she'd never see her sons again. When they arrived in Chicago, Chris had Sean and Josh telephone Elspeth from the Rock & Roll McDonald's to say that they were now living in Argentina. She nearly died.

"You can spend the whole day at Oceans of Fun," said Lauren. Chris couldn't tell if this was an invitation or wishful thinking. He woke up the kids, fed them some pancakes, and got them into the Windstar for the drive to the water park.

Just as Lauren predicted, they did end up staying all day. Razor and Sharon's favorite spots were the Wave Pool and the Monsoon, and this huge water slide that took about three minutes to navigate from top to bottom. Once you got past the Oceans of Fun ticket booth, you could ride as many things as many times as you liked. The Wave Pool would start gurgling every few minutes, and if you closed your eyes you could pretend you were frolicking in the Southern Ocean, right there in Kansas City.

"Surf's up," said Razor. He'd heard somebody say that on t.v. He caught a wave and body-surfed from one end of the Wave Pool to the other.

The Monsoon had this little roller-coastery tram that took you to the top of a high platform, where you'd wait for this hellish five-second drop into a big pond of cold water. The big thrill was the huge splash at the end. The kids liked the way they lost their breath on the way down, and they kept running back to ride the Monsoon over and over again for a couple of hours. After the first two rides, Chris sat down on a nearby bench and pulled the Cuffy Kamara brief from his pack. Razor lost his special Tilley hat in the Monsoon's waters, but it didn't matter. He and Sharon were having too much fun to care about anything. They high-fived Chris each time they ran past his bench.

On the way back to Lauren's from Oceans of Fun, Razor wanted to add to his Yu-Gi-Oh card collection. The card shop in Independence had a back room with a curtain, and behind it teenage boys wearing T-shirts with skulls and bare-breasted women were playing board games called "Warhammer" and "Imperial War Altar." The back room walls were covered with dark posters of demons and castles and hobbits and dwarves, none of whom looked the least like little Dopey. Miniature knights and dragons, named "War Lord" or "Dark Haven," were changing hands furiously, but it wasn't clear if this was part of a game or just a sideshow.

Chris felt like Dylan's Mr. Jones - he knew something was happening here, but he didn't have a clue what it was. He was pretty sure, though, that these kids would answer the call whenever George W. Bush needed a new supply of true believers to protect someone else's standard of living in some stupid war. They were honing their skills for modern warfare right there in Independence. Razor and Sharon bought their Yu-Gi-Oh cards and Chris drove back to Lauren's. Razor was happy, because the shop sold Japanese-edition cards that he couldn't get back in Sand River.

That night Brian cooked up some halibut on the grill. Alma Ruth and Lauren watched the kids swim around in their little halos as Chris flipped through some of Brian's old *Soldier of Fortune* magazines. After dinner, Brian was in a philosophical mood. He was an ex-Marine, now in the business of creating strip malls on any stretch of empty roadside property he could find, but his idea of real fun was talking about heavy-duty things, especially on the deck by his pool when the summer sun was going down. Obviously, Lauren had assigned Brian the task of getting through to Chris, and Brian had adopted a lateral-thinking approach

"Do you know the difference between an existentialist and a mystic?" he said out of the blue. Chris wasn't sure if it was a joke with a punch-line. He smelled trouble, and confessed that he didn't know the difference. A long silence followed. Brian passed a can of low-carb beer to Chris, and gripped another for himself.

"An existentialist tries to make himself larger than life," said Brian calmly, gazing across the expanse of his manicured back lawn. "A mystic tries to make himself smaller." Brian took a swig of his beer and smacked his lips.

He waited for Chris to respond to this opening gambit, but Chris just let the silence fill the warm summer air in Brian's back yard. This was a trick he'd learned from the Panda, who would just sit there like a bump on a log until his patient started rambling on again with the most personal details imaginable. The Panda had taught Chris that silence is a cup that has to be filled.

So Brian went into a long monologue comparing Camus' *The Stranger* with Thomas Merton's *The Seven Storey Mountain*. Chris found it peaceful just listening to Brian's melodious Missouri accent, and rested his head against a towel on the back of the deck chair.

Brian's voice reminded Chris of Australian cricket matches on the radio in the Wombat Forest. Chris had followed cricket since his years in the West Indies, and he loved the dulcet sounds of the international commentators.

"There's Alan Border at the wicket," they'd say. "He's doing a little gardening with the end of his bat." They'd make this crack about gardening a dozen times every match, and every single time they'd all chuckle as if it was the funniest thing they'd ever heard. Or they'd say, "Here comes Shane Warne with the next delivery. Oooh! A spinner that just missed the stumps. So close." The "oohs" were always sensual and just above a whisper. It didn't matter what they said. Chris just felt peaceful, as if nothing could ever go wrong again, so long as the cricket never ended.

Razor and Sharon were looking through Hooker photograph albums with Alma Ruth. They enjoyed the old pictures of Chris with his brother and sisters.

"You were so skinny, Dad," said Sharon.

"And ugly," said Razor.

Alma Ruth thought that was pretty funny and started to laugh, but her brain short-circuited into a past life as a school teacher and she said, in perfect English, "My land, honey, you shouldn't talk about your father that way."

There were black-and-white photos of Alma Ruth as a baby with her parents, photos of Alma Ruth next to Leonard in his sailor's uniform, photos of countless friends whose names Alma Ruth would never remember again. If Chris's old hitch-hiker pal Brenda Which Woman was right, Alma Ruth wouldn't be a noun in the Lakota language, any more than sex or death. Both she and the child in her photo albums were being born and dying right before Chris's eyes, and so were Razor and Sharon and everybody else.

It occurred to him that these photographs were Alma
Ruth's life's work, the one thing of value she would leave
behind for her children and grandchildren when she was
gone. For Alma Ruth, these pictures were priceless. She
wanted to make sure they found good homes.

Chris was pretty tired and turned in before anyone else.
This had been a strange day, almost an interlude, although
Chris couldn't figure out between what and what. Maybe it
was an interlude between Cardinals games. The Astros had
lost, while the Cardinals were idle, so even without lifting a
bat or a glove the Cardinals had moved back to within three-
and-a-half games of the division lead, and only three out on
the lost side. There were sixty-one games left in the season,
plenty of time to make up three games. You could do that in
a single series.

On his bed in the basement Chris found some more presents from Alma Ruth - seven neat binders filled with the
1950s baseball cards he'd collected in shoeboxes as a young
boy in Quincy, Illinois. A shaky Chinese note from Alma
Ruth told Chris that his younger brother Jeff had organized
the collection while Chris was in Australia. Jeff had put each
card in a plastic sleeve, nine sleeves to a sheet. There were
Warren Spahns, Henry Aarons, Duke Sniders, Roberto
Clementes, Willie Mayses, Mickey Mantles and Stan Musials,
plus hundreds of players with obscure names who'd made it
to the majors in the fifties. A note from Jeff said he'd sold two
Rocky Colavitos to pay for the binders. The three best Rocky
cards were still there, each one worth about twenty dollars.

Chris was stunned. He hadn't seen these cards in forty-five
years, and he'd assumed they'd been thrown away or sold at
a garage sale with his Okaw City letterman's jacket. As he
flipped the sleeves, he noticed that a couple of Ted Williams
cards had little punch-holes through Ted's name. Chris
remembered the blind kid, Marty Hutmacher, who marked
his cards in braille so he could tell what he was trading, especially when he was trading with Chris. In today's market, the
punch marks wrecked the value of the cards, but Chris hadn't

collected them for money. They were so cheap in the old days that he'd put them in his bicycle spokes to make motorcycle sounds as he rode the footpaths of Quincy College.

Chris placed his cards at the side of the bed and said the luminous mysteries of the rosary, the mysteries of light. These were the new ones, just added by the pope, and Chris was still getting used to them. They followed the public life of Jesus. The fourth mystery of light, the most luminous of all, was called the transfiguration. Jesus takes Peter, James and John to the top of a high mountain, where Jesus' face shines like the sun and his raiment goes whiter than snow. Moses and Elijah appear out of nowhere. Peter gets the crazy idea to build three tents, one each for Moses, Elijah, and Jesus, but nobody pays any attention to him. Then a big cloud comes along, and they hear God telling them to listen to Jesus. When the cloud lifts Moses and Elijah are gone.

Chris had no idea what this all meant, which made for a pretty good mystery. He'd seen Raphael's painting of this transfiguration at the Villa Albani in Rome, where Kazzie had taken him near the end of their Italian pilgimage. Raphael had all hell breaking loose down below as Jesus floats on the cloud and the three apostles hide their faces. It was a nice painting, but it didn't make any sense to Chris. Kazzie told him he should just accept its beauty and not worry about what it was supposed to mean.

Here in Lauren's basement, Chris yawned and finished off the mysteries of light with one he thought he could understand, the Last Supper. "This is my body," said Jesus. "This is my blood." No problem.

As he drifted off to sleep, Chris had a vision of his father Leonard coaching the Quincy Hawks baseball team on the green fields next to the college. In his selective memory, Chris sat in the Hawks' dugout in his little uniform, such a small boy next to the grown-up college players. They called him their mascot and their good luck charm, a forerunner of Dopey the Dwarf. They'd pat him on the head as they took the field. Chris wondered where that little boy had gone.

FRIDAY:
MORE SORROWFUL MYSTERIES

Since, tho' he is under the world's splendour and wonder
His mystery must be instressed, stressed;
For I greet him the days I meet him,
and bless when I understand.

G.M. Hopkins, *"The Wreck of the Deutschland"*

When you returned to Australia from the Cheyenne River
Sioux Reservation to marry Elspeth, the most remarkable
things happened, at least they seemed remarkable to you at
the time. In your brain you were still back there on the reservation with Thelma Medicine who wasn't dead yet, smoking
dope together and driving around in your banged-up Impala,
crazy Thelma Medicine who said she'd let you do that and
more but you'd have to marry her first, but that whole thing
was going nowhere and now you were here on the other side
of the world and you were getting married in three days to
Elspeth and gee it was weird. You went back to have a look at
your old office at the law school and you started to climb the
stairs and you couldn't make it, you got about half-way up
and you started to break down and sob and you had to stop
and Fred and Annemaree saw you, they were surprised to see
you, they thought they'd never see you again, and they took
your arms and helped you up the stairs and you stood at the
door of your old office and you tried to explain how you were
living on the edge on the reservation and someone you knew

*died every week and everything was so raw and now you were
back here and it had all happened in twenty-four hours like a
time-machine, first you were there and now you were here,
and here it was so calm and sedate and everybody was white
and you remembered how you used to be before the reservation and you weren't that way any more but you were getting
married in three days, and Fred and Annemaree said you
don't have to do it, but they didn't understand, it wasn't
about the marriage, it wasn't about the marriage.*

*And the wedding was going to be at Elspeth's mother's house
in St. Kilda, the same house where her father had died when
she was only fifteen, and none of your wives or girlfriends
ever had a living father, you chose them that way, half-
orphans, and you took a tram into the city to change over
some American money and there in the waiting area was this
guy, it was incredible, this guy with a leather belt engraved
with the word "Calgary" and wearing pointy cowboy boots
and a sweat-stained western hat, and he looked like an Indian
by God and you had to ask him who he was and he said he
was Charley, Charley from the Blood Tribe in Canada, and
they were out here, a group of them, to dance and drum at
the Moomba Festival, and you asked Charley to be your guest
at the wedding, your only guest, your best man even, but he
was flying out the next day, back to Canada.*

*So the day of the wedding came and you dressed in your dark
blue double-breasted suit from Taiwan but you wore your
purple cowboy boots too, with the little anteater ridges above
the toes, and Elspeth was in this white dress with a floral pattern and all of her relatives had come from all over Australia,
from Adelaide and Sydney and Perth and even Tasmania,
and the minister was a guy named Malcolm, an Anglican
because you and Elspeth couldn't get married in a Catholic
church because of the divorces, and everybody circled around
and Malcolm did the ceremony and he asked you if you'd take
Elspeth to be your wife and first your eyes welled up with
tears but they weren't tears of joy they were tears of madness
and then your face started to shake and Malcolm looked at*

you like he might have to call a doctor or maybe a shrink, and you started making animal noises, deep gutteral animal noises, not growls or moans exactly and not loud, something other-worldly, and Elspeth looked at you and she was so embarrassed, she was mortified, and you didn't dare look around at the others, and you said "I do" or "I will" or something like that, and Malcolm rushed through the rest of it and Elspeth said her part and it was done and you were married, but then you had to sit around with the rest of them and have cake and it was so embarrassing but everybody tried to act as if nothing had happened. And while you were sitting there eating your cake, a vanilla cake with white icing, an enormous bang came from the sky, an explosion, a single clap of thunder, but when everybody looked out the windows it was a clear sunny day without a cloud in the sky, and they all looked at each other and said "What was that," and nobody had ever heard anything like it, and you thought it was a sign of some sort, an omen, that you had done something very bad that could never be undone and that a curse was on the children she would have, Sean and Josh who would come later, because of what you'd done, but you didn't know exactly what it was, what you had done.

* * * * * * * *

On Friday morning, Chris and the kids got an early start without waiting for breakfast. Alma Ruth was still asleep, so Chris left her a note saying it was good to see her and he hoped she had a nice stay with Lauren and Brian. Lauren walked them out to the Windstar.

"Here," she said. "You forgot this." She handed Chris his black plastic rosary, the one he'd bought in Assisi. "You left it under your pillow."

Chris felt unclean, as if he'd been caught doing something shameful. No one in his family, not even Kazzie, knew about his daily sessions with the rosary. It was one of Chris's little secrets.

"Thanks," he said, and slipped the rosary into his jeans pocket.

Lauren frowned. "You know, Chris, it would be a lot better for everybody if you stopped saying your stupid rosary and started actually acting like a Christian once in a while."

Chris shrugged. He knew she was right. "I'm just sinning my way to God," he said. He'd used this line before, whenever he had to defend his bad behavior. "It's the price of admission," he added. He'd heard Father Con say that once, at St. Philomena's, and thought it sounded cool. No sin, no nothin'.

He kissed Lauren on the cheek as he got into the Windstar, which was very unlike him. He hated cheek-kissing and Hooker-kissing, and he wouldn't have done it if he hadn't been so embarrassed about his rosary.

"Thanks for everything," he said, making good eye contact. He could tell Lauren wanted to say a lot more, to pick up where Brian had left off last night, but she just waggled her fingers as they pulled down the driveway. Chris and the kids were back on the road.

They had a light breakfast at a gas station cafe in a little place south of Interstate 70 called Sweet Springs, then drove on to New Florence for lunch at Maggie's Restaurant.

"Look, Dad," said Sharon when she saw the exit sign. "Florence."

They'd been to the real Firenze during the Assisi pilgrimage, staying in a fifteenth-century palace that was now the Hotel Casci, close to the Galleria dell'Accademia and the Duomo. There were too many tourists at the Duomo for Chris, which got him in a grumpy mood, and he started telling anyone who would listen that Brunelleschi's cathedral dome was a monument to Catholic fascism. An old Norwegian couple found him amusing and insisted that Kazzie take their picture, with Chris, in front of the Duomo. Chris made a little V-sign with his fingers and raised them behind the woman's head as Kazzie snapped the photo.

As they walked away, Kazzie was furious. "How can you be so ignorant?" she said. "Florence is where the Renaissance started, you fool."

"Yeah, Dad," said Razor. "Besides, the Duomo's just a great big carnival. Look at all the street performers." A tall woman in white-face, dressed in velvet masquerade, posed stock-still in a frozen curtsy. Behind her were the enormous bronze doors to the Baptistry, with twenty-eight square panels depicting scenes from the bible in exquisite detail.

But Chris wouldn't look at the woman or the doors. He had himself so worked up that he wouldn't even go with the family to the Uffizi Gallery.

"But Dad," said Sharon, "it's got The Birth of Venus!"

Botticelli's goddess of love was her favorite. The whole *point* of *her* trip to Italy was to stand before The Birth of Venus and never, ever, forget that moment. She pulled Chris along as far as the Piazza della Signoria, but he wouldn't go another inch. A Canadian folksinger was busking on the stone steps outside the Uffizi, strumming on an amplified guitar and doing an Arlo Guthrie imitation with "The City of New Orleans." Chris sang along under his breath: "I'll be gone five hundred miles 'fore the day is done." He knew this train well. On a still night, he could hear its whistle from his home in Sand River.

"The lines are too long," said Chris, pointing to the Uffizi. He took a few photos of Kazzie and the kids in front of the Piazza's statues, then went back to the Hotel Casci to spend the afternoon reading about St. Francis and other stigmatics. By evening he'd cheered up, and the family had a pleasant walk along the Fiume Arno on Lungarno Terrigiani, bought some umbrellas at the Ponte Vecchio, and filled up on pasta in those last days before Chris's Atkins diet.

This New Florence in Missouri was about as un-Florentine as it was possible to get. Flat, stupid, waterless, and ugly. It made Chris long for Tuscany, Duomo and all. The only bright spot in Maggie's Restaurant was a photograph on the wall signed by Whitey Herzog, the White Rat, the best manager in St. Louis Cardinals' history.

Back on the road after lunch, Chris slipped the Rank Strangers CD in the Windstar stereo. This was the homemade disk that Sean had burned from the three Rank Strangers vinyls, the very disk that gave Sean his interminable ear-ringing and the hated red headphones. As Chris listened to his younger incarnation singing his own bluegrass compositions, Razor and Sharon watched *What About Bob,* another of the stolen DVDs from Blockbuster. They were just killing time instead of taking Chris's advice, which was that they admire the riveting central Missouri landscape.

"You should see this movie, Dad," said Sharon. "Bob's just like you!"

"I know," said Chris. He'd seen it before. Bob was a nutcase in the care of a Panda-like psychiatrist, whom he proceeds to destroy.

The Rank Strangers wall of sound percolated from the Windstar stereo. Chris sang along: "his childhood memories a-pounding in his brain." He'd played these recordings a thousand times, but he always listened as if he'd never heard them before, checking again to see if anybody played a wrong note in the studio. He liked his compositions, and wondered why he wasn't a famous songwriter. He wished again that he had a decent voice instead of sounding like an Illinois lawyer with a corn-cob up his butt, but at least he could listen to the CD without being embarrassed. The Australians in the band were great instrumentalists. They could make anybody sound good.

At the top of the hour, he switched to KMOX radio for the news. Nothing serious to report from Iraq or Afghanistan, but a lady was standing at the top of a tall building in downtown St. Louis, threatening to jump. The newscaster described this as a "breaking story," and promised to keep listeners up-to-date with developments. Chris switched back to the Rank Strangers and sang: "all these bridges that I been a-burnin', while the home fire's been a-burnin' still."

At the outskirts of St. Louis, he exited 70 and took Broadway south to downtown. He'd booked a room at the

Millennium Hotel on Fourth Street, but when they got there the street was blocked off with fire trucks and police on horseback. Of all the buildings in St. Louis, the woman in the breaking story was standing on top of Chris's hotel, twenty-six floors up, with her wings stretched and ready to fly. Rolling down his window, Chris could see her little face way up there, peeping over the edge as two firemen with mountain-climbing ropes crept closer on either side. There was a lot of commotion at ground level, but Chris couldn't see what was going on.

He parked the Windstar on Poplar Street and waited as the twins finished *What About Bob*. About an hour later, the police started taking down the barricades and motioned the traffic to start coming through. Chris crept into the Millennium driveway and parked in a disabled spot.

"You can't park here, Dad," said Sharon. "It's for handicapped people." Sharon was very strict about these things.

"We'll just be a minute," said Chris. "Just long enough to check in."

As Chris fooled around at the front desk trying to get the twins in for free, Razor and Sharon scanned the streets and sidewalks looking for a flattened body, but they couldn't find one.

"Did she jump?" Razor asked a bellhop, but he just stared straight ahead like a palace guard.

After check-in, they took their bags up the elevator to a fantastic room overlooking the Mississippi River and the Arch, then came back down to move the Windstar across the street to the parking garage. A Buick with a disabled plate had pulled up alongside the Windstar, and a man was working his way out of the driver's seat and into a wheelchair. He gave Chris the finger. Sharon was mortified, and hid her face.

After parking, they said goodbye to Dopey and left him in charge again. "Don't forget these, Dad," said Razor, handing the binoculars to Chris. "You might need them for the ball game." Razor and Sharon weren't thrilled about going to the Cardinals-Pirates game, but they were being nice about it.

What they really wanted was to swim in the Millennium's pool after the hot day of traveling.

As they walked back into the hotel lobby, Razor announced that his foot hurt. Chris had him take off his left sandal, and removed a little piece of blue glass from Razor's heel. They retraced their steps back to the sidewalk, and saw a few hotel employees with brooms and dustpans, sweeping the area outside the lobby. They hadn't even noticed them a few minutes before. A security woman in a dark blue uniform was stretching yellow crime scene tape from a ginkgo tree to a parking sign. Little chunks of blue glass sparkled on the ground. Chris looked up the side of the Millennium and saw a shattered second-floor window. It must have been knocked out by the rescue squad as they were preparing for the woman to jump.

Razor's foot injury was nothing more than a scratch, but Chris smelled an opportunity to get back part of the money he'd lost on the houseboat. With glass all over the place, liability was a no-brainer, so the only question was how much money Chris could squeeze out of the Millennium for Razor's scratch. Even a couple thousand dollars would pay for a lot of houseboat and gasoline. So he gathered Razor into his arms and walked to the concierge's desk.

"Look, my son cut his foot on that glass out there," he said solemnly. He pointed to the crime scene, and held up Razor's left foot. "I don't know how deep it is."

The concierge's name tag said "Winton D'Souza." Winton was very concerned, and told Chris to take the kids up to their room and wait for security.

They stayed in the room for half an hour, watching the barges chug up and down the Mississippi. Chris had Razor wash his scratch with a bar of hotel soap, and they all changed out of their sticky clothes. Finally, Sharon said "I'm hungry, Dad. Let's go eat."

This seemed like a better idea than hanging around waiting for the security guys to laugh at them, so they took the elevator to the lobby and snuck past Winton D'Souza. When they got outside they ran up Fourth Street to Walnut, past the old courthouse to a TGI Friday's north of Busch Stadium. Razor slowed them down by doing amazing cartwheels, demonstrating a heroic recovery from his crime-scene injury. They got to TGI Friday's just in time to beat the crowd that was gathering for the Cardinals game.

Chris had his usual fish dinner. Razor and Sharon got kids' meals of chicken nuggets and fries, and used TGI Friday crayons to draw pirate ships on the white paper tablecloth. Chris asked the waiter for some crayons of his own, and drew the most elaborate clipper ship Razor and Sharon had ever seen. It had three masts and twenty-seven sails, crows' nests and anchors, sharks in the surrounding waters and seagulls in the clouds above. Chris peopled his pirate ship with a one-legged captain and dozens of sword-brandishing sailors with parrots on their shoulders. He curled brass treads along the ship's ladders, installed a pulley system for the sails, and sketched wood fixtures along the slim deck. On the bow, he crayoned a woman with long red hair, wearing a green dress, with one breast bared for all to see.

"I didn't know you could draw, Dad," said Sharon, very impressed. Razor looked hurt and jealous.

"I can't," said Chris. "Just pirate ships. I'm the world champion at pirate ships." There was some truth in this. Chris was a klutz at the visual arts, with little taste and less talent. But at the age of six, in the little white house with the green roof, he discovered that his playmates were amazed at his pirate ships. Over the next fifty years, his style didn't change at all. He still drew the very same pirate ship he'd mastered as a six-year-old, always the starboard side, always twenty-seven sails and three tall masts, always a captain at the wheel and sharks swirling in the waters below. But as pirate ships go, this was a good one, worth repeating for fifty years.

Chris fantasized that his pirate ships were not unlike Philip Guston's harlequinade of hooded Ku Klux Klanners. He reminded Razor and Sharon that they'd seen some Gustons at the Art Institute in Chicago. Razor was fascinated by their cartoon quality, and couldn't believe that grown-ups actually got paid for painting such things.

"Sometimes it's good to keep working on just one thing," Chris told the twins as he added a golden belt-buckle to a tiny pirate boatswain. "You can carve out your own little niche, just like Philip Guston."

Until dinner came, Razor and Sharon tried to create pirate ships that matched Chris's, and it didn't take them long to produce drawings that were technically as good. But theirs were missing something, some pirate ship power that exploded from Chris's tablecloth. Razor's jealousy gave way to a grudging admiration.

"I'm glad you're my dad," he said. He scooted along the booth to give Chris a little hug.

After eating, Chris and the kids walked over to Busch Stadium to negotiate some tickets to the ball game. They passed an electric blues band in Kiener Plaza, which started Chris getting all nostalgic about Josh again, way down there in Australia banging on his drums and recording heavy metal CD's. But he didn't have time to get morose, because a scalper approached them waving a dozen tickets.

Chris was fussy about his choice of seats. His idea of going to a baseball game was that you had to be really close to the action. There was no point, he figured, sitting high in the upper deck or in the outfield bleachers. He wanted to see the players sweat, hear the ball snap into the catcher's mitt. He wanted to hear feet popping on the turf as runners circled the bases. He wanted to be a little boy in the Quincy Hawks' dugout.

The best price the scalper would give for three seats in the first-base field boxes, just behind the Cardinals' dugout, was three hundred dollars. But Chris figured he could make that up by threatening to sue the Millennium over Razor's left foot.

As Chris and the kids joined the line of fans going through the turnstiles, Razor wanted to know about the enormous statue in front of Busch Stadium. "That's Stan the Man," said

Chris. "Have a look at what it says below the statue." Razor
and Sharon both ran over, and Chris watched them move
their lips to commit the words to memory. When they came
back, Razor said, "Here stands baseball's perfect warrior."
Sharon added: "Here stands baseball's perfect knight."

"Good job," said Chris, impressed.

"Was he really *that* good?" said Sharon. "Nobody could
be *that* good."

"He was pretty good," said Chris. "But he didn't look like
that." The statue tried to capture the coiled Musial stance,
with the front foot forward, the front knee bent in, and the
head out over the plate. But the shoulders were way too
broad, and the bat was too high and too far back. It made
Stan the Man look like a cartoon character.

Inside the stadium, young Danny Haren was on the
mound for the Cardinals. He was a rookie with a 93 mile-an-
hour fastball. Kip Wells was pitching for the Pirates. Not
exactly Gibson versus Koufax, but good enough for Chris.
He just loved being there, the full moon whiter than ever
against the blackening St. Louis sky, the players and the
crowd shimmering in the liquid glow of the stadium lights. It
wasn't day or night, or 2003 or 1954. Busch Stadium on a
warm summer's night was timeless.

The surreal lighting carried Chris back to the old softball
field across the street from the little white house with the
green roof, to a night when Leonard poked one over the red
picket fence in left just as it started to rain. In those days, you
had to turn off the globes before a single raindrop hit, or
they'd explode. In the darkness of the gathering storm, the
other team complained that Leonard's ball had bounced over
the fence for a ground-rule double, but Chris had seen it. It
was a home run.

Here at Busch Stadium, the Cardinals loaded the bases in
the second and fourth innings, but couldn't score. This gave
Chris a feeling of foreboding. Maybe the Cardinals played
better if he just listened on the radio. But Haren was hanging
tough, and the game was still scoreless going into the fifth.

Razor and Sharon were absorbed with collecting plastic souvenir cups that fans were dropping in the aisles. "We've got a hundred and seven, Dad," said Razor. He'd collect anything.

"Great," said Chris. "They might be worth something some day." Each cup had a picture of a Cardinal's face, with the 2003 schedule below.

With one out in the bottom of the fifth, J.D. Drew hit a massive home run into the upper deck in right field. Fireworks exploded into the night sky, and even Razor and Sharon were jumping up and down with excitement. Chris high-fived a few old guys around him. They were all wearing red Cardinals hats and old Mark McGwire t-shirts. With Haren pitching like he was, one run might be enough.

But in the Pirates' sixth, Brian Giles led off with a double, and then Reggie Sanders hit a huge triple to left, scoring Giles. Randall Simon singled to right, and the Pirates had a 2-1 lead.

At that point, Cardinals manager Tony LaRussa started thinking way too much with his night law-school brain, and he motioned for a disaster named Estaban Yan to come in from the bullpen. All was lost.

"He shouldn't let this guy pitch," Chris said to Razor and Sharon, who were sorting their plastic cups. "Estaban Yan might as well write Hit Me on the horsehide."

Sure enough, Hernandez tapped a pathetic little roller into the hole at short for an infield hit, moving Simon to second, then Reboulet singled to right, scoring Simon. Three to one, Pirates. Only great plays by Rolen at third and Bo Hart at second saved Estaban Yan from a thirty-run inning.

The Cardinals came back in the bottom of the sixth with three runs of their own to retake the lead for a glorious moment, but the Pirates scored six in the eighth and it was Katy bar the door.

As the top of the ninth started, Chris took Razor to the fans' first aid room to have a paramedic look at his foot. Chris took down his name, Joe Murphy, in case he'd need this information later in his negotiations with the Millennium. Joe

FRIDAY: MORE SORROWFUL MYSTERIES

Murphy applied some antiseptic and a band-aid. "Looks good," he said.

The game didn't finish until eleven o'clock, and the kids were tired. On the way back to the Millennium, Sharon noticed a brass plaque posted on the outside wall of a parking garage across from the stadium, and asked Chris to read it.

"It tells about a famous Indian named Pontiac," said Chris. "He was the chief of the Ottawa confederation, and signed a peace treaty with the British back in 1765, before America was even a country. The sign says he died in 1769, and he's buried under this parking garage."

Razor had to think about that for a moment. First he was wondering why an Indian chief was named after a car, and he couldn't imagine why they buried him under a garage. Then he figured out that the garage must have come a long time later.

"St. Louis was just a little village in 1769," said Chris, "and this spot was a little cemetery at the edge of town." Still, Razor was mad about it, because he thought they should have moved Pontiac's grave before they put up the parking garage. "They should have had some respect," he said.

The twins went straight to sleep in the hotel room. Chris read an old *Mother Jones* magazine for a while, then some random passages from a Gideons bible: "Then the unclean spirits went out and entered the swine (there were about two thousand); and the herd ran violently down the steep place into the sea and drowned in the sea." It sounded like a Wave Pool full of piggies at Oceans of Fun.

No wonder the people of the Gadarenes prayed for Jesus the pig-killer to depart out of their region, thought Chris. There he was, ranting and raving and destroying their livestock. Any swineherd would have been furious with the Good Shepherd. No court in Israel would have accepted his defense that there were demons inside the pigs. Nor would the Good Shepherd get many character references from his flock. He wasn't exactly looking after sheep because they were *pets*. Sooner or later he was going to slit their throats.

Chris put down the Gideons bible and switched on the t.v. There were some reports on the Cardinals' debacle against the Pirates, and a late story on the day's suicide attempt at the Millennium Hotel. The reporter described the suicidal woman, Terrion Jackson, as "despondent." Terrion had jumped about eight feet from the top of the hotel to a lower roof above the revolving "Top of the Riverfront" restaurant, where she startled the well-heeled diners. Eventually she was rescued by two firefighters, John McLellan and Sherwin Caldwell, the same guys Chris had observed sneaking up on her with their mountain ropes. Terrion had been taken to a psychiatric hospital. Police said she would be charged with trespassing.

Before turning off the t.v., Chris flipped to the adult channel to sample the advertised porn. He hadn't seen one of these things in years, and took a detached interest. He thought of Miss Dottie Feeney's biology class at Okaw City High School, where he'd felt a similar dispassion while dissecting a frog.

The quality and detail of these dirty movies had certainly improved since the sixties. Right here in a Millennium Hotel room, overlooking the Mississippi River on a beautiful summer's night, there was little left for Chris's imagination.

He played scientist for half an hour as the twins slept, marveling at the creative ingenuity of the Tireless Watcher. If Chris had to come up with a brand new method for propagating the species, he doubted he could improve on what he was seeing. He whispered "beautiful" as these anonymous creatures carried on their frenzied choreography at the sides of swimming pools and in garish-colored bedrooms, accompanied by thumping music.

Still, he thought of how yucky it must be to actually make these movies, with the cameras and the re-shoots and the payment arrangements, the sales contracts with hotels and motels and sneaky roadside shops all over the world. He wondered what the performers did after the shooting was over. Shopped and ate, he guessed. Went home to some sort of family somewhere.

This was a Friday, a night for the sorrowful mysteries of the rosary, Chris's favorites. He went through them slowly, trying to make the words mean something for a change. Both the Lord's Prayer and the Hail Mary came from scripture, and offered a collective reconciliation. "Our" father would forgive "us" our sins. The mother of Jesus would pray for us at the hour of "our" death. Cheeto High Bear's death was Chris's, and Chris's was Fairy Belle Fanke's. The bell never stopped tolling.

Chris remembered his Dylan Thomas, "after the first death, there is no other," but he was too tired to think the whole thing through. Anyway, what did Dylan Thomas really know about first deaths or second deaths or a child's death by fire in London?

After Jesus' crucifixion in the last sorrowful mystery, Chris turned in his bed towards the window and the Mississippi. He whispered his Dylan Thomas slowly and softly, start to finish, striking every vowel and consonant and not caring for the meaning of the beautiful words. And he went to sleep.

ANOTHER SATURDAY: MORE JOYFUL MYSTERIES

A shared culture offers camouflage
behind which we can tend the covert fires
we feed our shames to, those things we most fear
to say, our buried, unspoken, common language —
the only one, and we are many.

William Matthews, *"The Place on the Corner"*

And sometimes the kids would want to know what your very
first memories were and you'd tell them and you'd always
start with Leonard's father P.Q. on a front porch in a rocking
chair and Leonard had you in his arms and he walked
through a grove of trees up to the white house and the front
porch and then he handed you to old P.Q. who held you in
his arms as he rocked in the chair but you weren't sure if this
was really a memory or if your mind was just piecing something together because P.Q. died before you were two but you
did have this picture in your mind. And then you'd tell them
about being in front of a Quonset hut playing with your
friends on a summer day and it started to storm and you kept
playing but then Alma Ruth came out the door and down one
step and picked you up and ran back into the hut and the
lights went out and her hair was very long and brown. And
later when you told these first two stories to the Panda he
said they were about sheltering and nurturing.
 And then things came together fast and jumbled, the chickens running in the back yard after Leonard chopped off their

heads, and Alma Ruth giving you baths in the kitchen sink with Lauren and lots of suds, and the time Leonard dressed up like Santa Claus but you figured out it was him and not really Santa Claus, and not much later you were a grown-up little boy and your memories were clear and no longer dreamy.

And as you grew you learned that Leonard would always fix things so that nothing could ever be right, ever, because when everything was wrong that was as it should be, because when he was a little boy everything was wrong and that was home and home is where the pain is. So when you tried to make him happy by doing something, anything, just the way he said to do it, exactly the way he said to do it, he'd think of some new thing after you were finished, something you'd missed, something he hadn't told you about, and because you'd left that out it was all wrong and you were just as worthless as he was and that was the way the child became the father of the man.

* * * * * * * *

Saturday was another day for kid stuff. They'd been pretty good sports, hanging around Busch Stadium as Chris indulged his neuroses. They began the morning with a long swim in the Millennium pool, then checked out and walked over to Union Station for breakfast. From there they walked up Fifteenth Street to the City Museum, where an old warehouse had been converted to a kids' paradise with tunnels and caves and bungee jumps and a children's circus and lots of hands-on stuff. Chris read *The New York Times* for an hour or so as Razor and Sharon ran around wherever they wanted, then he took a ride with them on the museum's ferris wheel.

Sharon found some polished rocks in the gift shop, and managed to walk right out the door with a bagful, just as she'd done with the Legos in Chicago. But this time Chris saw the wary eye of the gift shop cashier, so he took Sharon by the hand and walked back to pay for the rocks.

"You've got to be honest, Sharon," he said sternly, so the cashier could hear. He smiled and handed over three dollars.

Razor picked out a stuffed Garfield cat to stick on the car window, and a bumper sticker that read "Over the hill and gaining speed." It had a drawing of a hayseed driving to oblivion with a crazy grin on his face. "That's for you, Dad," he said.

Chris found an alternative on the top shelf: "Jesus loves you," it read. "Everybody else thinks you're an asshole." But Razor said he wouldn't ride in the Windstar if Chris put that on the bumper.

When they got back out on the street, St. Louis was hot and sticky. Chris and the kids darted from tree to tree, to stay in as much shade as possible on the walk back to the parking garage. They found some sprinklers in Memorial Park and ran through them for a while, getting soaking wet but deliciously cool. As they passed Busch Stadium, Chris flagged down an ice-cream van and bought the twins some Sno-Cones.

"There's an art to eating those," he said. "Don't put the straw all the way down to the bottom, and the flavor lasts longer." What a great thing it was for Razor and Sharon to learn these life skills from their father.

The twins wanted to go to the St. Louis Zoo next, which was fine with Chris. He hadn't been there in nearly fifty years, but it had been a staple of Hooker entertainment for generations going back to the 1904 World's Fair, which was a celebration of Thomas Jefferson's purchase of the Louisiana Territory from Napoleon one hundred years before.

All four of Chris's grandparents - Grigori, Fairy Belle, P.Q., and Alice - were at the World's Fair in 1904. Its theme was "Wilderness to Wonderland." The historian Henry Adams was rapturous: "Out of a medieval, primitive, crawling infant of 1838," he wrote, "to find St. Louis a howling, steaming, exploding, Marconiing, radiumating, automobiling maniac of 1904 exceeds belief."

There were photographs in Alma Ruth's scrap books of her grandfather and grandmother, the Fankes, standing next to a tepee with the Sioux Chief Tall Crane and Mrs. Tall Crane. Neither the Fankes nor the Tall Cranes looked very comfortable. An old post-card said the Fankes had spoken with the Apache Chief Geronimo at his booth in the Indian school, between Pueblo potters and Pueblo women grinding corn and making bread. Geronimo sold them a bow and a rubber-tipped arrow, and sang and danced for them.

Geronimo had taken Alma Ruth's mother, little Fairy Belle Fanke, on his knee and whispered, "I am a Christian now. All I want is to return to Arizona to die." Geronimo's bow was still in Alma Ruth's attic in Sand River, but Chris had lost the arrow as a little boy, shooting at clouds in the sky.

Chris and the kids took the Daniel Boone Expressway out to Forest Park, exited at Turtle Playground, parked in the hot sun and walked over to the zoo. Chris splashed Razor and Sharon with thirty-plus sun-screen.

They started with a ride on the zoo-train to beat the heat and get a look at everything. Chris managed to get the three of them on the train with only two tickets, by acting like a senile grandfather. He kept a transistor radio pressed to his ear to listen to the afternoon Cardinals game. He was pretty confident with Woody Williams on the mound, going for win number fourteen.

Sharon spotted the puffins & penguins display and wanted to get off the train. So they exited at the next depot and walked back in the heat. The puffins display was like heaven, because it was kept at forty-five degrees year round. Chris never wanted to come out. One of the puffins made the stay even more enjoyable by acting totally insane, skimming along the top of the water, flapping its wings and stopping on a dime with its big flat feet stuck out like a pair of water skis. Razor and Sharon wanted a couple of stuffed puffins from the gift shop, so Chris worked his magic. It wasn't much to ask.

Before leaving the zoo they had a ride on the carousel, then walked through the giant bird cage that had been built for the 1904 World's Fair. Except for the gold-crested cockatoos that reminded Razor and Sharon of their home in the Wombat Forest, they thought the bird cage was boring. They wanted to see the kangaroos, recalling the big six-footers in the morning mist of their front yard.

The zoo kangaroos were scrawny and unhealthy-looking by comparison, but the Americans standing around Chris and the kids didn't know that. Razor and Sharon were disappointed, as if they'd seen an old athlete playing past his prime. A couple of the kangaroos started mating shamelessly right in front of everybody, just like the strangers in Chris's hotel movie. Razor and Sharon were disgusted, and they pulled at Chris to leave.

"Just a little longer," said Chris. He was back in his frog lab. He watched alone until the kangaroos parted with sweet sorrow. "Beautiful," he said.

As they left the zoo, Mike Shannon's post-game wrap-up confirmed that Woody Williams and the Cardinals had won, 13-11, with Jason Isringhausen recording the save. Still, the Cards were three-and-a-half back of Houston going into the last third of the season. Chris was nervous.

They drove across the Mississippi on the McKinley Bridge and joined Illinois 3 heading north. At Alton, they stopped for a town festival and had coffee and hot chocolate at the Seafood Escape, which boasted that Lincoln had slept in one of the top rooms in 1858. Razor and Sharon had a look at the room, but weren't impressed.

"It's just a bunch of old stuff," said Razor. He thought he should have seen Abe's relics up there, or at least a talking statue. The kids were looking forward to getting to their campsite at Pere Marquette State Park.

They walked around the Alton festival for a while, but the crowd was full of grown-ups and everybody was drunk. Chris knocked a clown into a tub of water by hitting a target with a baseball, and that was enough family fun. They piled into the Windstar again, drove slowly up Route 100 with the Mississippi on their left and big river cliffs on their right, and entered the state park west of Grafton.

This was where the Illinois River joined the Mississippi, then both rivers rolled along as one for a few more miles until they were joined in a *menage a trois* by the Missouri, south of Alton. St. Louis must have been the best city in the world in those old Samuel Clemens days, with all the adventurers and river traffic coming to town from north, east, and west, then cruising down to New Orleans in a wild array of flotsam and jetsam.

Razor and Sharon found a great campsite next to a small creek that flowed into the Illinois River. Chris got a fire going and put up the tent as the kids explored the creek. They found a toad and a turtle, but Chris said they couldn't keep them. They had enough pets back home.

After the tent was up and the sleeping bags were in place, Chris and the kids went for a walk around the park. Chris had been here before, but it was back in the days of his very first pirate ships. As a six-year-old, he'd formed some of his earliest memories here at Pere Marquette State Park.

Somewhere there was an old swimming pool, where Leonard once entered Chris in an underwater race with big eight-year-old boys. Halfway to the finish, Chris was surprised to discover he could breathe underwater if he swam directly into the bubbles of the boys ahead. He didn't have to come up for air like the rest of them, and he won the race. Leonard was proud, but Chris was never able to manage the feat again. Whenever he tried to breathe under water, it just went up his nose and made him cough. Still, it had worked once, a miracle, and Chris never forgot.

He told Sharon and Razor about all the lizards he'd caught at Pere Marquette. Chris used to loop a string around a lizard's neck and pretend he had a tiny puppy, but some big kid would always sneak up and squash it. Razor was excited about finding lizards, and started looking for them under every rock.

They walked over to the Pere Marquette lodge, built by Roosevelt's Civilian Conservation Corp in the 1930s. Chris asked the receptionist about his old swimming pool, and she pointed him down the hallway. There was a heated indoor pool with a spa and sauna, but this wasn't what Chris was looking for. The pool he remembered was just a big white rectangular hole in the ground, so he went back to the front desk.

"Excuse me," he said to the receptionist, "I was looking for the outdoor pool. The old white one."

"Oh, that was filled in years ago," she said. "Back in the sixties. You must be an old-timer." She laughed, but winked and stuck out the tip of her tongue to let Chris know she was being friendly.

Chris and the kids went back to the indoor pool and stripped down to their underwear for a swim. This pool was for lodge guests only, not for sweaty campers in their underpants. But nobody else was using it, so they had a good time swimming laps and splashing around. It was refreshing after their muggy day in St. Louis.

After their swim Chris and the kids were full of energy, so they got in the Windstar and drove back along Route 100 to the village of Elsah for dinner. Chris had noticed the Italianate, Gothic and Greek Revival houses from the road, and wanted to investigate before dark.

Elsah was the sweetest little town Chris and the twins had ever seen. It was named after Ailsa Crag, the high cliffs of the Scottish coast, because the stone palisades along the Mississippi River reminded the founders of their home in Scotland. Elsah had only two main streets, Mill Street running north from the Mississippi and LaSalle Street heading back south. Every one of the houses and shops was freshly painted or made of ancient stone from nearby quarries. The Elsah Creek cut through the heart of town and emptied into the Mississippi under Route 100. Chris and the twins pretended they were churchmice, spiriting around a little Cinderella village just before the bell struck twelve.

On LaSalle Street, they found Jeremiah's Resale Shop and loaded up with presents for the rest of the family. They got two pairs of Italian leather shoes for Kristen, only six dollars a pair; a French woolen scarf in autumn shades for Kazzie; a brightly-colored London blouse for Jeshel; handcrafted pottery by Jan & Jon Wright for Sean; and four hard-to-find CD's by two of Josh's favorite bands, Candiria and Ghostride.

They learned from the shopkeeper that the recycled wares came from Principia College students up the hill. Principia was a Christian Science liberal arts college with an enrollment of about six hundred. Elsah also had a Christian Science church and a Christian Science reading room. Chris wanted to check out the reading room, so the kids played scrabble on the rug as he browsed through Mary Baker Eddy's *Science and Health with Key to the Scriptures*. Leonard had an old worn-out copy of this book in his Sand River attic, one of the few things his poor old father P.Q. had left behind.

"Agree to disagree with approaching symptoms of chronic or acute disease, whether it is cancer, consumption, or smallpox," wrote Mary Baker Eddy. "Meet the incipient stages of disease with as powerful mental opposition as a legislature would employ to defeat the passage of an inhuman law." An article in the *Christian Science Sentinel* observed that Jesus didn't commiserate with the man he healed at the pool of Bethesda. "Rise! Get up! Walk!" said Jesus, and the man picked up his bed and walked. Christian Scientists weren't inclined to feel too sorry for themselves.

Chris remembered now that he'd been to Elsah before, but as a nine-year-old good luck charm, not a tourist. Leonard's Quincy College baseball team used to travel down the Mississippi every now and then to kick the tar out of little old Principia. These baseball games were religious battles, the papists against the Christian Scientists. Every now and then Principia would win one, and the Quincy folks would be depressed for months until they had a chance to redeem themselves.

Leonard took special delight each time Quincy beat Principia, because it replayed the inner religious wars of his Morrisonville childhood, reenacting the singular early triumph of Alice over P.Q. Before each game, home or away, he'd go to the Quincy College chapel to kneel and pray. Chris would sit in the back of the chapel wondering what his old man was praying for. Victory? Respect? Forgiveness? Runs? All he knew was that some sort of deal was being done.

Leonard never forgot the death of his little nephew Jimmy Funk, his sister Sarah's son, which he attributed to Mary Baker Eddy. "They just let him die," said Leonard. "They wouldn't call the doctor. They said Jesus would rebuke Jimmy's fever."

None of these Hooker tensions was perceptible in Elsah in the summer of 2003. Chris and the kids enjoyed some local catfish and potato soup at "My Just Desserts" on LaSalle, where the drinks were served in glass jars. Sharon thought this was cool, and wanted to start drinking from fruit jars when they got home. "It would help the environment," she said. "We could recycle all our glass jars."

Chris laughed. "You did that for your first five years," he said. "You've just forgotten." Chris and Kazzie never threw out a jar in their seven years in the Wombat Forest. A glass jar was always good for something.

After dinner, Chris drove the kids back to their tent at the Pere Marquette campground. The night birds and crickets were making so much noise you had to talk loud even to someone right next to you. Sean would have hated it.

In the tent, Sharon found an all-night jazz station from St. Louis, 106.5 on the dial. They strung up the flashlight inside the tent and did some drawings on recycled sketch paper Chris had brought along, listening to Winton Marsalis and Miles Davis and Michael Brecker on the radio. Razor drew cool Japanese skaterboys on high-flying boards. Sharon drew fashion models with tears in their oversized eyes. Chris drew pirate ships, one after the other, each one exactly the same as before.

The weather had cooled, and it was hard for Chris to imagine anything closer to heaven than being in this tent with these twins on this night in Illinois. They stayed up past midnight, talking and drawing and listening to jazz until the kids fell asleep, Razor cuddling his new Garfield cat from the St. Louis City Museum and Sharon clinging to Dopey the Dwarf. Then Chris was alone in the darkness as the radio played, non-stop, a "deluxe edition" of John Coltrane's *A Love Supreme,* the original 1964 recording followed by the only live performance of the complete work, in France in 1965. Coltrane chanted his hypnotic four-note riff over and over again in Chris's tiny round tent - "a love supreme, a love supreme," as if in prayer.

Chris's in-built eschatology detector got revved up again at the mention of heaven and prayer, and he wished that this were another Friday night so he could say the sorrowful mysteries again, because that's how he was starting to feel. Maybe it was the jazz, which always carried him back to the little white house with the green roof where he listened with his parents to the radio in those days before television. He wasn't nostalgic for his crummy childhood, but he did miss the little boy he used to be.

Chris looked at Razor and Sharon sleeping so peacefully in the tent, and started wondering how Josh and Jeshel were doing. When Elspeth filed for divorce, Sean was only nine, the same age as these twins were now. Josh and Jeshel were even younger.

Chris tried to represent himself in the Australia Family Court, ignoring the lawyer's adage about having a fool for a client. He figured a simple child custody case in the land that gave kangaroo courts their name couldn't be as difficult as his magnificent Indian Child Welfare Act battles in the Cheyenne River Sioux Tribal Court, where justice was whatever Judge Karl Hawk Eagle said it was.

And Chris got on a roll in the Australia Family Court, in his own smart-aleck way, cracking some one-liners that even Judge Helena Mersey found amusing as Elspeth and her barrister stewed.

But Chris's fortunes, and those of Sean and Josh and Jeshel, were about to change. Elspeth's barrister, Chaim Nathan, stood erect to tender a copy of a recent American novel, *Groin Damage*, by an author with the unlikely name of Finbar Studge.

"Objection," shouted Chris. He was quick to his feet, and his right eye began to twitch.

"Yes, Mr. Hooker?" said Judge Mersey. "What is the basis for your objection?"

"Um, that book is hearsay, your honor," said Chris. "How can I possibly cross-examine Mr. Studge?" He looked quite pleased with this demonstration of legal prowess.

"Moreover, what could this American book have to say about a child custody dispute in Australia?" Chris liked this touch, a stab at anti-imperialism. Australians always fell for that. He sat down, casting his twitching eye at Chaim Nathan.

"Mr. Nathan?" said Judge Mersey.

Chaim Nathan rose again. "Your honor," he said in the measured tones of royalty, "this is not a garden variety custody dispute. Mr. Hooker's fitness as a parent turns on nuance and subtlety rather than specific incidents."

He adjusted his horsehair wig and brushed his palms against the sides of his black robe. "My client has testified to certain unusual tendencies, certain predilections that Mr. Hooker possesses, indicative of inappropriate behavior. She has attested to his instability. Mr. Hooker denies these allegations."

Chaim Nathan placed his right hand on *Groin Damage,* as if he were about to swear an oath to God Almighty. Hooker read the words "Finbar Studge" on the spine.

Nathan proceeded: "Mr. Studge's book is an internationally-acclaimed work of fiction. It has received a number of prestigious awards overseas, including the National Book Award and the PEN/Faulkner Award for Fiction." This was true, Chris recalled with some misplaced pride. Nathan pressed on. "A character who appears again and again is named 'Hooker,' and there is little doubt that he is my client's husband."

Nathan picked up *Groin Damage* and held it aloft, like a tent revivalist. Chris studied the handsome, thoughtful photograph of Finbar Studge on the back cover. Studge's wife had taken it not long before their divorce.

"More to the point, your honor," Nathan continued, "Mr. Hooker has *boasted* publicly that he *is* the man in Mr. Studge's novel." Nathan opened *Groin Damage* and removed an airmail envelope. He produced a hand-written letter with a folded newspaper clipping attached. Chris recognized the handwriting as his own. Nathan snapped open the clipping as if it were a cotton serviette.

"As an example, your honor, I tender this article from an overseas newspaper, the *Sand River Courier-Review*, which quotes Mr. Hooker at length bragging about his professed identity with Mr. Studge's so-called fictional character. I ask that this book, *Groin Damage,* be considered by the court for the purpose of impeaching Mr. Hooker's credibility, if not for corroborating my client's sworn testimony." Nathan smiled politely at Chris and took his seat. Judge Mersey gave an enigmatic smile, and directed her judicious eyes at Chris.

"Mr. Hooker?" she said.

Chris had reached the limits of his short attention span. On the yellow legal pad on the bar table in front of him, he had scrawled two lines from his favorite book of poems, Ted Hughes's *Crow:* "He stared at the evidence./Nothing escaped him. (Nothing could escape.)"

Chris half-rose into a question-mark and said softly, "It's prejudicial, your honor. Its prejudice far outweighs its probative value. And it's *fiction.* It won awards for *fiction.*"

Chaim Nathan was on his feet, chuckling. "Is Mr. Hooker suggesting he is not real, your honor? Would he have this court believe, despite his public assertions, that he is a product of Mr. Studge's imagination?"

Judge Mersey slowly opened her right hand to silence Chaim Nathan. She had heard enough.

"I don't suppose there would be any harm, would there Mr. Hooker, in the court's examining the book to determine what, if any, relevance it might have?"

Chris could see she was itching to get her hands on *Groin Damage.*

"Of course," smiled Judge Mersey, "the court will disregard any material that falls outside the parameters of permissible evidence."

"Of course," said Chris. He'd given up.

But Chaim Nathan wasn't finished. "Finally, your honor, may I draw the court's attention to the contents of the letter that accompanies the newspaper clipping?" He didn't wait for Judge Mersey's reply. "It is a letter from Mr. Hooker to my client, written while he was touring America with his bluegrass band." Nathan paused to give the following words their full effect, and cleared his throat: "The Rank Strangers."

"Your honor will recall that Mr. Hooker testified regarding his positive relationship with his family in America, and particularly with his father, a Mr. Leonard Hooker."

Judge Mersey nodded. Chris had certainly said this. Nathan proceeded.

"Mr. Hooker has expressly denied, *on his oath,* that he ever referred to his father in disparaging terms. Yet you will see, on page two, in Mr. Hooker's own hand, the following words: 'Elspeth, I'm so glad we've got the kids ten thousand miles away from my old man. He's an evil psychopath, and you can quote me.'"

Nathan's face flushed with great concern at the very thought of any lawyer, even one foolish enough to represent himself, committing perjury in the hallowed courts of Australia.

"Mr. Hooker?" said Judge Mersey. She'd stopped smiling.

Chris lifted his index finger to his right eyelid to stop the twitching. "No objection," he said. He didn't care anymore. After three more days of this crap, he ended up having every second weekend with Sean and Josh. Not too many fathers did much better. It could have been worse.

Here in the Hookers' tent at Camp Pere Marquette, Elvin Jones's tympani sounded through the radio and into the night, setting the stage for "Psalm," Coltrane's final soliloquy. When it was finished and all was quiet, Chris said the joyful mysteries of the rosary, and then a quick prayer for every person he could think of who was once alive but now was dead.

He said one for Russell Kamara, another for Cheeto High Bear. He even said one for Baruch Shulman, who'd died of stomach cancer after his murder trial, and Jillian Daley Shulman of course. The list was long, including many races from many countries. Chris was only halfway through his litany of ghosts when he joined the twins in slumber.

ANOTHER SUNDAY:
MORE GLORIOUS MYSTERIES

We shall not cease from exploration
And the end of all our exploring
Will be to arrive where we started
And know the place for the first time.

T.S. Eliot, *"Little Gidding"*

And you dodged the Viet Nam draft by hiding out in South
America in Guyana and Venezuela and Brazil and Surinam
but when you came back they still wanted to draft your
skinny ass because your number was low and the war wasn't
over yet so you applied for conscientious objector status and
they gave it to you because you were crazy and wouldn't make
a decent soldier anyway and this c.o. stuff would come back
to haunt you in the future you'd see. So you went back to the
little university in Charleston for some graduate studies to kill
time until you went to law school and every night throughout
the summer you'd take a chair out to the lawn facing the
girls' dorms which were twelve floors high. There you'd sit
with your Martin D-28 guitar and you'd play the songs you'd
written in South America and you'd sing to the dorm win-
dows and one-by-one the lights would come on first in one
room then another and it was funny because pretty soon
you'd have a big audience but each girl would be listening
alone in her room and not connected to the other girls on the
different floors or even down the hall so each one would feel

*like you were singing to her alone, and none of them knew
who you were as you sang in the darkness to their silhouettes
in the windows high above the lawn.*

*And your sister Lauren was in the convent then and she
had this Okaw City boy she knew Roger Diggle a friend of
yours who was in Viet Nam and she wrote to him a few times
and he wrote back but the nuns wouldn't let her see his letters because they thought she'd lose her vocation if she
started thinking about boys so she stopped writing because
she thought he wasn't answering. And then he got killed by a
grenade and the nuns brought her the news with this big
stack of his unopened letters and she wanted to kill them for
what they'd done even though the letters didn't have much to
say, they were just dumb letters from a boy in Viet Nam, and
she quit the convent and got married right away after that.*

*And later you went from South Dakota to D.C. to lobby
for the Cheyenne River Sioux's water rights and you went
out to the Viet Nam Wall and you couldn't believe how many
names there were on that wall 58,000 of them but that was
just a number and when you saw all the names it was different, it was like there were a million, most of them young and
all of them dead and this was all that was left of them this
unworthy little chisel in the granite, and you found old Roger
Diggle's name and you touched it and you hadn't known that
his middle name was Floyd and as you stared into the black-
ness around his name your own face was reflected back to you
but you were thirty years older and Roger Diggle would
always be a kid and what had you done with your extra time
and what difference did it make anyway?*

* * * * * * * * *

On Sunday morning, Chris and the kids had a big breakfast at the Pere Marquette lodge as tiny hummingbirds heli-
coptered outside the window, close enough to touch. This was
the last day of the trip. Chris planned to visit Hannibal,
Missouri, and Quincy, Illinois, then zip across the middle of

the State of Illinois for home. He had to drive to Chicago O'Hare next week to meet Kazzie and Kristen's flight home from Australia.

After breakfast, they packed the tent and sleeping bags and hiked up the trail to McAdam's Peak. Razor kept looking for lizards but couldn't find any.

"They must have died out," said Chris. "There used to be thousands."

"This reminds me of the Wombat Forest," said Sharon halfway up the trail. From the time Razor and Sharon could walk, they went on wood-gatherings with Chris and Kazzie, deep into their surrounding eucalypts. The twins' job was to gather kindling in canvas bags as Chris chain-sawed through fallen trees and Kazzie split the blocks of wood into fours. There were no gum trees here at Pere Marquette, but the sunlight flickered through the ashes and oaks, and the undergrowth tugged at their pants and shoes just as it had back home in Australia.

"It makes me think more of Cinque Terre," said Chris, breathing just a little heavily. He'd climbed the path behind a thousand-year-old stone church in Vernazza one afternoon, waved goodbye to the family on the little stretch of beach below, and walked alone in the hills to Monterosso al Mare. On his left were the blue waters of Mare Ligure, just as the brown Illinois now caught the morning sun as he climbed with the twins to McAdam's Peak. He imagined himself back in Italy, sipping cappuccinos at Vernazza's Hemingway bar.

Razor never did get his lizard, but Sharon found a huge praying mantis that was nearly as good. Chris took some pictures of the mantis crawling all over the kids' faces and hair. After conquering McAdam's Peak and walking back down the trail, they said goodbye to Pere Marquette and headed north along Illinois 100 and the Illinois River.

This was the least-populated part of Illinois. A few miles north of Nutwood, an old guy with a blue handkerchief around his head and a flowing gray ponytail passed them on a motorcycle.

"Organ donor," said Chris. This was a family joke started by Kazzie. In Australia, all the motorcyclists wore helmets. So she was surprised when she came to America to see all these yahoos on their Harleys showing how macho they were by slamming their heads into pavements at eighty miles per hour, all in the name of freedom. Razor and Sharon waved to the Organ Donor, and he waved back.

Nobody passed through this backwater without a reason, except Chris. And even Chris had a reason of sorts, because Calhoun County was the quickest way to Hannibal, Missouri. Just before they reached the Hardin bridge, they stopped at a roadside stall for some peaches and nectarines. The fruits were sweet and dripping, and Razor and Sharon loved them so much that Chris bought a couple bags of each.

There was some roadwork on the bridge, and traffic was reduced to a single lane, controlled by one of those temporary stoplights. Chris caught a red light and waited for the oncoming flow of traffic to finish. His was the only vehicle heading west. Just as the light was about to change, Chris looked in his rearview mirror and saw a big red dog crossing the road behind him, and a motorcycle heading straight for the dog. The motorcyclist couldn't stop, and a hellish collision took place. The dog exploded and flew to the side of the road as the motorcyclist went into a horizontal skid, stopping a couple of yards behind the Windstar.

Chris jumped out, thinking this was just perfect, another accident on the last day of the trip. The motorcyclist turned out to be Organ Donor, the guy the kids had waved to a few miles back. His jeans were shredded and blood was splattering from his head and elbows and right knee. But he stood up and said, "Don't worry! I'm ok."

This wasn't necessary information for Razor and Sharon, who had run to the dog. Sharon was patting it on the head and saying "poor doggie," but it was deader than hell. More to the point for Razor, this dog was a real mess.

"Look at his eye, Dad," he said. One of the dog's eyes was hanging out of its socket. Razor wanted Chris to grab the camera. He was fascinated with the physical details of death - the gorier the better.

Sharon was more taken with the very idea of mortality. She thought death was a personal insult. And at the age of nine, she'd developed a knack for writing dark poems in her secret diary, relying heavily on her American Heritage dictionary. Chris kept tabs on her work every now and then, just to stay in touch with the state of Sharon's mental health. One of her better poems, written when she was eight, was called *Be Like Water:*

> How brief we are
> and amorphous, as single drops of rain
> that run into each other and find a flow
> and lose a self and go into deep crevasses
> and fill a space of slain myths. Through all
> of this, I can hear you breathing in sync
> with the lungs of the sky.
> I say to you: be like water for it never tries
> to be higher than it is.

Be Like Water was followed in Sharon's diary by a drawing of a little stick creature wailing away with oversized teardrops.

After the drama on the houseboat, Sharon added *Demons in a Low Country Summer* to her growing portfolio:

> In the late July dusk,
> an ashen dome stretches over
> the western sky with recurring
> waves of rain. The wind carries
> the water in terraced increments
> across the lake, and any left-
> over light squeezes out until night
> takes over to crescendos of thunder.

Chris didn't know whether to laugh or cry. After reading Sharon's private thoughts, he snuck her diary back into her schoolbag so she wouldn't know he'd been prying.

Organ Donor tested his motorcycle. It was a little banged up, but started ok. He revved the motor and took a quick test spin over by the fruit stand. He was ready to roll. With a wave of his hand he zipped across the Hardin bridge and out of sight. Chris and some other drivers tended to the dog. They borrowed a shovel from the fruit stand and dug a shallow roadside grave. Sharon and Razor threw a couple of nectarines on top to give the doggie a good sendoff, and asked Chris to read St. Francis's "Canticle of the Creatures," which he kept with him on a holy card in his wallet. He'd picked it up at the Basilica di S. Francesco during the Assisi pilgrimage.

"Praise be to thee my lord with all thy creatures," he read. "Praise be to thee for our sister bodily death . . . the second death can do no harm . . . O bless and praise my lord all creatures." The other drivers kept their heads bowed.

Chris had a captive audience, so he decided to add a few words of his own. He cleared his throat, bowed his head, and closed his eyes.

"We will never know how many pups this unnamed dog has left behind," he said softly, picturing himself at the pulpit of St. Philomena's. "We can only know that her species has been reproducing for centuries at a rate twenty times faster than our own." Chris was setting the stage for one of his favorite themes, the marriage of science and religion. Several of the drivers started sneaking looks at their watches.

Chris's theory was that dogs, not to mention monarch butterflies and gray finches and goldfish, had souls. But more importantly, they also had a lot more mutation opportunities than humans, because it took humans twenty years or so to start a new generation. So it stood to reason that animals had evolved at a faster rate. Just because they let people push them around and have their way with them, that didn't make them inferior. In fact, in the gospel according to Chris, animals' silent acquiescence in the face of human dominance and cruelty was proof of *their* higher nature.

"St. Francis knew that the highest spirituality belongs to the creatures," said Chris, a little louder. He was getting carried away. "He knew that *we* may have dominion over every living thing that moveth upon the earth, but *their* prayer is the praise of God, the only form that does not return to self, rising to infinity and content simply to be expressed."

Out of the corner of his eye, Chris noticed some of the drivers inching toward their cars, but a couple of girls from the fruit stand were standing still and sobbing uncontrollably. He quickly crescendoed to a closing flourish.

"This praise of God has a thousand voices, because all of creation proclaims it! It is in the song of the skylark outlined against the sun, in the chirp of the locust in the heat of the day! Yet again, it has no voice, for this highest form of praise is in the silent adherence of the will to the most high God!" Chris spread his arms wide, like Terrion Jackson at the top of the Millennium Hotel.

One of the sobbing girls approached Chris after the service and said, "That was so beautiful." Her t-shirt stated her membership with the Calhoun County girls' volleyball team. Chris gave her his best preacher-style bear hug, handed back her shovel, and climbed into the Windstar.

The bridge light was red again, so Chris and the kids had to wait for another line of cars from the east. When the green light came on, Chris slipped into the single lane and crossed over the Illinois River.

"Bye bye, doggie," said Sharon. She opened her diary and started writing another secret poem.

Once across the Hardin bridge, Chris turned north for Kampsville and Illinois 96 along the Mississippi. At Atlas, Illinois, he turned left onto Highway 54 and crossed over a free bridge to an oxymoron called Louisiana, Missouri. Then he got onto Missouri 79 for Hannibal, the boyhood home of Samuel Langhorne Clemens. More significant for Sharon, though, was that Hannibal was also the home of the Unsinkable Molly Brown, a heroine of Sharon's who'd survived the sinking of the Titanic.

Titanic was Sharon's favorite movie. She'd seen it a dozen times, and had Chris buy her the DVD for her eighth birthday. Every time Leonardo DiCaprio and Kate Winslet stood at the bow of the great ship with their arms outstretched like the wings of cruising sea-birds, Sharon would always stand and do the same. She could quote almost every line from the movie, and her favorite was Molly Brown's: "Now there's a sight you don't see every day." Molly says these words as she sits in the safety of a lifeboat, watching the Titanic lift to vertical before its final descent. Sharon would always join her.

Downtown Hannibal was dead for a tourist trap on a weekend. Chris took the kids to Sam Clemens's boyhood home on Hill Street, showed them the fence Tom Sawyer supposedly whitewashed, bought some Indian head pennies at the Mark Twain Museum & Gift Shop, and had some catfish at Bubba's. After lunch, they had a look at the J.M. Clemens Law Office, where Sam's father presided as justice of the peace in the 1840s.

"That's where Muff Potter was tried," said Chris in a very authoritative voice, hoping other folks would hear his knowledgeable commentary. Razor and Sharon knew who Muff Potter was, because Chris had read them an expurgated version of Tom Sawyer, several times.

Sharon was tired of boys' stories, and wanted to see some girls' things. So they went to the home of Laura Hawkins, Sam's childhood girlfriend who became Becky Thatcher in Tom Sawyer. Everything had been restored to just the way it was when little Laura was alive. Then they drove over to the birthplace of Margaret Tobin Brown, the unsinkable Molly. There were rags to riches photos tracking her life from Hannibal to Denver to Europe, and a whole room dedicated to the Titanic voyage.

Sharon started singing "the heart must go on" at the top of her voice and wouldn't stop, pretending to be Celine Dion and hoping everybody would notice her, which they did.

"Look," said Chris trying to shut her up, "it says here Molly Brown was on her way back to Hannibal when the Titanic went down."

"Just think," said Sharon. "Such a great woman, and she started here in this little town." Then she started singing again.

After saying goodbye to a Molly Brown lookalike who was handing out Tootsie Rolls, they took Route 36 to a bridge over the Mississippi and got back onto Interstate 72 in Illinois. They were heading north for Quincy and a childhood home closer to the Hooker family tree.

The Cardinals' broadcast was coming in loud and clear on KMOX, but the news was grim. The Cardinals were behind 3-1 in the bottom of the ninth. This year's team was not known for coming from behind. Even though the Cards had two runners in scoring position, the light-hitting reserve Orlando Palmeiro was pinch-hitting, and Chris wasn't holding his breath for a rally. He steeled himself for another heartbreaking defeat.

But Palmeiro lined a single to right, scoring Edgar Renteria and Kerry Robinson to tie the game. Chris was ecstatic, but Sharon and Razor were in a parallel universe watching *Lord of the Rings* on the DVD. Even better for Chris, Albert Pujols was coming to the plate. The Cardinals were tied, and there was a chance to win.

Palmeiro advanced to second base on a passed ball. Just as the outskirts of Quincy came into view, Pujols lined a shot to center and the Cardinals had their very best victory of the year, 4-3. A manic smile came over Chris's face as he pounded his palms on the steering wheel. In the post-game interview, Palmeiro told Mike Shannon that he gave thanks to his lord and savior, Jesus Christ, for seeing fit to give him a base hit, and Mike quickly got him off the air.

After almost fifty years, Chris was still able to wind his way back to his old school, a block from Quincy College, without a wrong turn. He parked the Windstar on the street outside St. Francis Grade School.

Through all these years Chris had remembered this school being named after St. Francis of Assisi. This was a point of pride for Chris, a source of identity, and he fancied his pilgrimage to Francis's crypt as a completion of some circle of destiny. He'd stood in silence before Giotto's frescoes of scenes from the life of Francis. He'd walked beneath the precious cross in the lower church transept. He'd prostrated himself before the stone pilaster covering the saint's remains. He'd knelt in meditation at the Cappella delle Relique di San Francesco, where Francis's personal belongings were on display. He'd taken to wearing the T-shaped wooden cross of the Franciscans, and even bought a pair of second-hand leather sandals at the Ostello Della Pace youth hostel.

Now he was surprised to learn he'd been wrong all along. His old grade school was named not for Francis of Assisi, but for Francis Solano, a Peruvian missionary. Solano's name was carved in stone above the school entrance. Chris pulled out his pocket Penguin book of saints to look up this imposter.

Francis Solano was worthy enough in his own way. In fact, he had a lot more in common with Chris than Francis of Assisi ever did. Solano had lived with the Indians, just like Chris. He and Chris both spent some time in South America - not a riveting connection, but more than Chris had with Assisi. And one of Solano's claims to fame was that his ship from Spain had to be abandoned in a storm, which had Chris musing about sainthood as he recalled the hurricane winds at Table Rock Lake.

Still, "Francis Solano" didn't have the same resonance for Chris as "Francis of Assisi." This fifty-year error would take some accommodating. Chris nervously fingered his wooden cross.

He took the kids for a tour of his old stomping grounds. Above the school door, under Francis Solano's name, was an ambivalent motto Chris had never noticed before: "God's will, the end of Man." Chris wasn't sure which way to take it. Was the purpose of human life to do the will of God? Or was God willing the end of everybody, including Chris?

As they walked around the school, Chris had a rush of time-travel. Once again, bad boy Joey Sohn stood at the top of the stairs, like Leonardo DiCaprio on his way to the *Titanic* ballroom, except that Joey was making obscene gestures with both middle fingers in the direction of Sister Adelbert, the fifth-grade teacher.

Chris remembered playing during recess after a big rain, making speed-boats from popsicle sticks and racing them in the gutter. The old basketball hoops were still standing where they'd always been, rising above the asphalt where Chris had to sink five in a row of every kind of shot before he'd let himself go home. He tried to explain the significance of each memory to Razor and Sharon, but they wanted to do something a lot more fun than reliving Chris's Quincy childhood.

They crossed the street to what used to be College Avenue, where Chris lived with his parents and Lauren and Rachel in a little apartment above a bookstore. Except now the avenue was gone, replaced by a terraced walkway that connected the old college buildings to a fancy new library. The library stood where the Hookers' bookstore used to be, and Chris's upstairs apartment could be revisited only in his mind.

If he could have, he'd have walked the twins through the apartment's rooms, and shown them where he climbed the cherry tree to get into the bathroom when his parents forgot their front door key, and the stairs Alma Ruth ran down, holding him by his ankles and banging his head on the steps to dislodge a piece of jawbreaker candy that got stuck in his throat.

"My dog Skeeter is buried under that library," Chris said absent-mindedly.

"Just like Chief Pontiac!" said Sharon.

"No," said Razor, "he's buried under a garage." The Ottawa Chief had made a big impression on Razor.

The three Hookers were at the very spot where Chris had stood fifty years before, next to the chapel entrance, watching his parents return in triumph in the back seat of a shiny new convertible as confetti fell around them and people cheered. But everything was gone. The cherry tree, the yard, the dog, the youthful parents, the apartment, the little sisters, the little boy.

A few people started strolling up the walkway for the Sunday afternoon mass at the college chapel. Razor and Sharon started inching backwards in the direction of Francis

Solano's school and the refuge of the Windstar, but Chris said, "Come on guys. You could use a dose of church." They rolled their eyes in unison, just like twins. "Oh, c'mon," he said. "It's been a week. It won't kill you."

The chapel was right across from the library, inside the old red brick college buildings. Chris and the kids climbed the smooth stone stairs and opened the ancient wooden doors. Along the inside walls were photographs of dozens of Franciscan priests who'd run the college over the years. Chris recognized some of the black-and-white faces, and they hadn't aged a day. But now they looked severe and scary, not at all like the friendly men he remembered from his childhood.

Chris and the kids followed the Quincy folks through the chapel doors. As he passed under the choir loft, holding each twin by a hand, he heard the usual ruffling of missals and murmuring of good afternoons as people settled into their pews.

Chris took a few more steps and froze. All of a sudden he felt about three feet tall as his eyes ran up the wall behind the altar. Staring down from the domed ceiling, heralded by a sinister choir of smiling seraphim, was a gigantic mural of the familiar face of Jesus, a puzzled look descending from his huge gothic eyes. Chris had stood here before, but he hadn't given a single thought to this smothering icon since the Hookers uprooted themselves from the banks of the Mississippi after Leonard got fired all those sad years ago. But this face, this particular image on this remote chapel ceiling, had never gone away entirely. It used to scare the bejesus out of Chris when he was a little boy living across the street above the bookstore. And here it was again.

This particular Jesus had burrowed into whatever soul Chris had back then in the fifties, and stayed even when he didn't know it was there, somewhere deep inside where he knew with absolute certainty that there was no other, nothing at all beyond the perimeter of the skull of Christian Leonard Hooker, nothing but this black hole of Chris inside, sucking all light into itself as it had always done, without time or touch or escape or hope of escape, where Chris was suspended in nothing and there would be no death from this life, no reprieve and no one to reprieve, where he heard the doggies bark and the cat died down and the crow stropped his beak as Chris wrapped his tiny arms around his shaking puppy in a shallow grave now crushed beneath a hundred thousand books.

Chris wasn't thinking he was Jesus. He was thinking that Jesus was *him.* Once upon a time he was frightened of what he might become. Now he laughed softly in this college chapel aisle. The joke was on him. Nothing escaped him. Nothing could escape.

"Relax, Dad," said Razor, tugging at Chris's sleeve.

"Yeah, Dad" said Sharon. "People are staring at us."

This was true, because Chris was quite a sight, quaking in the aisle in something like rapture, his eyes fixed on the ceiling, two little kids clutching their father's trembling hands.

Chris thought he heard the seraphim cry out to one another, "Holy, holy, holy is the lord of hosts! All the earth is filled with his glory!"

The frame of the door shook and the chapel was filled with smoke. Chris said aloud, "Woe is me, I am doomed! For I am a man of unclean lips, living among a people of unclean lips, yet my eyes have seen the lord of hosts!"

Then one of the seraphim in the form of Cheeto High Bear flew down to Chris, holding a glowing ember from the sun dance. He touched Chris's mouth with it and said, "See, now that this has touched your lips, your wickedness is removed, your sin is purged."

Then Chris heard a voice from high above the chapel altar saying, "Whom shall I send? Who will go for us?"

And Chris ejaculated softly, under his breath: "Here I am. Send me."

No doors really shook, of course, and there was no smoke, and nobody saw any flying seraphim or burning embers except Chris. He looked down at Razor and Sharon and snapped out of it as if nothing had happened. And nothing had. He led the twins to their seats in a front pew to the left, and behaved himself during the mass. People soon forgot he was even there.

This was the Seventeenth Sunday in Ordinary Time. The reading from 1 Kings 3:5 had Solomon praying for an understanding heart to help the people distinguish right from wrong. God liked this prayer, because Solomon didn't ask for a long life or riches.

The next reading picked up where last week's left off, with another excerpt from Paul's letter to the Romans. "For those he foreknew he also predestined to be conformed to the image of his Son," said Paul, "so that he might be the first-born among many brothers and sisters."

This freaked Chris out, and he snuck another glance at the ceiling. It had to be more than coincidence, didn't it, that he too was a firstborn son, and his mother's name was Alma, the virgin?

The final reading was another parable from Matthew, where the kingdom of heaven is like a treasure buried in a field. A man finds the treasure and hides it again, then goes and sells all that he has and buys the field. This parable made a lot of sense to Razor. It was a lot better than last week's mustard seed.

"That's just what I'd do, Dad," he whispered. "I'd hide the treasure."

But Chris was lost in thought, speculating on the legal implications of the hidden treasure. What if the real owner turned up? Would the man who bought the field still own the treasure? Or could the original owner make an enforceable claim? This had the makings of a good lawsuit.

It all depended on whether the treasure was lost, or mislaid. The case law was pretty much the same in Australia or America or Guyana.

Chris busied himself with a legal brief in his head, citing *South Staffordshire Water Co. v. Sharman*, [1896] 2 Q.B. 44, and *Bridges v. Hawkesworth*, 21 L.J. (Q.B.) 75. His brief declared that the finder of a lost article is entitled to it against all the world except the true owner, but the owner of the *locus in quo* is presumed to be the owner of an article found on his land. Razor might be out of luck if the real owner ever turned up.

The mental brief reached the conclusion that the finder of heaven would have a lot of trouble keeping it all to himself. Chris imagined himself in ancient Israel wearing a wig and black robes, making this learned argument to Judge Solomon himself, whose heart was so wise that he had no equal.

The Franciscan priest's homily in the Quincy chapel was more down-to-earth. He said the treasure was within each of us, but we had to journey before we even reached the field. There would be wild animals and ogres along the way, disguised as God. "The glamour of sin" would lure us into trouble. If you finally reached the field, you would have to dig, but the first layer of soil would be deeper and harder than you imagined, and you would be weak and helpless. Even if you finally found the treasure, you would not recognize it at first. And when you did, you would be in for a big surprise.

Razor and Sharon were so annoyed, because the priest wouldn't tell everybody what the surprise was. "That's not fair, Dad," said Sharon.

"It sucks," said Razor.

After the homily, Chris swallowed the body and blood of you-know-who yet again. He couldn't tell if there was murder or innocence in his heart, and he wasn't sure if it mattered.

As they left the chapel, Chris and the kids walked around Leonard's old baseball field, surrounded by stone walls, where Chris had run the base paths as a boy and where he'd flown a kite so high it was only a speck against a threatening sky. Those old stone walls had once defined his universe.

"Grandpa used to coach over there," said Chris, pointing to the baseball diamond. He pictured Leonard in his Hawks' uniform, making mysterious hand-signals from the dugout to call for another suicide squeeze.

And just like that it was time to head back home to Sand River. Some turbulent weather was brewing in the east. Chris and the kids strolled hand-in-hand back to the Windstar and headed straight into the storm.

"Hold onto your hats," said Chris, but he might have saved his breath. Razor and Sharon already had their headphones on, watching *Spy Kids II* on the DVD.

In front, Chris unwrapped an Atkins bar and slipped a CD into the car stereo, a collection of Italian love songs. He selected Puccini's *Nessun Dorma*, and pressed the repeat button so he could listen to Pavarotti over and over again as he rambled down Highway 72 through the level heart of Illinois.

Once out of town, he pulled his black plastic rosary from his pocket, the one from Assisi, and mumbled the glorious mysteries to himself. "Gee," he thought as the lightning flashed and the wind and rain battered the Windstar, "this was a good vacation."

EPILOGUE

You should let yourself go a bit.
You might have written a better book.
Or at any rate the right book.

Tom Stoppard, *"Arcadia"*

You found yourself wondering why Finbar Studge seemed to hate you so. You must have done something. It didn't bother you that he hated you, not much anyway, but it was curious. His most famous character, with your surname and your clothes and your jobs and your wives, kept getting meaner and meaner and meaner, but no matter how mean he made him, Studge's readers still liked him, which drove Studge crazy.

In an e-mail exchange, Studge told you he'd tried to write a short story explaining why he hated Hooker so, but when the story was done it didn't add up, the hatred still didn't make any sense because your offenses were not big enough. "You remember what they were," wrote Studge in his e-mail, "you remember, because they really happened."

There were two things, and each mixed sex with the death of Studge's father, Harry Chalmers Studge, when Studge was seventeen. You remembered where you were when you got the news. You were playing tennis at Halloway Park, and Leonard called you over to the swimming pool and spoke to you through the cyclone fence. At first you went home and you told

Alma Ruth and she told you to go over to the Studge's house and be with Fin and you couldn't do it, you were catatonic, you didn't know how to act or what to do or what to say, but eventually you drove over in the Rambler station wagon and you and Studge sat for a couple of hours in the car in front of his house and you remembered him saying "We always wondered how it would feel if one of our fathers died, and now it's happened and I'm still wondering how it feels."

And two months later it was time for Studge to go off to college in Indiana, and you drove over with him and his mother Rosa and you sat outside the college with them on a picnic table talking to a young priest who used the word "provincial" and you'd never heard that word before and had to ask him what it meant. And after you and Rosa left Studge behind you drove back for Okaw City but she wanted to stop at the Starlite Motel and she got a room for herself and another for you right next door, and it was strange because the whole drive from the college to Okaw City was only three hours and why did you have to stop for the night? And after an hour or so she knocked on your door and asked you to come to her room and you did, and she said that she just didn't want to be alone and she wasn't crying exactly but her face was all sad and lonesome and crazy and her husband was dead and her son had gone off to college. And nothing happened, you just sat there and talked with her, you can't even remember what either of you said, you just sat there all skinny and eighteen and she talked and after a while you said good night and went back to your room and that was that. But then a year or two later you wrote a letter to Studge and you thought you were being funny or pushing the envelope or something and you said, "Hey Studge, you know that night your mother and I took you off to college, well we stopped off at a motel and she invited me into her room and I went, and it was real good" and now Studge's e-mail said that he went right off the deep end after that with years of therapy and later when he took his mother to see "The Graduate" and Dustin Hoffman hops into bed with Mrs. Robinson, Rosa got all flushed and had to walk out of the movie so Studge always wondered just what had gone on in that motel room, but it was nothing it was just the way you told it, nothing happened, and you couldn't really have done anything with his poor mother even if she'd wanted to, she was just lonely and wanted someone to be in the room with her and you were skinny and ugly and wouldn't have known what to do anyway, you were just bragging and being stupid.

So that was one thing. And the other was this party, a few years later, where Ellinghaus came up to you, an old high school buddy of yours and Studge's, and Ellinghaus said that Studge's dad had an affair twenty years ago with a nurse and there was a child, a secret lovechild right there in town and her name was Sophie, and didn't you ever notice how much Sophie looked just like Fin, and there was a resemblance in the eyes, and you passed it along to a few other people at the party just the way Ellinghaus told it, and the next day it got back to Studge and he phoned Leonard to say what in the hell was Chris doing anyway spreading these rumors and Leonard came up to you and said, "Harry Studge is dead, Chris, what in the world are you doing?" And in his e-mail, Studge said he wasn't really mad at you because of the rumor but he really just wanted to know if it was true about Sophie and he'd checked it out and all of his father's friends told him there was no truth in it whatever, but that was the second thing that Studge had against you but when he tried to write about it and to explain to his readers why he hated his Hooker character so much it just didn't add up, it just didn't add up, especially when it was only you and nobody else in real life who came over the night his father died and sat with him in the Rambler station wagon outside his house for a couple of hours.

* * * * * * * * *

A week after cowering before Jesus H. Christ in the Quincy chapel, Chris and the twins had to pile in the

Windstar again and drive to O'Hare to pick up Kazzie and Kristen. "It's déjà vu all over again," said Razor, under the impression that Chris had never heard this line before. Razor had picked it up on the St. Anthony's playground, and said it whenever anything happened twice.

Kazzie was affectionate after her two-week respite from Chris. Kristen was still listening to her Discman, but she had a new CD by an Australian group called "My Friend the Chocolate Cake." Kazzie and Kristen were full of stories about "home," as they always called Australia. Josh's heavy metal band was taking off, but Kazzie wasn't sure Chris would like the music.

"They shout a lot," she said. She had a homemade CD Josh had put together in his garage, playing all the instruments himself with overdubbing. Chris was impressed. Josh played the drums, bass, lead guitar, and yelled. Metal or whatever, it was pretty complicated to keep all those notes and rhythms together, as Chris knew well. Some of Josh's songs were in weird times, like 5/4 and 7/4. Chris kept getting mixed up as he tapped his foot on the floorboard, trying to find the first beat of each bar.

Jeshel was directing and starring in a school production of "Cat on a Hot Tin Roof." Razor wanted to know if Jeshel was the cat, and Sharon asked if Jeshel's play was the same as the Cat in the Hat.

"You'd be proud of her," said Kazzie to Chris. "She's tall and beautiful and very smart, and for some reason she really likes you." Chris took that as a compliment. Jeshel had probably been better off growing up without him. He entertained the notion that this was an example of his outstanding parenting skills.

Most of all, Kazzie had taken a liking to Miriam Slade. "You're lucky you had an affair with her," she said. "Good choice." She sounded envious. Chris wondered again what Kazzie had been up to in Australia, but quickly put such wicked thoughts out of his mind.

They pulled over at a roadside rest stop, and Chris could tell it was sinking in for Kazzie that she was back among the

Illinois cornfields, far from the Wombat Forest and Acland Street and the Great Ocean Road. But she tried to stay cheery. She bought a bag of peanuts and some decaf from a vending machine, smiled and said, "Let's go home." She hugged Chris a lot, and squeezed the twins as if she couldn't believe they were real.

Kazzie climbed into the back seat of the Windstar and read a couple more Taro Yashima stories, *Umbrella* and *Momo's Kitten*. Chris stared ahead at the highway and listened to Kazzie's voice, thankful to have at least part of his family back together. Taro Yashima went straight to his heart and made him feel like a nine-year-old. Everything was ok.

Chris took Dopey the Dwarf from the dashboard and tossed him back to Kazzie. He was in the process of telling her all about the newspaper accounts of the prison van that had crashed near Ashkum two weeks ago, when they saw some lights flashing ahead.

"Not another one," said Sharon.

"Déjà vu all over again," said Razor.

But it wasn't quite. This accident had happened quite a few minutes before. The police and ambulance were already there. Chris didn't have to wallow in angst about stopping to rescue somebody.

A red S-10 pickup truck was pointed northeast in Chris's southbound lane. A semi-trailer was in the same lane but pointed southwest, and a shattered green Subaru was sitting in the median. The pickup driver was still sitting in his truck. The ambulance was over by the Subaru, and paramedics were scrambling about desperately.

Chris rolled down his window to hear what was going on. "Welcome back to Illinois," he said to Kazzie.

Just then, the pickup driver jumped out of his truck and ran towards a cornfield next to the highway, just like the guy had done in Morrisonville a couple of weeks before.

"Told ya, Dad," said Razor. "It's déjà vu." A big difference, though, was that this pickup driver had a butcher's knife in his right hand.

A few seconds later they heard a piercing squeal coming out of the field, like some wild animal caught in a leg-trap, and three policemen ran from the Subaru into the cornfield. Chris closed his eyes and saw a Dallas school book depository and a black convertible, imagined himself crawling up a grassy knoll towards a picket fence where three shots had come from.

One of the policemen came out of the cornfield covered in blood. He motioned for the paramedics across the median. It didn't look like the policeman was hurt, so all that blood must have been somebody else's.

Kazzie put down Taro Yashima and covered Razor's and Sharon's eyes with her hands. Kristen took off her head-phones and stared into the cornfield. The paramedics raced across the median with a gurney and disappeared behind the corn. A cop directing traffic waved his hand for Chris to pull around the semi and move along. "Show's over, folks," he said. Chris eased past the semi and moseyed on down the highway, thinking this show was anything but over, but he'd never have a chance to see the end.

They got back home and life went on. August and September weren't as hot as usual for central Illinois. Chris settled his claim against the Millennium Hotel for fifteen hun-dred dollars, which paid for the houseboat and the Cardinals' tickets. He started preparing for the next semester at the law school. In addition to his course on Indigenous Law, Chris was teaching a new subject called "The Kennedy Assassination and the Law."

Kazzie received news that she'd been given a job promo-tion at the hospital. Illinois started to seem a little better for her, but it would never take the place of the Wombat Forest.

Sean switched from philosophy to pre-med, and Kristen emerged as a star setter on the high school volleyball team. The twins joined the YMCA basketball league, with Chris as their coach. He took the games very seriously, always looking for an edge.

"The smallest thing can turn a game around," he would say, hoping the kids would understand this as a life lesson. He bought a silver whistle, and a white clipboard with a basket-ball-court diagram, where he made lots of Xs and Os to show the fourth grade players how to set picks and cut to the hoop.

But Chris's heart was on defense, not offense. "Stay between the basket and the kid you're guarding," he'd shout. "Block out for rebounds." Razor was a ball of fire, playing out of control most of the time. Chris liked that. Sharon specialized in defense. Her favorite move was to strip the ball from bigger boys every chance she got. Then she'd swing her elbows until they backed off. They'd glare at her as Chris applauded.

"Way to go, Sharon," he'd say. "Good hustle."

Cuffy Kamara's death sentence was commuted on the basis of briefs filed by Boynkin & Sneed and Chris, but they still had to try to get Cuffy transferred to Australia to serve his time. The Florida newspapers hadn't breathed a word about Chris's involvement with Yolanda Possum Kamara. Chris spoke with Cuffy by telephone, telling him how well he'd known Yolanda and his father Russell. They made an appointment to meet in Cuffy's prison cell sometime in March, which was nice for Chris because it coincided with the Cardinals' spring training schedule in Jupiter, Florida. He'd even have a chance to catch up with his childhood friend Finbar Studge, the writer. He hadn't seen Studge in almost forty years, since their Okaw City days.

The Cardinals started September in first place in the National League Central, but faded badly in the last month of 2003 and finished third, behind the Chicago Cubs and the Houston Astros. But at least Albert Pujols won the batting title by a fraction of a percentage point over Todd Helton. The Cardinals' manager, Tony LaRussa, got suspended for a game in the last week of the regular season, so he couldn't wear his uniform and sit in the dugout. He had to wear street clothes and sit in the press box, watching the game from on high like a regular fan. Chris watched him do a t.v. interview in the sixth inning.

"It's so much easier up here," said LaRussa. "You sit here like God, and you can see everything that's going on." He said he could see why it was such a great game for the fans, who were always saying what-if and why-didn't-you and all that. He promised never again to get angry with broadcasters or sportswriters who second-guessed him. "I second-guessed everything myself from the first inning. Why did you make that pitch? Why did you pull off the ball? Why didn't you get a better jump?" Chris started thinking he'd been too hard on old Tony, and felt bad about it. It was only a game.

In the post-season, the Cubs knocked off the Atlanta Braves, and Cubs fans were tremulous in the hope that this might be their time, their first World Series crown in ninety-five years. But first they had to get past the Florida Marlins in the National League.

Out of the blue, Chris got a phone call from his old law school buddy from Blue Mound, Tim McFarland, inviting Chris to Game 6 of the National League Championship Series in Chicago. McFarland had landed a consulting job with the new governor of Illinois, Rod Blagojevich, who was a big Cubs fan. The seats were five rows behind home plate, and Mark Prior looked like a colossus on the pitching mound. His curve ball was unhittable, breaking about two feet right in front of Chris and Tim.

"Some pitcher," said Tim McFarland. "They call him Messiah Mark."

The Cubs and Messiah Mark went into the eighth inning of Game 6 with a 3-0 lead, and were only five outs from the World Series, when the ancient Curse of the Billy Goat asserted itself right before Chris's eyes. A 26-year-old fan named Steve Bartman, sitting in the front row along the left-field line, was moved by the Tireless Watcher to tap a soft fly ball from the waiting glove of Cubs outfielder Moises Alou, and the Cubs imploded. Moises slammed his glove to the ground in disgust, Messiah Mark lost his concentration, and the Marlins proceeded to score eight runs.

After the game shattered the Cubs' hopes, Bartman got vicious death threats on Chicago radio, prompting Governor Blagojevich to issue an official state-wide call for calm. The governor's one-sentence statement was drafted by Tim McFarland: "Nobody can justify any kind of threat to someone who does something stupid like reach for that ball." McFarland's clumsy prose didn't enhance his stature as a literary stylist, but Chris was so jealous of his brilliant legal stratagem, defending a guy on the basis of how stupid he was. Chris was kicking himself, wishing he'd used this tactic in the Australia Family Court when Elspeth was beating him to a pulp.

Three months later, the Bartman ball, as it came to be known, was purchased by one Grant DePorter at an auction for $113,824.16. DePorter promptly announced, "There will be no pardon on this ball." He planned a public execution of the baseball at Harry Caray's restaurant on Kinzie Street in Chicago, opposite the Redfish Cajun restaurant where Chris and the kids had played with their stolen Legos before houseboating in the Ozarks. Bartman was publicly invited to the destruction site, but his whereabouts were unknown.

Alma Ruth's brain remained in steady and irreversible decline towards its use-by date. "Rebot" became her word for "Reader's Digest." Kazzie was "Kurza." Razor was "Rackie." She told Chris she thought he was itchie rot, which meant he was smart. Some days were better than others. Chris would drive her over to his house during the week so she could hang out while the kids did their homework. She spent most of her time folding socks or running a damp cloth over kitchen counters.

But on the way home one night, she spoke so slowly and clearly, in English, that Chris wondered if she'd been faking all along. "Death," said Alma Ruth. It was a complete sentence. Chris wasn't sure how to respond.

"Be sure to come to my play," said Alma Ruth. She waited for Chris to figure out what she meant. "I'll jump out of my shoes if you don't come to my play." She was talking about her funeral, which was just around the corner.

"Jumping out of your shoes wouldn't be so bad," said Chris. "You'd sure ruffle the pillows of the church."

Alma Ruth laughed, even though she didn't understand the old Con McGrady pun about the pillows. She had an old habit of laughing at jokes she didn't get, and nobody could make her laugh like Chris could.

Chris said he wasn't sure he'd even come to her funeral. He only made the Hookers nervous, and he'd managed to avoid every family funeral up till now.

"Oh, no," said Alma Ruth. "You've got to be there. You can sit next to Carol." Alma Ruth had it all organized in her mind. She would be the hostess, and wanted everybody to be comfortable. Despite their differences in age and politics and style, Carol was the most Chris-like of the Hookers, because (like him) she'd made an art form of keeping Hookers a safe distance away.

As they pulled into the driveway, Alma Ruth said, "It won't be long. I don't have time to do very much." She paused, and Chris looked out the car window at the empty swing in the side yard. One summer afternoon in that yard, when his little brother Jeff was only six years old, Chris hit a baseball straight back at him that just missed his smiling face. It knocked three branches off the cherry tree behind the house, and Chris was horrified at the close call. The cherry tree had been gone for many years. A circle in the grass was all that was left of it.

"Too bad," said Alma Ruth. "I've got to go home." She fumbled around for the door handle, pressed the window button by mistake and said, "Oh my" as the window came down.

Chris was back in the swings of his childhood, arching high in the playground across the street from the little white house with the green roof. Someone was standing right behind him saying, "Let the cat die down."

"We *are* home," he said. He pressed the button to raise the window.

"No," Alma Ruth said, shaking her head. "I've got to go *home.*" She said goodbye and made Chris promise again to come to her play.

Chris told her he wished her father Grigori Bekyeshova

were still alive. "Wouldn't that be something?" he said. "You couldn't talk, and he couldn't hear. The two of you would have driven Leonard nuts."

Alma Ruth's slipped back into Chinese, saying that she'd already *done* that. Chris watched from the Windstar as she shuffled up the driveway into her sad little house. When she got inside, she waved through the picture window.

Old Leonard wasn't haunted by the ghost of Grigori Bekyeshova, but he did have an operation that autumn, for a stomach ulcer. Afterwards, he reported a near-death out-of-body experience. He was ecstatic.

"I watched the entire operation from the ceiling," he said. "And then I went down a curved hallway towards a beautiful light, and my mother and her sisters were there. When I got to the end of the hallway there was a man holding a sheet with numbers on it and he kept telling me what number I was. I told him I had to go back because it wasn't quite time for me. When I returned, it felt like plunging into a pool of ice water, and the nurses told me I'd been mumbling a sequence of numbers over and over."

Leonard said he couldn't wait to get back to the lighted hallway. He said it was like being reborn. His whole high school baseball team was waiting for him. First base was open.

The oak leaves started falling into Chris's back yard swimming pool. He couldn't get the pool guys to come over and close it down for the winter, so all through October he had to scoop out big gobs of soaking leaves with a net. This got him all grumpy, because it was too cold to swim, but still he had to keep the pool clean. Razor and Sharon loved the leaves, especially the ones that collected a foot deep on the back-yard trampoline. They made for great jumping games.

One Sunday morning in October, Kazzie said "Look, Chris, here's a newspaper story on that wreck we saw on the way home from Chicago." She handed Chris the local section of the *Courier-Review*. The car crash Chris and Kazzie and the kids had passed on Highway 57 turned out to be the weirdest one of all.

The *Courier-Review* reported the findings of the coroner's jury. The driver of the Subaru was a 24-year-old professional rock climber from Maine named Jesse Miller. He was in the wrong place at the wrong time, and now he was dead from massive head injuries. He and his sister Angela were traveling together in the Subaru, on their way to a new home in Colorado. After the crash, Angela was treated for minor injuries and released from Landen Hospital. She told the coroner's jury they were just driving along the highway when a red pickup swerved into their car.

"We didn't even know the guy," she said. "Jesse tried to keep control, and got the Subaru back on the highway. But then the truck swerved again, and forced us into the median." The red truck continued to pursue them, slamming into the Subaru a third time, pushing it into the path of an oncoming semi. After the crash, Angela tried to help Jesse until the ambulances arrived, but he was pronounced dead at 2:07 p.m., just about the time the Hookers were pulling into their driveway in Sand River.

The rest of the story was told by a Kankakee police officer, Kenny Fischbach. He arrived at the scene and saw the truck driver running from his truck into a cornfield. He and two other officers ran after him. When they found him in the corn, he was sitting in a little bald spot in the field, pounding on his legs and squealing.

"Look at my is-land," said the truck driver, pointing to the empty patch around him.

"Don't you mean eye-land, pardner," said officer Fischbach.

"No, man. This *is* land," said the truck driver. Then he took a butcher's knife in both hands and sliced his own throat.

"Clean as a whistle," Fischbach reported. He identified the truck driver as an ex-convict named William "Toolbar" Freyfogle. "My uniform was covered in Mr. Freyfogle's blood when I came out of that cornfield."

The paramedics pronounced Freyfogle dead at the scene, from sharp force injuries to the neck. Toxicology showed he had cocaine in his system, according to the coroner's report.

A further police investigation revealed that Freyfogle's elderly parents, Don and Shirley, were found dead in their home in Okaw City, Illinois, later that same evening, apparently due to blunt force trauma. A baseball bat was found in the driveway. Mr. and Mrs. Freyfogle had been dead for two days. Police said Toolbar was the only suspect in the murder of his parents. The red pickup he was driving was registered in their names.

Kirk Freyfogle, a social worker in the Okaw City school system and a younger son of Don and Shirley, found his parents' bodies. At the inquest he said, "The only thing I feel bad about is the 24-year-old man," referring to young Jesse Miller. He declined any further comment.

A business associate of Don Freyfogle, Okaw City Comptroller Herschel "Red" Nitze, recalled the Freyfogles as an exceedingly kind and loving couple. "Don commuted to work at Kraft Foods in Sand River for thirty years, and Shirley taught kindergarten here in Okaw City," he said. "I saw them at the farmer's market not long ago. They were just nice, nice people."

After enjoying his morning newspaper and some Atkins pancakes, Chris strolled over to St. Anthony's church for Sunday mass. He went early enough to catch Monsignor Reilly's pre-mass confession, or reconciliation as they called it these days. Chris had a yearning for some spiritual sheep-dipping, prompted by another article in the Sunday morning *Courier-Review*. Pope John Paul II had issued an encyclical with "a stern reminder that divorced Catholics who remarry cannot receive communion." The pontiff also warned Catholics not to take communion in non-Catholic churches.

Chris had been breaking both rules for years. When he wasn't having bread and wine at St. Anthony's, he was riding his little blue Honda motor scooter down to the Power House Memorial Church of God in Christ, for communion from the enormous black hands of the Reverend Israel Cumberbatch. Chris would be the only white guy in the church, hugging and kissing in the frenzy of gospel music and Israel's microphone-swallowing sermons.

Chris thought he'd cleared up all this communion business years ago with crazy Con McGrady in South Melbourne, after marrying Kazzie. Father Con gave him the green light on communion, saying he couldn't imagine Jesus turning Chris away from the table, so long as he came with a clean heart. "Even the church recognizes the primacy of your conscience," said Con. "And don't forget, Chris - God needs us as much as we need him." But Con was the kind of priest who used the f-word from the pulpit, rocking left and right as he quoted everyone from Jack Kerouac to Dorothy Day. Still, Con's imprimatur was good enough for Chris.

But now the pope was issuing press releases saying Chris had committed about seven hundred *more* sins in the meantime. In a rush of piety, Chris thought he'd better straighten this out with Monsignor Reilly.

Here at St. Anthony's, Chris entered the confessional, knelt, and made the sign of the cross. Behind the screen, old Reilly began the ancient drill: "May God, who has enlightened every heart, help you to know your sins and trust in his mercy."

"Amen," said Chris, followed by his opening line from the drama: "Bless me, Father, for I have sinned. It's been six months since my last confession." Reilly waited for the opportunity to absolve.

Chris paused. What the hell was he doing? He already had the answer from Father Con, all those years ago. Why get a second opinion just because of some newspaper report, when you already had what you wanted? He *knew* Reilly, and Reilly would go along with the pope no matter what. Chris changed his mind about confession, and decided to let sleeping dogs lie. He cleared his throat.

"I'm sorry, Monsignor, I don't really have anything to confess."

Reilly rearranged his priestly robes behind the screen. "Then why are you here, my son?" he said. He sounded weary and slightly disappointed.

"It's just a mistake," said Chris. "Sorry to bother you." He got up to leave.

"Stay a moment, my son," said Reilly, and Chris obeyed. He knelt back down before the screen.

Reilly departed from the script. He could tell it was Chris on the other side of the confessional, from the half-baked Australian accent. "Look Chris," he said, "the *defining* sin of modern times is the loss of the *sense* of sin." He reminded Chris of St. John's observation: "If we say we have no sin, we deceive ourselves, and the truth is not in us." Reilly proposed a little prayer together.

"Repeat the following after me," he said: "Mary, mother of Jesus and my mother."

Chris didn't want to do this, but he played along, and echoed the words.

Reilly continued. He sounded a lot happier now that something was happening. "Your son died on the cross for me."

Chris said the same.

"Help me to confess my sins humbly and with trust in the mercy of God," said Reilly.

"Help me to confess my sins," Chris repeated, "humbly and with trust in the mercy of God."

"That I may receive his pardon and peace."

Chris let out a long sigh. These were beautiful words, "pardon" and "peace." He wanted those things. How nice it must be to have them.

"That I may receive his pardon and peace," Chris whispered.

When they'd finished their prayer, Reilly said, "Are you sure that's all, my son?"

No, thought Chris. There *was* something else on his mind, something that had been bothering him for a long time, even before Father Con. Chris wasn't even sure it was a sin, but it felt like one. Chris wanted to make it go away.

"There is another thing, Monsignor," he said. Chris heard Reilly settling back, sensed Reilly's air of victory through the screen as he readied himself for Chris's coming clean.

"A long time ago," said Chris, "I violated the sixth commandment with a married woman. She initiated the affair, but I went along. Her husband found out, and he murdered her."

Chris had Reilly's attention. No one said a thing. The Panda's old friend silence went to work, demanding to be filled.

"I confessed to the affair," Chris finally added, "but I never confessed to anything else. I never knew what else to say."

The cup of silence was only half full. Reilly didn't get too many murders here at St. Anthony's. He crouched in wait, but this time Chris outlasted him. Reilly had to break the ice.

"Are you truly sorry for this, my son?"

"Yes, I am," said Chris. "Yes, Monsignor, I am."

Reilly quickly returned to the safe haven of his script. "Then pray the act of contrition," he said. He was back on auto-pilot.

Chris spoke the words he had learned so long ago at St. Francis Solano in Quincy, words he had never managed to forget, in South America or South Dakota or Australia or Italy:

> O my God, I am heartily sorry for having offended thee, and I detest all my sins because of thy just punishments, but most of all because they offend thee, my God, who art all good and deserving of all my love. I firmly resolve, with the help of thy grace, to sin no more and to avoid the near occasions of sin.

He was a nine-year-old boy again, sitting in his father's dugout.

Reilly forgave Chris for something, then assigned an unusual penance. Chris was to take a seat in St. Anthony's and simply look at the cross of Jesus above the altar.

"That's it?" said Chris. He was used to saying Our Fathers and Hail Marys.

"Yes, my son," said Reilly. "Just look at the crucifix and think about it." He told Chris to go in peace, and the sacrament of reconciliation was complete. Or nearly complete. Chris still had to do his penance.

Chris thanked Monsignor Reilly and left the confessional. He took a seat in his usual section of St. Anthony's, near the front and to the left. The church was beginning to fill with the morning mass crowd as the organist worked her way through Samuel Barber's *Adagio for Strings.*

The crucifix in St. Anthony's was big, but otherwise unremarkable. Chris had seen thousands of these crosses, on church walls all over the world, or dangling from the bottoms of hundreds of rosaries. Jesus was deader than hell, and nailed in place on a shaved tree. He had a deep wound in his right side. He wore a crown of thorns. Above him were the mocking initials INRI - "Jesus of Nazareth, King of the Jews," the Romans' final joke. This icon of redemption through bloodshed was nothing like the sprightly crucifix that spoke to Francis of Assisi in the Chiesa di San Damiano.

Chris saw wood and stone. He saw art, and a terrible beauty. He saw Terrion Jackson perched atop the St. Louis Millennium, wings spread above the unsinkable *Titanic* in the icy waters twenty-six floors below. He saw a figurehead on a pirate ship. He saw Russell Kamara and Jillian Daley Shulman, and a youthful Finbar Studge. He saw his own children hanging from the arms of that cross, and Leonard, and Alma Ruth, and Cheeto High Bear - everyone he could think of. And every single one of them appeared as an angel who had come into his life for better or worse, a character in a Hooker novel that was still being written by someone, somewhere.

And now he squinted and saw the lines. They'd been there all along, but Chris had never noticed them before. They were so plain, so simple, yet obscured by the overwhelming image of the death of God.

For Miriam Slade, reality was a mandala and time was an illusion. No matter where you started you always circled back to the same place again and again and again. You never left and you never returned. There was no beginning and no end, because such abstractions only masked the face of the Watcher.

These linear extensions of the crucifix were different. They unfurled from a center of nothing, in the four sacred directions of the Lakota, never turning back on themselves, pointing farther than the eye could see. You would never come back to where you started, no matter how many breadcrumb sins you dropped along the way.

Or if you *started* in the heavens or from the netherworld, your lines would converge in a point so small it couldn't be seen. Chris entered the lines and became a speck of dust, a mote. Then he turned his face and was forever. Either way, it was the same great mystery. Wakan Tanka.

But Chris's penance was not complete. These lines were only two dimensions of this crucifix, demanding a third and a fourth.

"Eloi, Eloi, lama sabachthani?" cried Jesus, as Chris lifted a sponge to the cross, soaking his mouth with sour wine and gall. Then blade in hand, like the captain of a pirate ship, like a convict in a field of corn, Chris pierced the side of Jesus, and blood and water flowed as from the ribs of a Rainbow Serpent.

Now it was finished, thought Chris. Now his penance was done. Now he could let the cat die down.

St. Anthony's had filled with parishioners. It was the 29th Sunday in Ordinary Time. The first reading was from Isaiah 53:10-11:

> If he gives his life as an offering for sin,
> he shall see his descendants in a long life,
> and the will of the Lord shall be accomplished
> through him.

Paul's letter to the Hebrews followed, declaring that Jesus had been "tested in every way, yet without sin." The lector smiled, and closed the book.

"Some test," thought Christian Leonard Hooker, as he fumbled with his rosary beads in the pew. "Some test."

He was at peace. It was a Sunday, and the mysteries were glorious.

Editor's Afterword

So there you have it. Christian Leonard Hooker's solipsistic morality play.

After editing Chris's manuscript, I took it to Kinko's and had fifty copies made. I distributed them to some of our old high school classmates, and to those of Chris's family and acquaintances I was able to locate in Australia, South Dakota, the Caribbean, and Illinois. As the last envelope slipped from my fingers into the mailbox, I felt a sense of purgation, then immediately felt guilty for indulging in such selfish thoughts. This was for Chris, after all. It wasn't for me.

I tested the commercial waters by sending *Houseboat* to a few New York City literary agents I knew. Only one of them, Seamus Rogan of the Heritage Agency, took the trouble to reply:

> Chris comes off like an outlaw Jesus, busting through the world with an egomaniacial abandon that somehow seems endearing. That said, I must disappoint by saying I'm not the right agent for *Houseboat.* Chris compares his memoir to *The Dharma Bums* and *Catcher in the Rye.* However, the relative plotnessness of those books was supported by an overabundance of tightly observed characters. Chris's *Houseboat* tells only Chris's story. Perhaps this choice could work if he lived in an environment the reader could immerse himself in. The Summer of 2003, however, may be too near the present to be its own sharply focused world. I wish you the best of luck in placing *Houseboat,* and wish our response could have been different.

Two weeks later, I received a FedEx package containing five of my edited manuscripts, four of them unopened. They were accompanied by a brief note from Chris's widow, Kazzie Sorenson Hooker. "Dear Mr. Studge," she began:

> While I thank you, and the children thank you, for trying to keep Chris's memory alive, and for all the work you've obviously put into this project of yours, I must ask you to produce no more of these books. Chris's disappearance was a very big deal here in the St. Anthony's community. The children and I are trying to move on with our lives, and have no wish to dwell in the past. The revelations in Chris's "novel" are too personal, and we hope to continue living in this small Illinois community without such embarrassments.

> By the way, Chris *did* receive your last e-mails, and he was trying to take your advice by expanding sections on Miriam, Elspeth, Yolanda and others. In his heart, he really did want to see the world through someone else's eyes.

> But next to his laptop I found this handwritten note: 'Studge. Don't think I can do it. The whole point of *Houseboat* is the failure to communicate at all levels - spiritual, personal, artistic, parental.'

> Chris had a knack for portraying his shortcomings as a matter of integrity. His neuroses were well-protected.

> Another thing that might interest you: one of Chris's cute little epigraphs quotes from the James Taylor song, "Enough To Be On Your Way," from the *Hourglass* album. Six months before he

died, Chris and I went to a James Taylor concert
at the Assembly Hall here in Sand River, and
Chris kept calling out for James to sing that song.
I was so embarrassed. But James wouldn't do it.

Chris's choice of epigraph surprised me, because
the words he quoted weren't even his favorites
from that song. He loved to sing along with the
chorus: "Home, build it behind your eyes, carry it
in your heart, safe among your own."

All that being said, Mr. Studge, I hope that you
understand my concerns, and that you will
respect my wishes.

Kind regards,
KSH

I folded Kazzie Hooker's note and went for a walk in my
neighborhood. Married couples were leveling their yards and
planting their trees. Children were playing with hoops and
jump-ropes. Dogs were jumping after flying frisbees. It was a
beautiful sunny afternoon.

I wasn't sure what to do with the returned manuscripts.
They sat on my desk for a couple of days, then I tossed them
in a dumpster. This probably wouldn't have surprised Chris,
and in all likelihood he wouldn't have been disappointed. He
may have had such an ending in mind all along, as he played
his music to himself.

I thought once more of his South Dakota hitch-hiker,
Brenda Which Woman, and her undelivered promise of dan-
ger and sex. In the Lakota world of Wakan Tanka, Christian
Leonard Hooker was never, ever, a noun. And truth be told,
he wasn't much of a verb.

                                        Finbar Studge

Long long ago, on the other side of the world, author Gary Forrester was an acclaimed bluegrass musician. Many of the events and themes of his writing were already present in his songs. As David Latta wrote in his book *Australian Country Music:*

"Bluegrass is an international music. Gary Forrester, leader of The Rank Strangers, already knew this fact, but it wasn't really rammed home until their first album, *Dust on the Bible,* was narrowly beaten in an international bluegrass album of the year competition in Nashville by a group from Czechoslovakia... The most striking aspect of the albums, apart from their frequency, is the exceptionally high standard of songwriting. With the exception of a handful of songs, the three albums have come from the pen of Gary Forrester. Writing within the tightly constrained boundaries of the bluegrass melody, Gary's lyrics juggle a stinging social commentary with great wit and passion... The Rank Strangers have a musical immediacy that typifies the best of bluegrass and recalls such players as The Stanley Brothers and Bill Monroe... [They] occupy a unique place in the bluegrass culture... In 1989 the band, with Di McNichol, toured the United States with the high point being an appearance at the International Bluegrass Music Association Fan Fest at Owensboro, Kentucky"

A CD of the original bluegrass songs mentioned in this novel, together with a number of other songs written and performed by Gary Forrester, may be obtained by contacting:

AfterImage
509 South Chaucer Boulevard
Monticello, IL 61856
or by emailing afterimage@verizon.net

www.garyforrester.com